Also by S.Y. Thompson:

Under the Midnight Cloak
Now You See Me
Fractured Futures
Destination Alara

Under Devil's Snare

S.Y. Thompson

*Mystic Books
by Regal Crest*

Texas

Copyright © 2014 by S.Y. Thompson

All rights reserved. No part of this publication may be reproduced, transmitted in any form or by any means, electronic or mechanical, including photocopy, recording, or any information storage and retrieval system, without permission in writing from the publisher. The characters, incidents and dialogue herein are fictional and any resemblance to actual events or persons, living or dead, is purely coincidental.

ISBN 978-1-61929-204-8

First Printing 2014

9 8 7 6 5 4 3 2 1

Cover design by AcornGraphics

Published by:

Regal Crest Enterprises, LLC
229 Sheridan Loop
Belton, Texas 76513

Find us on the World Wide Web at
http://www.regalcrest.biz

Published in the United States of America

Acknowledgments

Writing is a passion. It must be or we wouldn't spend hours in solitude working on such a lonely, albeit satisfying, craft. However, as much as an author invests solitary time creating characters and worlds, no one creates a novel alone. I'd like to acknowledge and thank the readers, my friends and family as well as the other fiction authors who inspire me. My heartfelt gratitude to Linda North, who is always available anytime I need help brainstorming. No one is a better friend or beta. Heather Flournoy, who is the best editor ever, I learn so much from you each time we run through the process. Finally, thank you to my Regal Crest family.

Fantasy, abandoned by reason, produces impossible monsters.

~Francisco Goya

Chapter One

WITHOUT A CLOUD in the sky, the sun shone bright blue overhead. Already past its zenith, it headed quietly toward the horizon. There was a chill in the air despite the sun's presence, testament to the waning fall season. Birds still sang gaily in the trees and nearby a bee's wings beat as it flew about in the fruitless search for pollen. On a normal day, all of these things would combine into a glowing testament to the circle of life. This wasn't a normal day and considering where they stood, these usually bright things felt obscene.

"Did you touch anything?"

Uttered quietly, the question hardly disturbed the air. Jamison Kessler recognized the softly spoken words as respect for the dead. Eight people stood in the clearing, including her, and with her heightened senses she knew where each stood without looking. She absently noted the rigidity in their bodies, the seething anger and unspoken grief. The crime scene technicians waited patiently. They'd already collected evidence and now gave law enforcement officials space to gather their impressions. Once the coroner arrived, they'd collect more evidence from the body. They wouldn't touch the victim until then.

"No, but I know it was the same guy."

Jamison had met the detectives from the U.S. Park Police only an hour before. It was the first time since working at the park that she had needed to call in the big guns and wasn't happy to do so now. Normally, the park police were stationed at the more populated areas and content to leave the local rangers alone to perform their duties. Jamison's instincts told her that each of the detectives were self-assured and had been doing this type of work for years.

Their leader, Patricia Hex, was of average height and build with dark brown hair and keen sable eyes. Everything about the woman's appearance said she was "average" but Jamison sensed there was much more to her than met the eye. Although she seemed a little more forceful than necessary, Jamison thought she had an air of compassion and quiet strength.

"How do you know it was a guy?"

Jamison's slightly lopsided smile held no amusement, only bitterness. "I don't, but you know the stats as well as I do."

"Yeah, white male typically between the ages of twenty-five and thirty-five. Yadda, yadda..."

In point of fact, Jamison didn't know anything except that another young woman had met a grisly end. Standing a few feet from the body, Jamison couldn't help but scan the slight form lying under a blanket of leaves and brush. Only the head lay exposed and from the short distance, it was almost possible to believe that she merely slept. The killer had combed the blonde hair straight back from the forehead and applied fresh lipstick. Jamison had witnessed the same scenario two weeks before, the details exactly the same. Only the victim had changed. Sometimes, Jamison wished her species' abilities included selective amnesia.

"I took a report over the phone from a young woman who said she found a body in the woods. I came out here myself to check the scene. Rangers Thomas and Latimer secured the perimeter while I contacted you. My next call was the local coroner's office, but I guess you had the pleasure of beating them here."

Jamison couldn't keep the sarcasm from her voice. Her ire wasn't directed toward the Park Police or the investigative team's leader, Detective Patricia Hex, but frustration got the better of her. Compounding her frustration, even her enhanced Panthera senses couldn't detect any trace of the killer on the victim. Someone was smart enough to use forensic counter measures and Jamison wasn't above calling out Mickey Mouse if he could help solve these crimes. This unfortunate woman was the second murder victim in only a few weeks and Jamison felt things were beginning to spiral out of control.

Hex snorted in response. "You know very well that Park Rangers share jurisdiction with the criminal investigative division of the U.S. Park Police, but what's *she* doing here?"

Detective Hex's brown eyes rested on a small, uniformed woman squatting beside the body. Sheriff Samantha Macke's wide brimmed Smokey cast her face in shadow so that even Jamison couldn't see her expression.

"I know all about jurisdiction, Hex, but this is way above my pay grade. I'm a park ranger and I deal with four-legged predators. Whoever is doing this didn't leave any clues on the first victim and I'll go out on a limb and bet you a month's pay that it's the same this time. Sheriff Macke may be a local cop, but she has experience with murder investigations and I trust her."

"Unlike us, huh?"

Jamison's eyes met Hex's fully for the first time since the detective had arrived on scene. The lack of progress in finding the killer and now this second murder had her nerves on edge and her anger overflowed. "We don't have time for a pissing contest, Detective Hex. If you have a problem with Macke, tell me now and we'll just forget I ever called you."

Hex's dark eyes narrowed as she assessed Jamison for a few intense moments. Jamison wondered if she would walk away over a jurisdictional issue. If she did, Jamison didn't want her help anyway. She didn't need someone who would give up so easily. The victims deserved better.

"I only meant that you don't really know us, my team that is. It's only natural that you'd want someone here that you're familiar with, but we're here and we're going to need your cooperation. Now if you'll excuse me, we have a crime to investigate."

Hex drifted away, calling to her crew. The second in command of the Major Crimes Unit, Jack Chase, wore an Armani suit but had the sense to wear comfortable shoes in the woods. Jamison thought he'd probably changed from a more expensive pair in the car. While she watched, Hex and Chase conferred and after a few minutes, he started sauntering around the crime scene with a camera. Since the forensics team had already taken photos, Jamison assumed the detectives wanted their own. The final member, Leann Seaver, scanned the area for anything forensics might have missed but had yet to place a single placard indicating a clue. She also carried a tablet, sketching an image of the scene with a stylus as she went. No one attempted to lift fingerprints from the scene, probably because there wasn't a single object in the clearing capable of holding a print except possibly somewhere on the victim. They'd all leave that for the medical examiner.

The Harmon County Medical Examiner's van rolled to a stop at the edge of the firebreak. Jamison felt a sense of relief wash over her when Doctor Laura Paul exited the vehicle. Her red-gold hair sparkled in the sunlight as she turned her head to meet Jamison's gaze. Her senses expanded and silent, mental communication ensued.

It's all right. You'll find who did this.

The message from her longtime friend carried a wealth of feelings including reassurance and regret for the loss of life. Jamison gave Laura a small, almost imperceptible nod. She turned her attention back to Sheriff Macke while Laura pulled on a sterile set of coveralls, preparing to approach the scene.

Chase stopped taking pictures and removed a note pad from his inside coat pocket as he headed for Sheriff Macke. From a distance of thirty feet, Jamison eavesdropped shamelessly. "Did you investigate the previous scene, Sheriff?"

Macke stood slowly and tipped her head to look at Chase. She was a small woman, but Jamison never considered her less than formidable in her natural law enforcement element. "Yeah, I was there."

"Was there anything that stood out at the previous crime scene, any details that might help us catch this killer?"

"I can assure you, detective, if there was I'd already have the son of a bitch in custody."

Unperturbed by the terse response, Chase nodded and stepped out of the way for Doctor Paul. Laura glanced at Macke before kneeling beside her and taking a medical probe from her small, black bag. Jamison looked away. She didn't want to watch Laura insert the liver probe. Standard operating procedure required Laura to use the device to help determine time of death, but Jamison could tell from the smell of decomposition that the woman had been dead for a few days.

Unlike Jamison, Chase seemed fascinated by the procedure. He leaned over slightly, eyes riveted as Laura carefully brushed leaves away from the woman's abdominal region with her gloved hands.

"I assume you performed the autopsy on the first victim, Doctor Paul. Do you still have the other body?"

"No," Laura admitted. "Ranger Kessler, the forensics team and Sheriff Macke checked the body over for any evidence. I conducted the autopsy and then released the body to the family after completing my pathology report."

"What were your findings?"

"The victim, Pauline Nielson, died of exsanguination."

"She bled to death."

"Precisely. The killer used a very sharp, single-bladed weapon to inflict two deep lacerations. One of the cuts transected the femoral artery in her groin and the second severed the brachial artery inside the left upper arm. She would have bled out in less than a minute."

"Like a hunting knife, maybe?" Detective Chase jotted down a few words. "Did you find any trace from the killer?"

"Nothing, nor did Ms. Nielson have any defensive wounds and there was no sign of sexual assault."

Chase nodded and frowned, clearly not liking the answer. He handed Doctor Paul a white business card, realized she didn't have any free hands, and carefully slipped it into her coverall pocket. "My fax number is on there. Would you mind sending along a copy of your pathology report on the first victim and anything you may find with this one?"

Jamison watched as Sheriff Macke backed away a few paces to give the medical examiner room to work. Her dark eyes kept track of every move. To be effective, Jamison knew Sam needed to ensure everyone followed strict procedures to prevent any tainting of evidence.

"Of course, I'll see to it as soon as I get back to the office." Laura frowned slightly and looked at Jamison.

Laura silently communicated her anxiety to Jamison. Both had concluded from the first attack that the victim must have known the attacker or it was someone she trusted. Since she hadn't defended herself, it was the only thing that made sense. Detective Hex squatted beside the unfortunate victim, bagging evidence. Hex removed debris from the body slowly, making sure to preserve everything. She confiscated every twig, leaf and pill bug. Jamison's nose twitched while she observed.

Jamison couldn't help but feel that she should have found something to bring the killer to justice before this second attack. She should have been able to put a swift end to this, which was why she carried so much guilt over the latest murder. That she had to call in outside help from the U.S. Park Police was just further proof of her failure.

"She's still wearing her cell," Detective Hex commented, handling the device with gloves. The phone went into another bag. "Maybe we'll get lucky and she'll have some identification on her."

"That would be nice," Doctor Paul said. "Jamison, I mean, Ranger Kessler helped identify Ms. Nielson. She had registered with the Paul Smith's Visitor's Center as a camper a few days before she was found."

Jamison felt Laura flinch almost imperceptibly. She must have felt Jamison's displeasure. Jamison wanted the Park Police to prove how good they were by finding out all this information on their own instead of having it spoon-fed to them. Hex raised a disapproving eyebrow in her direction but remained squatted beside the medical examiner.

"I'll assume you were going to tell me about that later."

Jamison shrugged in response. "It's a matter of public record."

"We'll need to check out her campsite."

"We already did." Jamison frowned and shook her head. "We didn't find anything. Whoever did this killed her somewhere else and moved the body."

"That's nice. Still, humor me and let us examine the scene for ourselves."

Jamison let out an aggravated sigh. She needed their help and couldn't afford to keep the detectives at arm's length. While being territorial was part of her animal psyche, she had to overcome her baser instincts. She had expected the detectives to want to check the campsite, but it wouldn't really do them any good. Still, what did she know? Jamison wasn't a homicide detective and acting like a jerk didn't accomplish anything.

"That crime happened two weeks ago and it's rained since then, but whatever you say. Thomas can take you over there when you're ready."

"I think we've done everything we can here." Hex stood and moved toward her team to compare notes.

Ranger Brenda Thomas looked her way when Jamison called her name. She stood at the far edge of the perimeter tape to keep out any curious tourists. So far there were none, but it was late in the season. Her alert expression and competent demeanor impressed Jamison. Thomas was coming up on her one-year anniversary as a park ranger and had come a long way from the shy, introverted woman she'd been the first day.

"You're doing a good job, Brenda."

"Thanks, Chief."

Jamison almost told Thomas not to call her "chief" but she wasn't in the mood for their usual banter. "I need you to show the detectives to Ms. Nielsen's old campsite."

"I'm on it."

Forensic experts reentered the scene to finish looking for potential evidence. Ranger Latimer glanced around and Jamison could see the concern on his face. A little more experienced than Thomas, Latimer seemed more interested with maintaining the integrity of the scene, but his worries were unfounded. Two more park personnel blocked the only treks leading into this part of the woods to ensure no unauthorized personnel made it through.

"Your thoughts?"

Jamison lifted an eyebrow as Sheriff Macke stepped to her. "That I want to strangle the bastard who did this."

"Agreed, let me rephrase. Do your...instincts...tell you anything about this crime that I don't know?"

"Not really. I can tell you that she's been here for about four days. The cool weather we've had has helped preserve the body. I also know she didn't die here, there's not enough blood. Beyond that, I'm just as baffled as the next person. I smell bleach and disinfectant."

"So someone is smart enough to clean up after themselves. I'm surprised the critters haven't gotten to her yet." There was nothing frivolous or disrespectful in Macke's tone, just an honest appraisal. "Maybe we'll get lucky and find something that will lead us to the perp."

"Maybe, but I doubt it."

"Shit, Kessler. Don't sound so hopeful."

"Look, Sheriff, no disrespect but we didn't find anything on the Nielsen woman and unless this freak got careless, I doubt we're going to find anything this time. The only way we're going to know who did this is through good old-fashioned police work, something at which I know you excel."

Jamison sensed Macke's anger flare. The sheriff wasn't a huge fan of the Panthera and barely put up with them. Macke wouldn't even have known about the shape changers if her previous partner hadn't been one. It was only on Nicky's deathbed that she had told Macke the truth.

"Are you being a smartass, because if you are..."

"No, I'm being sincere. I know we don't always see eye to eye, Sheriff, but I brought you in on this for two reasons. One, as local law enforcement you deserve to know when federal officers are investigating a crime in your jurisdiction."

"And the second reason?"

"The second reason is that you're damn good at your job."

Macke's ire faded and she let out a tense breath. "Fair enough, until this is over you're my new best friend. Everything I find out I'll share with you, but I expect the same in return."

"Deal."

"Good, now let's get the hell out of here and let these people do their jobs. You look like you haven't slept in a week and I don't want to have to fill out the paperwork when you keel over."

Jamison accepted the attempt at humor with a wan smile and followed Macke out of the clearing. They parted ways as Jamison climbed into the Park Service's Range Rover. She headed for her office at Paul Smith's Visitor's Center, her thoughts far away. On days like this, Jamison wished she was still a *pieta*, the Panthera version of a private eye. As a *pieta*, she'd be free to investigate these crimes exclusively. Since becoming an elder and accepting the promotion to captain for this region of the Adirondack Park, she sometimes felt she had the weight of the world on her shoulders. She wanted nothing more than to shirk the balance of her responsibilities and concentrate on catching whoever was victimizing these women, but the Panthera Council would never accept that.

Gravel crunched under the Range Rover's tires as she pulled into the Paul Smith's Visitor's Center parking lot. Jamison shut off the engine, but sat for a few minutes. The sunset over the mountains was a masterpiece of orange, red and purple hues. Through the backdrop of pine, sycamore, ash and maple trees, Jamison thought this the most beautiful area in the world. That someone would come here to stalk and kill innocent women filled her with a quiet rage that threatened to bring her beast out of confinement. She wanted to change into her jaguar form and stalk the killer as he had stalked his victims, to feel her claws rend the flesh from his bones. Jamison realized that desire came from her animal side, from the part of her that cried out for the justice of the natural world. Unfortunately, that time in history of taking life to avenge another had come and gone.

This killer had a human face and Jamison couldn't allow her cat to seek retribution. She would investigate using her higher reasoning. She would find out who had committed these crimes and she would bring them to justice. Human justice. If her abilities gave her an advantage along the way, Jamison was fine with that. She took the keys from the ignition and climbed out of the vehicle, locking the door before she slammed it shut.

A light still burned inside the office. Jamison's secretary, Jeanie Kraus, looked up from the document she was reading when the door opened. Jamison met her eyes through the black-framed glasses and noted the compassion in her gaze. Jeanie seemed to have aged in the last few weeks, and Jamison could have sworn there were a few more strands of gray in the beehive hairdo. Sorrow deepened the lines beside her mouth making Jeanie appear older than the fifty-six Jamison knew her to be.

"Was it...?" Jeanie's voice trailed off. She hesitated and then tried again. "Are you all right?"

Jamison nodded once. The gesture felt stiff, forced. "Have the others checked in?"

"Yes. Ranger Thomas said they've arrived at the original campsite and the detectives are setting up lighting equipment so they can check the area. I think she's in for a long night. Ranger Latimer said the forensics team is mopping up. He doesn't think they'll be much longer."

Unsurprised by the update, Jamison only grunted. She rubbed her eyes and couldn't help thinking what a nightmare all of this was. Jamison considered telling Jeanie to go home, changing into her jaguar form and heading into the woods in search of two-legged prey. However, the killer seemed to be on a two-week cycle and unless he escalated, scouring the woods would prove a waste of time.

"Why don't you go on home, Captain Kessler? You look beat."

"I'd rather be here, Jeanie. I just don't feel right going home to rest while this murderer is still out there."

"I know," Jeanie allowed. "But you're not going to do any good by exhausting yourself and I'm sure Lee will want to know that you're okay."

The mention of her partner brought the first real smile to Jamison's lips. Even now Jamison could picture Lee's flashing blue eyes. "Okay, you win. Why don't you head out, too? It's getting late."

"I'm right behind you."

"No, now." Jamison wasn't about to take a chance with Jeanie's safety, regardless of the killer's time cycle. "I'll walk you to your car."

Chapter Two

"I KNOW YOU'RE worried about her. I am too, but what can we do? It's not like there isn't reason for her to be upset."

Lee Grayson grumbled her response into the phone. She'd called Jamison's twin sister hoping to commiserate over the latest series of events. Instead she had to listen as Dinah came up with perfectly reasonable excuses for Lee to let Jamison have some space. That her partner now dealt with two unsolved murders in the span of as many weeks made Lee want to do everything in her power to help. Since that was impossible unless she found the guilty party herself, there was nothing for her to do except worry. Jamison was hardly sleeping at all, and when she did, it was not well. When she wasn't searching for clues during her daytime working hours, she was in cat form prowling the forest. Somehow, she blamed herself for these deaths and nothing Lee said would ease that guilt.

"I guess, but do you have to be so logical about it?"

Dinah laughed and her voice sounded a little tinny through the phone speaker. "It's only normal to want to protect the person you love but until this thing is over, you're just going to have to allow Jamison to deal with things in her own way. Just be there for her. That's the best thing you can do."

"Fine, but that doesn't mean I have to like it."

"Of course not. Are you on your way home?"

"Yes, Cleo and I have been up on Regis Mountain taking some sunset pictures for my next showing."

"How is my girl?"

Lee glanced over at the beagle in question and smiled. "Right now, she's passed out and snoring. I swear I'm going to have drool all over my leather seat."

"When is your next show?"

Lee understood that Dinah was attempting to distract her from worrying about Jamison. Although it wouldn't really help, she still felt grateful. "In about six months. Jasmine is really riding me to get some new proofs to her."

"Jasmine, that's your agent in New York, right?"

"That's the one. Hey, I'm pulling onto Mafdet Lane now and I need to get Cleo's dinner. Is it all right if I call you tomorrow?"

"Call me anytime, Hon, and remember that we're still on for that helicopter ride up to Wolverine Summit next week."

As she cleared the tree line, Lee spotted a white rectangular box on the manor's front porch and felt another smile tug her lips. As busy as she was, Jamison still found time to show Lee she was thinking of her.

"I'm looking forward to it." Lee ended the call just as she rolled to a stop. Cleo roused herself, stood up and shook her entire body. When she finished she looked over at her master as though wondering why the door wasn't yet open.

"Are you finished?" When the dog cocked her head to the side, Lee grinned and opened the door.

Cleo didn't wait for an invitation. She climbed across Lee's lap and bailed out of the Mercedes. It still surprised Lee a little that she could hear Cleo's paw pads strike the ground under the thick grass. She heard the small bits of sand and gravel slide against each other as they accommodated the dog's weight. Being Panthera had its advantages but there was also a downside. When Lee tried to sleep at night, Cleo could wake her up simply by scratching. The sound was like sandpaper rasping through the inside of Lee's brain. She still hadn't adjusted to all of her body's changes. Lee hadn't even known about the Panthera before her arrival in Harmon a year ago. The discovery that she was one was an added shock. It seemed that being around the community and the rampaging behavior of a lion shifter had triggered her own latent abilities. Now, all this time later, she still had difficulty with transforming by effort of will alone. Perhaps eventually she would develop more control, but she wasn't overly worried.

After grabbing her camera bag from the floorboard, Lee followed the dog toward the house. She glanced around the yard, not really expecting anyone but somehow still unsettled that she and Cleo were alone. With Jamison at work and Lee's apprentice, Lindsay, in school that wasn't a surprise, so she shook off the feeling. Climbing the steps onto the manor's wide porch, Lee picked up the florist box from the swing. For a second it felt like something moved inside. She dismissed the notion as the product of an overactive imagination and pushed open the front door.

Greeted by the comforting sight and smell of home, Lee felt the tension of the day vanish. She cruised through the circular foyer and dropped the flowers onto the dining room table. She wanted to see what Jami had sent her, but Cleo wasn't that patient.

"Yeah, yeah, I'm coming," Lee responded to the barking.

Seeming satisfied that her master wasn't ignoring her dietary needs, the dog padded into the kitchen. She waited beside her bowl, brown eyes following Lee's every move. Lee poured kibble into the dish and filled a second container with fresh water. Then Lee poured herself a glass of iced tea before heading back into the dining room. A smile of anticipation curved her lips as she set the tea down and reached for the flowers. It wasn't like Jamison to send her flowers so soon. The last delivery had only taken place a few days ago, but she wasn't complaining.

Lee was already planning where to display the bouquet and wondering where she'd stashed her other vase when the bow came off.

She peeled back the lid and reeled back from her first glimpse inside.

"Jesus Christ!"

The words ended on a very cat-like hiss. A snarl passed her curled lips but she didn't notice, too riveted in disgust by the prize awaiting her. There *was* a bouquet of long-stemmed roses inside the box. They were dead and already starting to crumble. The other objects packed inside with the foliage were what held her attention.

Snakes twisted obscenely through the shoots, twining and undulating over each other. Predominately dark brown or green, the snakes had three yellowish stripes down their sides and back. Lee spotted beetles in an array of colors mingled in the tangle of serpents. They competed for space with the serpents until one attempted to escape confinement by crawling over the box's edge. Regaining her wits, Lee slapped the insect back inside. She grabbed the foul parcel and strode for the kitchen door, bypassing the beagle who barely glanced up from her dinner. Lee didn't stop until she reached the edge of the woods where she tossed the whole mess, box and all, into the brush.

For long moments she stood there shuddering. When she could think again, Lee wondered why in hell someone would send her something so awful. There was no way Jamison would do such a thing. Then again, Lee assumed the flowers were for her. It was possible someone was sending Jamison a message. She hadn't actually seen a card. Regardless of the intended recipient, Lee still had the same question: Why?

She watched the snakes eventually slither away. The shadows from a fading sun couldn't make the sight any less disturbing. Cleo left the house through the dog door and soon joined Lee's side. When her master didn't respond to her presence, Cleo lay down in the grass and rested her head on her paws. She didn't show any interest in the package.

Lee was still there when Jamison pulled up in front of the house. She heard the engine shut off, but the door didn't open. Lee realized Jamison could see her standing to the side of the manor near the woods and probably wondered what she was doing. She sensed her partner's concern but, still new to her Panthera abilities, couldn't always communicate telepathically. Finally, the door opened and she heard hesitant footsteps as Jamison exited.

She heard Jamison's hiss of revulsion halfway across the yard. Suddenly Jamison was beside her and a comforting hand rested on Lee's shoulder.

"What the hell?"

Lee smiled but there wasn't any humor in the gesture. "That is a truly excellent question. At first, I thought they were from you, but unless your romantic streak has taken a turn to the dark side..."

Jamison removed her hand and Lee felt her shifting around. When she stepped toward the mess, Lee saw she had tugged on a pair of black leather gloves. Jamison knelt down and picked up the florist box, taking the time to flip the remaining live contents into the weeds.

"The fact that these are harmless garter snakes doesn't really make me feel any better," Jamison confided. "Someone intended this as a threat."

"Yeah, but who are they threatening, me or you?" Lee felt a chill and crossed her arms. "Usually I'm the one receiving flowers."

Standing, Jamison turned toward her and shrugged. "I don't know, but I'm going to need a sample of your fingerprints for elimination purposes. I doubt any shop delivered these and maybe we'll get some prints from whoever did."

"Okay, I understand you're looking for whoever dropped off that box, but can't you leave that nasty thing out here? I'm not sure I want it in the manor."

"I understand, baby, but I can't leave it here. I can't risk exposing any evidence to the elements. I'll have to run it over to the lab and I don't want to wait until morning. We're using the M.E.'s office for our investigation since the facilities are closer than driving to Lake Placid and we have everything we need here in Harmon."

Jamison's compassionate tones didn't make her feel any better when Lee caught on to what her partner was thinking. "Do you think this is related to your case somehow?"

"It must be. The timing is just too coincidental. If we're lucky, we'll find some prints and our suspect will be in the system."

"But you don't really believe that, do you?"

Jamison shook her head. "I wish I could say yes, but whoever is committing these murders is far too careful. Still, it's worth a shot. If nothing else, our suspect just made a critical mistake."

"How so?"

"They just made it personal." Jamison didn't wait for Lee to respond. "I'll be back as soon as I can."

The focused and angry expression told Lee that whoever did this was about to have a firestorm rain down upon them. She watched Jamison remove her cell phone from the holster as she walked toward the truck. The call was answered quickly.

"This is Ranger Kessler. I may have something. Meet me at the Harmon Medical Center. You'll find the morgue in the basement."

Lee could hear a female voice respond on the other end of the call, but Jamison flipped the cell closed without really listening. She jumped into the truck and roared off down Mafdet Lane a few moments later. Standing in the dark, Lee suddenly had the impression that she wasn't alone, that something malevolent crept upon her from the shadows. There wasn't really anything there, just a sense of paranoia caused by the recent delivery. She'd have felt better if Jamison just stashed the box in the pickup overnight and took it to the lab later.

Taking another look around the yard, Lee almost expected to see

Benny. The raccoon, admittedly not a pet, nevertheless served to help Lee feel centered. When she first became medicine woman to the Panthera the little guy had come out of nowhere when she needed him most. Jamison had explained he was her counter, an icon meant to balance her emotions. Indeed, he usually made an appearance when she least expected it but always when most essential. Apparently, this wasn't one of those times.

With a sigh and shake of her head, Lee started back to the house. Benny had been absent more and more over the summer and she hadn't seen him in weeks. Maybe he had a new family to care for and she was no longer the priority. Somehow she felt neglected.

Cleo followed her back into the house and Lee closed and locked the back door. She proceeded throughout the manor making sure she secured all doors and windows, both upstairs and down. A sensation of disjointed reality settled over her as she moved. Flashes from the previous year zipped through her head, not just the good times since meeting Jamison, but also the incident with a brutal, lion-shifting butcher that almost killed them all. Among the victims was Lee's former girlfriend, Debra Mason.

Lee had never seen Debra's body; the coroner wouldn't allow it, but her imagination had helpfully filled in the blanks. She still struggled with those reconstructed images a year after the fact. She hadn't been able to help Debra and thought she'd always carry the blame for Debra even being in the area. In the end, Lee could only attend the funeral and try to suppress tears she had no right to shed. Seeing Debra's mom and dad and the small gathering of New York's well-dressed upper elite grieve for the tragically short life made her feel like more of an outsider. She had returned to Harmon as quickly as she could, back to Jamison where she felt safe, but Lee would never be able to escape the remorse she bore.

Lee shook her head, forcing the unwanted images away.

"Sorry, girl, I didn't mean to zone out on you. Must be the...flowers...that pushed me over the edge." Lee stroked the dog's hard skull and smiled when Cleo contentedly closed her eyes. "Come on, I need to get cleaned up before Jami gets back."

Lee felt a little unsettled that she couldn't let go of the events from last year. She hadn't really seen much of the carnage, her only involvement being Debra and then later trying to save Jamison. That meant she couldn't have post-traumatic stress or anything. Right? Maybe it really was just that monstrous gift on the front porch that brought it all back in combination with the current case on which Jamison worked. Regardless, she determined to put it out of her head.

Gathering up clean clothes, Lee headed for the shower. She tried to focus on the here and now. Scrubbing under hot water, Lee considered what to make for dinner. She wasn't really hungry, but Jamison would need her strength and she wouldn't eat without Lee. Thoughts of her partner brought her mind back around full circle and again Lee remembered Debra's crushed red convertible.

Lee turned the heat up and scrubbed harder. She tried to think of nothing but the massive condensation ring that must be on the dining room table from her abandoned glass of iced tea.

Chapter Three

JAMISON LOOKED UP as the door to her office opened unexpectedly. She had a relaxed office policy, but knocking was still considered the polite thing. While she hadn't anticipated the door actually opening, Jamison had picked up on the sounds of another helping themselves to coffee and moving about the outer office for the last few minutes.

"Come on in."

Voice loaded with dry sarcasm, her tone had the desired effect. Ranger Thomas froze for an instant and a look of mortification ghosted across her face. The expression reminded Jamison of the rookie Brenda had been a year ago. It quickly vanished, leaving behind a haggard twenty-three-year-old with tired, bloodshot brown eyes. Her long mousy brown hair, usually shiny and neatly groomed, looked windblown with brittle wisps that escaped the clasp at nape of her neck.

"Sorry about that." Brenda rubbed her eyes and eased into the chair in front of the desk. She took a quick sip of lukewarm coffee from a paper cup. "I guess I'm too tired to think clearly. The Feds kept me out until two last night. What are you doing here anyway, Captain Kessler?"

"I work here, remember?"

"Yes, but you don't live here," Brenda bantered in return. "It's Saturday. Won't your partner worry?"

Jamison ignored the question. Lee wasn't happy to have her working today, but Jamison couldn't stay home and do nothing while a killer stalked her woods. "Brenda, you can call me by my first name, you know."

"One day, Chief." Brenda flashed a self-deprecating grin. "I was raised to show respect to my superiors, and that's hard to get over."

"Fine, I guess I can understand that, but at least don't call me chief."

Brenda drained her cup in one long swallow, giving Jamison the impression she was trying to cover her expression. Jamison wanted to think Brenda tried to hide another smile at her boss's reaction to the friendly moniker, but was more concerned with her use of the word *superior*. Did Brenda mean it in reference to someone she considered better than herself, or simply to point out a higher rank?

Or maybe Jamison was overthinking the situation and making too much of it. "I take it you all didn't have any luck last night?"

Brenda grunted and placed the empty container on the front of Jamison's desk. Her eyes focused on the wood grain, but there was no mistaking the tightness on her face or the frustration in her voice. "No.

We didn't find anything useful."

"You look all in. Why don't you go home and get some sleep?"

"I appreciate that, Chief, uh, Captain, but it's my normal shift. Don't worry, Bobby Adams is supposed to relieve me at three and then I'll head home. Speaking of being on duty, I should get back to work." Brenda stood up and grabbed her cup, leaving behind a slight smudge of humidity that slowly vanished. She ambled toward the exit and then turned back. "Have you heard anything new this morning?"

Jamison shook her head. "Not yet. I don't really expect to unless Hex and her people find something or another body turns up."

"Another body? That's kind of soon isn't it? I mean I thought our guy was on a two-week cycle."

"He is," Jamison confirmed. "Personally, I hope it stays that way and that we catch the killer before he strikes again. Unfortunately, we don't always get what we hope for and we don't really have enough information to be sure of anything."

"So at this point, we're just guessing."

Jamison nodded.

When she didn't reply further, Brenda shrugged. "Just don't spend all day here. It's not good to get too immersed."

"Thanks, I'll try to remember that and don't worry, Lee will be here to get me in a few hours."

"She has the truck?"

"Yeah, I guess the equipment she needed today wouldn't fit in the Mercedes."

"Gotcha. See you later, Chief."

After she was gone, Jamison realized she hadn't told Brenda about the delivery to her house yesterday or how the horrible gift might be tied to the case. She decided that was a good thing. Some details needed to be kept to as few people as possible. Besides, the flowers might not have anything to do with the killings. It was possible Lee had offended someone in her capacity as *Kadin*, although Jamison didn't seriously consider that possibility. She found it more likely that the message was intended for her, a warning to back off from the murder investigation. Despite any conflicting doubts, Jamison had no intention of dropping the case. If anything, that personal delivery to her home made her angry that the suspect had drawn Lee into the mix and made Jamison more determined than ever to find the guilty party.

Jamison stood up, getting ready to grab some keys and head off into the park. The cell phone vibrated against her hip just as Jamison reached for the lockbox. Glancing at the number, she frowned. Not Lee and not one she recognized. Jamison answered at the same time she removed the Range Rover's keys from the wall-mounted chest.

"Kessler."

"Good morning, Ranger Kessler. Detective Hex here. I hope I'm not disturbing you."

"Not likely. I'm at the office."

"Good, then now is a good time to tell you what we've found."

"Which is?" Hoping Hex was about to prove what a good decision she'd made by bringing in the U.S. Park Police, Jamison's heart beat a little faster.

"Absolutely nothing."

Jamison snarled quietly when she inadvertently slammed the lid on her thumb. "Well that's a big help, certainly worth a phone call at nine o'clock on a Saturday."

"I thought you said you were at work."

"So not the point, Detective."

She could have sworn Hex laughed. "All right, all right. I processed the flower box and didn't find any prints. No partials or smudges either. The lab is going to run it for any other trace that might lead back to your anonymous admirer but I seriously doubt they'll find anything. Nothing found at either crime scene leads anywhere either so unless we can track down a witness, we're out of luck."

None of this was a surprise. "Thanks for getting back to me so quickly. I'll call you if I find anything else."

"Hold on, Kessler. You're crazy if you think you're just going to blow me off. I assume you're not at the office filling out paperwork?"

Jamison rolled her eyes. "No, I'm getting ready to interview the campers near the latest dumpsite. Maybe they saw or heard something."

"Great idea, I'll be there in just a few minutes and go with you."

"I can hardly wait."

Hex didn't respond to the sarcasm. "My people are already talking with everyone living just outside the park near access road Forty. Has your M.E. identified the victim yet?"

Jamison felt relieved that none of those people Hex planned to speak with were Panthera. "Not that I know of, but Doctor Paul didn't get the body until late yesterday. As soon as she knows, I'll know."

The crunch of gravel told Jamison that Hex had arrived. She stepped onto the wooden porch and locked up while the detective approached.

"Could you be more cliché?" Jamison asked in greeting.

Hex grinned and glanced toward her rental car. "I couldn't resist."

Jamison dangled her car keys. "Let's take mine."

Four campsites and two hikers later they were no closer to finding the killer than before. No one had seen or heard anything they considered unusual. Jamison settled quietly into the Range Rover's driver's seat trying to figure out her next step. A cool breeze drifted through the cab when Hex opened the passenger door. Jamison pulled her coat shut but didn't speak.

"Feels like that cold front is here," Hex observed. "So now what?"

Jamison looked up slowly, lost in thought. She was impressed Hex didn't push, but gave her time to sift through possibilities. "We didn't find any tire tracks at the crime scene."

"Right, nor was there any mention of them in the report from the first victim."

"And the only tracks at Pauline Nielsen's campsite were from her own vehicle."

Frowning, Detective Hex said, "As much as I enjoy the back and forth, where are you going with this?"

"We believed both victims either trusted or knew their attacker because there weren't any defensive wounds but what if there's more to it than that? What if the killer snuck up on them from behind at their campsite?"

Hex considered the information briefly. "And then killed them somewhere else before getting rid of the body? Kessler, if that's true this is one strong son of a bitch. He'd have had to carry the Nielsen woman through the woods for what, two miles to the dumpsite? I'm sorry, no one is that strong."

"And you're thinking like a tourist." Jamison leaned across the seat and opened the glove box, unfazed when the lid dropped onto Hex's thigh. Rummaging inside, she pulled out a battered park map.

"What are you onto?"

Rather than answer, Jamison spread the map out between them. Her finger traced a few lines before she answered. "Here, look at this. Pauline Nielsen's campsite was here, near Deerlick Falls. If you take the park road to where we found her at Carry Falls Reservoir it's probably a mile or a mile and a half."

"I see where you're going." Hex's eyes glittered in excitement as she leaned over the map. "The woods are pretty heavy around the campground, but this looks like some sort of trail. Hiking?"

The trail Hex spoke of would only be a short distance through the trees. "Yes. The path is pretty rough for a regular vehicle, but any four-wheel drive could manage and it would cut the distance to a fraction."

Hex reached for her cell. "I'll have Detectives Seaver and Chase check the area, but Kessler, that's still more than a stone's throw over uneven terrain between the campground and the hiking trail."

Jamison's phone rang and she climbed out of the Range Rover so she wouldn't interfere with Hex's call to her people.

"Hi Jamison, it's Laura."

"Hey, how are you holding up?" She could hear the weariness in Laura's voice, but was much too far away to sense anything.

"Not well. I don't mind telling you, this has me baffled. Why here, Jami? Murders happen all the time in New York but this isn't a big city. Honestly, between what happened last year and now this, I have to admit relocation is starting to sound good."

Startled, Jamison didn't know what to say. "Tell me you're kidding. Where would you go?"

"There are other Panthera groups," Laura pointed out. "Maybe

Oregon could use a pathologist."

"Laura, you're one of my closest friends. I've known you my entire life. Please tell me you're not seriously considering leaving."

"Oh, I don't know. I'm just so frustrated. Promise you'll catch this bastard soon."

"I'll do my best but you're going to have to give me something, Laura. Have you found anything I can use?"

"No. There is no trace, prints or semen. There's no sign of sexual assault or any marks on the body other than the two transected arteries. Everything is identical to the first murder down to the shade of lipstick the killer applied postmortem. I'd be willing to speculate that it's from the same tube, but we can't know that without further testing. At least Detective Seaver was able to identify the second victim through phone records a few minutes ago."

Jamison absently noted Hex had exited the Range Rover and come around to stand beside her. "Who is she?"

"Lauren Reid, a thirty-two-year-old nurse from Stark. Seaver talked with her sister. Apparently Lauren was on her way to Lake Placid for a job interview. I wouldn't even know that much, but I overheard her telling Sheriff Macke."

Jamison shot a disapproving look at her companion. "I'm surprised she told her anything without running it by the boss first."

"Hey," Hex objected.

"You know how the sheriff is," Laura continued. "She hasn't left since we brought the body in. I think she even camped out in the hall overnight and she wasn't going to let Seaver get away with shutting her out."

"What's she going to do now?"

She listened while trying to ignore Detective Hex, who had moved well into her personal space and leaned close in an attempt to hear Laura. Being pressed up against a soft, attractive woman wasn't a hardship but Jamison had no romantic interest in Hex. She took a step back and bumped into the side of the vehicle. Undeterred, Hex moved close again and Jamison had nowhere to go. Fortunately, Laura finished her update and Jamison ended the call.

"Detective Hex, do you mind?"

"What? Oh, you think I'm coming on to you?" The disbelief in her tone stung Jamison's ego a little but she recovered quickly.

"No, I don't think that. I know you're just trying to listen in, but I don't appreciate having my personal space invaded. You're just going to have to trust that I'll share whatever I find out."

Hex took a deliberate step back, surprising Jamison when she blushed lightly. "You're right. Sorry, I guess I'm just used to being in charge and doling out the information."

"Let me guess, first in your class?"

"Classic overachieving only child," Hex confirmed. "Plus, you know as well as I do how hard it is to succeed in a male dominated career. I've had to work twice as hard and put in more time than anyone else just to get this far."

"I'm sure that's true, but I don't think you'd be leading this investigation if your superiors didn't have faith in your abilities."

Hex offered her an unguarded smile, the first authentic gesture Jamison noticed since the team's arrival. "We'll talk about who's really in charge later. Tell me what you found out."

"Lauren Reid, a thirty-two-year-old nurse. Apparently, she was only passing through. Sheriff Macke and Detective Seaver are running down her information now, the route she took, any enemies...you know the drill."

"What about the forensics?"

"Doctor Paul said there wasn't anything useful, not even sign of sexual assault."

Hex frowned and placed a foot on the front bumper. Her eyes rested on the ground, arms folded over her chest. She seemed tense, almost pensive.

"Maybe when we find the car we'll get lucky." Jamison felt like she was saying that a lot lately.

"That's just it," Hex huffed, dropping her foot to the ground and pacing a few steps away before turning back. "No one kills without leaving a trace, and why no assault? It's basic serial killer psychology. The kill, or at least the procedure used, is always a ritual and there is always a sexual component. Always."

"Our killer isn't a serial, at least not yet. He needs one more to earn that distinction. Still, you have a point. What if our suspect is impotent?"

"In that case the murder weapon would substitute. Our victims would have been stabbed, probably repeatedly."

"But they weren't. They were sliced across two major arteries to ensure bleed-out as quickly and painlessly as possible."

"Bingo. It doesn't make any sense."

"Well, one thing's for sure. We're not going to figure it out right now and we need a break. Maybe with some rest and fresh eyes we'll see something we're missing. Let's head back to the office."

After they were on the way back to the visitor's center, Jamison asked about Hex's call to Detective Seaver.

"She and Chase are going to check it out once she finishes with the sheriff. They'll get back to me as quickly as they can. How's your partner doing, by the way? I imagine she's pretty rattled after opening that box."

"Lee?" Jamison smiled, keeping her eyes on the road. "She was a little upset, but I think she's okay. She's tough, a real city girl. She only moved to the Adirondacks last year."

"I can see why she stayed. The scenery is amazing."

Jamison's eyebrow rose as she detected innuendo. She took Hex's comment as an opening to share details, but Jamison wasn't about to give a virtual stranger information about her private life. She had to remember this woman was a trained federal investigator. She needed her assistance to find a murderer, but Jamison's primary responsibility was to the living, specifically the Panthera. Regardless of what happened, she couldn't allow knowledge about a shape changing community to get out. Letting her guard down about private matters could lead down a road from which there was no return.

Deliberately adopting a playful tone, Jamison asked, "Why Detective Hex, are you flirting with me?"

Hex raised both hands and laughed. "No way, Kessler. I never mess with anything that's not mine and that goes double for women."

So who was the eye-candy Hex had hinted at a moment before? At least they wouldn't have to dance around the sexual orientation question. "Speaking of women, it looks like mine is already waiting for me."

Jamison pulled into the parking lot and stopped beside her Chevy Silverado. The bed was partially filled with photography equipment and she spotted Lee sitting on the front stoop to the building.

"Wow, I want one."

Jamison didn't detect any disrespect. The words were so quiet she doubted Hex knew she'd been overheard. Lee stood and waved, offering a bright smile and Jamison forgot about Hex. Jamison smiled back at her partner and started across the parking lot. Pine needles littered the old, cracked cement and the pungent smell wafted into the air as she crushed them underfoot.

"Have a good day?"

"Yes, thanks. I got some great shots using a remote camera and tripod. Thanks for loaning me the pickup. All that stuff wouldn't possibly have fit into the Mercedes."

"No problem. Lee, this is Detective Patricia Hex. She's with the U.S. Park Police and is helping us on this case."

Jamison heard another vehicle pulling into the lot. She recognized the engine's sound and didn't bother to look around. From the teasing glint in Lee's eyes, Jamison knew she was in for it later. For some reason, Ranger Thomas had developed a bit of a boss-crush on Jamison and Lee never missed an opportunity to kid her about it.

"I guess I should let you get to whatever remains of your day off," Hex said. "I think I'm going to track down Sheriff Macke and Detective Seaver, see if they need any help."

"It was very nice to meet you," Lee said.

Hex waved and strode across the parking lot toward the dark blue sedan. Leave it to a federal agent to pick out a car that screamed "government vehicle." She moved with purpose in her steps and Jamison thought she already had a plan of attack in mind. She found it heartening that regardless of any prior misgivings, Hex seemed open and willing to work with local law enforcement. Now if only Macke proved as receptive. Jamison knew firsthand that the sheriff could be rather hardheaded when the mood struck. After all, Sam hadn't warmed up to the Panthera since she found out about them, and that had been eight years ago.

Hex drove away and as Jamison turned back to her partner, she absently noticed that Ranger Thomas still hadn't exited the Jeep. She was probably filling out paperwork. Jamison turned to Lee and offered her another smile before leaning down to kiss her properly.

Chapter Four

STEPPING INTO THE knee-high brush, Lee selected a large tree and dodged behind it. This area was perfect for concealment. The canopy of branches and leaves overhead helped to cast more shadows that Lee happily took advantage of. She felt a little embarrassed and couldn't refrain from glancing around before pulling the shirt off. She stripped down, folded her clothes and left them tucked between the tree's exposed roots.

"You don't have to hide you know."

Lee started slightly when the girl spoke and squatted down farther without thinking. She forced herself to relax. They went through this every time their lessons took place in their more natural forms. "Sorry, Lindsay. I wasn't raised being a shape changer like you were. Some taboos are hard to overcome."

Stripping naked in front of a sixteen-year-old was definitely one of them.

"I understand, *Kadin*. When the elders named me to apprentice with you, Mother explained."

Her tone was so serious Lee found it amusing. She could picture Lindsay standing calmly on the trail already prepared to shift but patiently waiting for her mentor before she changed. Maybe Lindsay should be teaching her. Their people considered Lee a spiritual leader, just as her late aunt before her. Part of her newfound abilities included being able to see future events as they related directly to the Panthera. That gift wasn't always reliable, and Lee couldn't tap into it anytime she wanted. She doubted anyone ever had that much control, but she suspected it was harder for her since she hadn't even been aware of such powers a year ago.

Lindsay was another story. The girl had shown signs of exceptional insight since she learned to speak. Lee thought she would grow to become a strong medicine woman, and it fell to her to instruct Lindsay as much as she could. One day, the girl would replace Lee as the community's *Kadin*. These jaunts to the woods where they converted to pelt allowed them both to tap deeply into their animal psyche.

"What did she explain?"

"That you lived as a human and didn't know you could become something else. I'm sorry you had to go through that."

"Lindsay, it wasn't a hardship. A person can't miss something they don't know exists."

"I guess so, but would you miss it now if you had to go back?"

Lee didn't hesitate to respond. "There's no way I could ever go back. Finding out about the Panthera and that I am one is one of the best things that's ever happened to me. Why don't you go ahead? I'll be right out."

"Okay."

It wouldn't take Lindsay but a moment to transform into a jaguar adolescent, but Lee needed a minute. Unless it was a life or death situation, she couldn't change very fast. She closed her eyes and slowly the tension drained from her body. Lee stood, feeling the muscles in her thighs flex as she concentrated on the feel of crisp air against her skin. Nipples hardened in the cool breeze. Goosebumps broke out over her arms and a thin line of snow-white fur traced down between her breasts and over her abdomen. She felt the blood singing in her veins as endorphins surged. Bones lengthened, tendons slid over thickening muscle.

She relished every sensation as her body seemed to shrink in and simultaneously grow denser. Lee's chin shrank as her cheeks and nose rounded. She panted at the excruciating pleasure when her spine compacted and she dropped to her newly formed front paws, unable to remain standing on two legs. Slightly darker rosettes decorated her white pelt and she sank her claws into the damp earth. The life of the forest suddenly rushed in and she felt more aware of the world around her, more *there* than she ever felt as a woman. She sensed the rabbit hiding in the den beneath the great tree where she had shed her human trappings, heard its heart beat in terror from the predator's presence.

Lee flung her head back and roared from the simple joy of being alive and then turned toward the lanky cub. While she was more in tune with the environment, Lee didn't lose all sense of upper reasoning when she shifted. Sharing her soul with the jaguar inside allowed her to draw perspective and she realized that being naked in front of Lindsay before the change had no significance. The Panthera were a part of nature and each of them were family. There was no shame. She knew this each time she assumed pelt form, but somehow she always forgot that truth when she became human again.

Come.

Loping off the trail and into the wilderness, Lee heard Lindsay crash along behind her. The cub was young and foolish. She would draw attention to herself by not minding her surroundings. Hunters stalked the Adirondacks and would happily take a trophy with Lindsay's gold and black pelt. If shot and killed as a feline, her body would retain that form. Today Lee would teach the youngster the art of stealth. She had barely finished the thought when the cub swatted at Lee's swishing tail. Then Lindsay leapt playfully onto her back. Lindsay's jaws wrapped around the back of her neck and teeth bit into her flesh, though not hard. Lee easily tossed the cub off and cuffed her across the head.

Play later. Learn now.

Lindsay's eyes danced merrily, but she dipped her head in

acknowledgment. Communicating telepathically allowed the transmission of ideas more than words, but Lee felt sure that the girl took her lessons seriously. An idea occurred to her and Lee struck off through the woods headed for the lake. People were always fishing from the banks and Lee could show the cub how to conceal herself, to hide in plain sight. It could be a dangerous exercise if anyone spotted them, but they were Panthera and would not shy away from a task because of fear. Without the incentive of a real situation, Lindsay would not be properly motivated. Lee considered the best way to implement her plan and then set about teaching the young cub her next lesson.

"WHAT ARE YOUR plans for the day?"

Lee nodded toward the stuffed manila envelope sitting on the edge of the dining room table. "I need to run into Harmon and mail that to Jasmine."

"Are those the pictures you showed me last night?"

They sat sipping coffee in preparation of starting the day. Sunlight streamed through the window, casting a warm glow throughout the room. There wasn't a cloud in the sky and Lee thought it was going to be a gorgeous day. It was just too bad she couldn't spend the time with Jamison. Nothing out of the ordinary had occurred in the last week, but with every day that passed Lee could feel her partner's tension level elevate as though she awaited an emotional or physical blow. Lee felt like she was walking on eggshells lately with Jamison and longed for some time to reconnect. It wasn't that Jamison was cold, just distant.

"Yes, I want to send them overnight. Plus I want to add delivery confirmation."

"Smart." Jamison didn't really sound all that enthusiastic.

"Lindsay did really well yesterday. I'm always so impressed with how well she catches onto things. It's almost intuitive with her." When Jamison didn't respond, Lee added. "We practiced the art of concealment near Meacham Lake but things really got interesting when she pounced in among a group of campers and ate one of their kids."

"Hmm."

"Then I shaved her head before sending her home."

"That's nice."

"Jamison, you're not listening to me." Lee hesitated briefly, not wanting to push. Finally, she asked, "Jami, are you all right?"

Jamison blinked and looked up from the spot on the table she'd been staring at for the last five minutes. "Of course, why wouldn't I be?"

"It's just that with all that's happened lately, I haven't seen a lot of you. Then, when we do spend time together, it doesn't feel like you're really there."

"I guess I just have a lot on my mind."

"Have you been able to find anything that might help you find whoever killed those women?"

Jamison frowned and Lee realized how close to the surface her emotions were. She could feel the anger rising up in Jamison like a storm surge. "Don't you think I'd have told you if we had? I'm sorry if I haven't been spending enough time with you, but I thought you'd understand that some things take priority."

"That wasn't what I meant." Stung by the unexpected attack, Lee defended herself. "I'm just worried about you. I wish there was something I could do to help."

Jamison started to speak and then closed her mouth. She glanced down into her cooling coffee and took a moment before she met Lee's gaze. Lee still sensed the barely contained gall, but at least Jamison tried to contain her temper. "I know. Trust me, I wish you could. Unfortunately, it doesn't seem like anyone can. Hex and her crew are less than useful and Macke didn't like any of the Panthera before all of this started. The people who are supposed to be solving this thing can hardly stand to be in the same room."

Lee clasped Jamison's wrist and squeezed reassuringly. She couldn't take her hand since Jamison clutched the mug so tightly. "And it doesn't help that you're coming up on the two week mark and there could be another victim any day."

"Exactly." Jamison took a deep breath and pulled away from Lee's grasp. "So forgive me if I'm not the best company."

The comment hurt and Lee wasn't the type to sit idly by while someone deliberately attempted to bruise her feelings. Slowly she stood and looked down at her partner.

"I love you, Jamison, and I'm here for you. But you have no right to speak to me that way. When you can be civil again, let me know."

Leaning across the table, Lee snatched up the envelope and stalked out of the room. She left the house, refraining from slamming the door, unaccountably even more pissed that Jamison didn't make an effort to stop her.

Lee stomped across the yard wondering where Cleo had gotten off to. Had even the dog abandoned her? She decided she didn't care and strode to her gold Mercedes SLK. She lowered the convertible top and roared away from Mafdet Manor headed down Blue Mountain Road. With the wind blowing her blonde hair back from her face, Lee started to relax and consider that maybe she'd overreacted. Jamison had a right to be distracted, all things considered. Lee took a deep breath and decided she would apologize tonight at dinner.

Trying to get her mind off the disagreement with Jamison, Lee thought again about Lindsay. She really had caught on to what Lee tried to get across with their exercise in cover and concealment. In her mind, Lee could still see the tawny cat stretched out so low to the ground that she was almost completely hidden in the high grass near the lake. At one point Lee grew concerned that someone would spot Lindsay because she had moved to within twenty feet of the people fishing from the pier. Lee had remained watching from the shadows of the tree line, aware that her white coat would stand out like a searchlight at midnight. It was only at her mental insistence that Lindsay returned to her side. Lee felt the girl's desire to close the distance to the tourists even more than she had, but that was pushing things too far. There was a difference between teaching a lesson and tinkering with folly. One moment of panic from a frightened park visitor could bring down devastating repercussion for all of the Panthera.

Lee frowned, thinking that her next session with the gifted young apprentice should entail the true definition of discretion. She still needed to introduce Lindsay to Benny, too. Lindsay understood that an icon provided balance for a *Kadin*, an emotional tether when visions became stormy. The raccoon was Lee's icon and provided a balm when her jaguar threatened to react physically to a situation rather than consider the consequences. Lindsay would someday have to find her own counterpart.

Spotting the road sign that announced the Harmon city limit, Lee concentrated on her driving. She rounded the bend on the roadway and began to slow for the red streetlight. The brakes felt a little mushy and she made a mental note to have the vehicle serviced. She was about due for an oil change anyway. Lee made the planned stop at the post office and then decided to stop by Andy's Café for another coffee before heading home.

The aroma of fresh coffee, homemade pastries and bacon made her mouth water before she ever stepped inside. Lee noticed the café's namesake standing behind the counter and sauntered over with a smile. Flour smudged one chubby cheek and a few wisps of hair had escaped from Andy's ponytail, but her friendly grin was firmly in place. Andy wiped her hands on the apron around her waist before offering one to Lee over the top of the counter.

"Lee, what brings you around so early in the morning? I figured you'd be off somewhere in the forest with a camera and your canine companion. How is the old girl, anyway?"

"Old is right," Lee bantered back. "It's all I can do to talk her into a long walk these days."

Andy's grin faded and a look of concern darkened her brown eyes. "Is she sick or something?"

"Oh no, just getting up there. She's nine this year. Sometimes I still can't believe she's that old. I've had Cleo since she was a little thing."

"I've got just the thing to perk her right up."

Without awaiting a response, Andy turned and headed into the kitchen. She returned less than a minute later with a bulging brown paper bag.

"Andy, you're going to make her fat." Lee reached for the parcel even as she protested. The gift was hardly unusual and fast becoming a ritual. Almost every time Lee stopped in, Andy sent something home for the beagle.

"Nonsense, what canine doesn't like a good bone now and then? Now, what can I get for you?"

"The biggest mocha you have."

"Ah, one of *those* mornings. I'll fix you right up."

Lee checked out the display cases while Andy brewed her drink. They appeared recently stocked and her empty stomach made itself known. She couldn't decide between fresh bear claws, apple fritters, chocolate caramel cheesecake with walnuts, or tiramisu. There were also éclairs, assorted cookies and even caramel apples in deference to the season, but Lee was more interested in something she could eat in the car without making too much of a mess.

"Hey, Andy, how about one of those apple fritters and a slice of caramel cheesecake to go?"

"Got a sweet tooth?" Andy asked, setting the paper coffee cup on the counter.

"I missed breakfast." The fritter was for her, but Lee thought the cheesecake might serve as an apology to Jamison for their earlier squabble.

Andy slipped on a pair of sterile gloves and reached into the backside of the display case. Lee noticed that she selected the largest of the fritters and an ample slice of the cheesecake. While she packaged up the items, Andy said, "Dinah has a sweet tooth, too. A little unusual for our folk, if you know what I mean. Our tastes tend to lean toward the savory."

Lee did know what she meant and it concerned her that Andy spoke about the Panthera so casually. She glanced around and realized there wasn't anyone close enough to overhear. She relaxed marginally. "It must be a Kessler family trait. I'm not much on sweets myself, but I get a craving sometimes. However Jamison, just like her sister, loves sweets. Speaking of your lovely partner and my sister-in-law, where is Dinah today?"

Andy shrugged and Lee saw lines of tension around her mouth for the first time since walking into the café. "Flying some newlyweds around the area in that death machine she calls a helicopter. I guess they thought it would be romantic or something."

"Right, well, a girl has to earn a living." Lee didn't really know what else to say and felt somewhat awkward. She'd gotten to know Andy since moving to Harmon, especially since the woman dated Jamison's sister, but she wasn't comfortable discussing personal matters in a crowded restaurant.

Lee paid Andy and left the café, trying not to mention anything else that might be delicate. She placed Jamison's cheesecake carefully onto the passenger seat, set the coffee in the cup holder and pulled the fritter halfway out of the paper bag before starting the car. Using the sack as a napkin, Lee gripped the fritter and took a healthy bite before backing out of the parking space.

The sugar kick was just the thing she needed. Lee polished off the whole pastry before turning from Main Street onto Blue Mountain Road headed toward the house. She chased the sugar bomb with a healthy sip of the mocha and the chocolate added to her rush. For the first time all morning, she forgot about the cross words with Jamison and enjoyed the wind in her hair. The drive back to Mafdet would only take about ten minutes.

Maybe she'd take Cleo over to St. Regis Mountain for the morning. The beagle loved to play in the small creek up there. Cleo still wasn't comfortable with Lee's alter ego and they were working on the situation. It made sense the dog wouldn't be completely at ease around a jungle cat, but the beast was part of Lee now and it was important to her that Cleo make peace with that fact. The quiet of St. Regis would allow her to expose the beagle to her cat again.

Lee noticed a sign indicating a sharp curve ahead and tapped the brakes. The Mercedes did not respond. Lee tried again and the brake pedal sank to the floor. The car picked up speed as she headed downhill and into the turn. Her heart hammered against her ribs. Lee gripped the steering wheel with both hands and pressed the pedal against the floorboard as hard as she could with her Panthera enhanced strength. It was a waste of time. She sailed into the turn at full speed. The car tipped onto the two outside tires and barely managed to retain traction. Lee couldn't help notice the sharp drop-offs on each side of the elevated pavement.

An alternating turn around the next bend caused the vehicle to bounce down hard onto all four tires as she negotiated the curve. She managed to stay square on the roadway though she drifted onto the oncoming lane. A lone vehicle was headed straight at her and she could hear the other driver's horn blaring a quarter of a mile away. Lee wrestled with the wheel and navigated back into the proper lane with only inches to spare between herself and the other car. As she passed the frightened driver, Lee had the impression of a single female occupant whose mouth hung open in astonishment.

The fun wasn't over yet. Blue Mountain Road zigzagged at this stretch like a snake and there were several more curves before it straightened out again. Lee wanted to believe that the Mercedes could handle the turns even without brakes, but combined with her speed it simply wasn't so. She noted the caution sign suggesting twenty-five miles per hour at the next bend and glanced instinctively at the speedometer. A fatalistic sense of dread swept over her when she saw the vehicle's current velocity. Somehow, the Mercedes had crept up to sixty-two.

Lee hit the curve, gritted her teeth and tried to ride out the storm.

The Mercedes skittered a little as it slid off the shoulder and slammed into the guardrail. Metal shrieked, the car shuddered and she felt it begin to slow. She shot past the barrier and the vehicle left the roadway entirely. Here, the shoulder fell sharply away, becoming a drop of about fifteen feet. Strapped in by the seatbelt, Lee sailed over the ditch and watched as the front of the car dipped toward the ground. She heard the crash as the bumper impacted granite and turf, felt the bridge of her nose strike the steering wheel even as the airbag exploded and punched her in the face. The car flipped forward into the air, but she couldn't see anything.

Suddenly, the Mercedes slammed into an immovable object and Lee felt her knees hit the dash. Motion ceased and Lee rejoiced that she wasn't crushed under the weight of the car. For only a second, she smelled spilled mocha. Then something hard struck the back of her head and everything went dark.

Chapter Five

"CAPTAIN KESSLER, YOU have a call on line one."

Jamison stifled her first response, which was to snap at her secretary for interfering with her brooding session. She wasn't in the mood to be polite right now. All she'd thought of the last two hours was how she'd allowed Lee to leave the house with anger simmering between them. To make matters worse, Hex hadn't contacted her for two days and Macke seemed to have fallen into a black hole. Every time Jamison called the sheriff's office, the dispatcher told her Macke was in the field. All in all, it was shaping up to be a hell of a day.

"Can't you handle whatever it is, Jeanie?" Jamison asked through the tenuous connection of a speaker phone.

"I don't think so. She says her name is Lindsay Drake and it's about Lee."

The hair stood up on the back of her neck and Jamison dropped her feet to the floor from where they rested on her desk. She reached for the handset. "Thanks, Jeanie, I've got it." Jamison pressed the flashing button and connected the call. "Lindsay, this is Captain Kessler. What's wrong?"

Lindsay stammered a little. "M...maybe nothing, ma'am, but I had a bad dream about the *Kadin*. Only I don't think it was a dream, you know?"

Perplexed, Jamison worked through the ramifications. Lindsay shared a spiritual connection with Lee and they spent a lot of time together. On top of that, Lindsay had experienced visions on and off since she was very young. Jamison had to trust that she had reason to worry.

"Exactly what did you see?"

"I just remember that she was driving her gold car and she had an accident."

Jamison felt the air whoosh out of her lungs. She took a deep breath and asked, "How bad of an accident? Was it a tire blowout or did she break down somewhere?"

"No, not like that." Lindsay's voice grew more confident as they spoke and Jamison could hear her concern. "She crashed."

"Lindsay, this is important." Jamison swallowed against a suddenly dry throat. "Do you know when or if the accident has happened yet? Was it day or night in your dream?"

"Geez, Captain Kessler, I'm not a crystal ball. But I can tell you it was daytime and it felt like it already happened. I tried to call her, but it keeps going to voicemail."

Jamison was already out of her chair and reaching for the Range

Rover's keys. Lee only shut off the phone when actually on a shoot. There was nothing like that planned for the day and Lee would have answered Lindsay's call. She wasn't the type to ignore someone to whom she had a responsibility.

"Can you tell me anything that might pinpoint where she is?"

"No, I just kept seeing one of those yellow road signs shaped like a triangle. It said twenty-five, like a speed limit for one of the curves around here."

Jamison's eyes closed briefly. Harmon sat amidst the Adirondack Mountains and there were numerous winding roads with speed limit cautions. If it was anyone but her partner concerned, Jamison wouldn't know where to start. Fortunately, that wasn't the case. She easily pictured the spot Lindsay spoke of because she knew Lee's plans for the day included a run into the post office. The area Lindsay mentioned was on the return trip from Harmon to Mafdet, less than four miles from the house.

"I'm on my way to check on her now, Lindsay. You did the right thing in calling me."

Jamison ended the call and zipped out of the office, aware of Jeanie's curious expression but too worried to stop and explain. She drove recklessly, far beyond the speed limit and way past caring about such mundane things as breaking human laws. Her mate was threatened and that was all that mattered. Normally a fifteen minute drive from the park office, Jamison closed in on the area inside of eight. One look at the black and white patrol units blocking traffic from both sides told her it was more than just a fender bender. An ambulance had parked as far as possible onto the shoulder, but the driver's side still occupied part of the highway. No one was in the vehicle that Jamison could see.

"Oh Great Mother, please."

Grateful that the deputies had stopped the traffic, Jamison pulled into the empty oncoming lane and gunned the engine. She drove onto the miniscule shoulder beside a crumpled guardrail, shoved the vehicle into park and leapt out. Leaving the door open, Jamison plunged over the side of the roadway and down the slope toward Lee's ruined Mercedes. The front of the vehicle had folded back in on itself and rested against the trunk of a massive tree. There was no part of the car that remained dent-free. It didn't take a mechanic to see that the vehicle was totaled.

The convertible top was down and Sheriff Macke and two other uniformed officers surrounded the car and seemed to be trying to get someone out. EMS was on scene, a man and a woman, lending their efforts. Jamison spotted a large red trauma kit resting on the grass near the crash site.

She sprinted up the other side of the ditch and over to where she assumed Lee was pinned inside the car. An officer looked up, saw

Jamison and spoke a few words to Macke. Macke glanced over her shoulder, met her eye and took a step toward her.

"Slow down, Kessler. Ms. Grayson is unconscious, but alive. A passing motorist saw the whole thing and called nine-one-one."

"We have to get her out."

"What do you think we're trying to do? The seatbelt's stuck."

Jamison ignored her aggravated tone and resisted the impulse to rip the offending restraint from her lover. Lee's head rested against the door. Blood coated her face and soaked into her shirt. Her nose sat off center, clearly broken, and there was a laceration across the bridge of it. Her cheeks and the area under her eyes were already starting to blacken. Jamison's fingers trembled when she reached out to stroke Lee's face.

"Oh honey, I'm so sorry," she said quietly.

"Here," Sheriff Macke said. "Try this."

She handed a folding pocketknife over Jamison's shoulder. Though the blade proved quite sharp, Jamison still had to saw through the thick strap. When it abruptly let go, Jamison passed the knife back to Macke and started to lean inside the vehicle to lift Lee over the door. One of the EMS technicians stopped her.

"Ma'am, don't. She might have internal injuries. We need to get a c-collar on her and try to prevent further damage. Please, step back and allow us to do our jobs."

Jamison struggled against the urge to lash out. Her beast insisted that she chase all of these strangers away from her mate and take Lee somewhere safe, even if it required slaughtering a half dozen people. Jamison felt a rumble start deep in her chest, too low a decibel for humans to hear.

A strong hand clamped on her shoulder and sharply pulled Jamison around. Sheriff Macke grabbed her by the upper arms and shook her, hard. "Stop it." Her voice was low and harsh, directly in Jamison's ear as Sam pulled her close. "Get yourself under control before you do something you'll regret."

The appeal to her higher reasoning worked, for the most part. Jamison clenched her teeth and beat back the desire to shift. Her teeth felt longer and her vision had sharpened considerably. She closed her eyes to hide the partial change and concentrated on drawing deep, even breaths. After a few beats, she stepped away from Macke and nodded once.

"I'm good. Thanks." Her voice sounded rough, but otherwise Jamison was in control. She could hear Lee's strong heartbeat and steady breathing.

By the time she turned back, the EMTs had snapped a cervical collar around Lee's neck for support. They lifted her gently out of the vehicle, over the door and straight onto a backboard in case of spinal injury. After strapping her down, the female technician started an I.V.

Her partner approached Jamison to ask for Lee's age and any known medical issues and then returned to Lee's side.

Working quickly and efficiently, the two stabilized Lee for transport to Harmon Medical Center. Once they had Lee secured onto the board, Jamison announced that she would ride with Lee in the ambulance. This time it was the female technician, Amy according to her nametag, who contradicted her.

"I'm sorry ma'am but there's no room for a passenger. We could use some help getting our patient to the blacktop though."

"Lee, her name is Lee."

Amy raised an eyebrow in response and Jamison grunted in irritation. Did she intimidate no one? Pushing aside the exasperation, Jamison acknowledged that the ambulance attendant was right. Regardless of her personal protective feelings, Lee was the priority and she refused to become an impediment to the trauma team.

The terrain prevented them from wheeling Lee upon a gurney to the pavement. "We'll have to carry her on the backboard," Jamison announced. "Everyone grab a side."

Jamison took a front corner handle while Amy took the other side. The other EMT took the rear along with one of Macke's officers. The remaining deputy took the lead carrying the trauma kit. Sheriff Macke walked beside Jamison, ostensibly ready to jump in if necessary. After a bit of struggle and all hands working together, they lifted Lee across the ravine and up the incline. With Lee finally on the gurney, they loaded her into the ambulance. It dismayed Jamison that she had yet to regain consciousness and her chest hurt when the doors slammed between them.

"You're in no condition to drive," Sheriff Macke said. "I'll take you over to the hospital and have a uniform bring your car."

"I told you I'm fine."

"No, you're not. We need to talk anyway." Macke turned to her crew of deputies, forestalling any reply Jamison would make. "Let that traffic through. Gomez, I need you to drive the Park Services vehicle over to the hospital and leave it in the parking lot. Give the key to the charge nurse."

"On it, Sheriff." Gomez pegged another deputy to follow in a cruiser so he'd have a ride back to the office.

Macke gave further instructions for someone to call a tow truck. Jamison chafed to get moving and started for the sheriff's car, hoping that her impatience would communicate itself. As they drove away from the scene Jamison forgot about Macke's announcement that they needed to talk. She was more concerned with Lee.

"The Mercedes will be towed to Wally Hunter's garage."

"Sheriff, the last thing I'm worried about is the insurance company. I don't think filing a claim is all that important at the moment."

Sam's irritation was clear in the glance she leveled at Jamison. "I'm also posting a couple of guards on it, just in case."

Jamison's teeth clenched together to prevent her gasp of surprise. "You think this is related to our case?"

"I think this is related to that little delivery your partner received last week."

"Hex had no right to tell you about that," Jamison began.

"You're right. She didn't," Macke snapped. "You should have told me. We had an agreement that we would work together and share any pertinent information."

"How could I possibly know if that was related? And you're leaping to conclusions, don't you think?" Jamison didn't really believe that. Now that Sheriff Macke had pointed it out, the car wreck did seem a little too concomitant. The floral delivery last week presented a clear threat, they just hadn't known toward whom. On the heels of Lee's accident that answer now seemed evident.

"Maybe, but I don't believe in coincidence."

Jamison thought quietly about everything that had been going on for the last month. There were many unexplained happenings, but she found it hard to fathom it was all interconnected. "You realize this might have nothing to do with the killings. We might actually have two separate crimes in progress."

"What, you think your girlfriend has a stalker?"

"It's possible. Think about it. Lee is a well-known nature photographer for magazines and documentaries. She even sells her prints at galleries. She's been all over the world. Isn't it within the realm of possibility that someone, completely separate from the murders, has fixated on her?"

With that question to chew on, the two rode the rest of the way in silence. Jamison watched the back of the ambulance, feeling a small measure of her tension drain when the vehicle pulled into the hospital's emergency entrance. Triage nurses and orderlies already waited for the technicians to unload their patient. The sheriff pulled into the lot and as soon as Macke slowed enough, Jamison opened the car door.

"Hey, wait a minute!"

Macke slammed on the brakes and Jamison struggled with the sudden shift in momentum before bailing out of the car. She had the courtesy to push the door closed behind her and then jogged across the parking lot toward the ambulance. Jamison was there before the gurney wheels locked into place.

"Is she awake yet?"

"Ma'am, you need to step back and let us do our jobs." The nurse stood a full head shorter than Jamison but stepped in front of her without hesitation.

Each time Jamison tried to go around her, the woman blocked her path. "Let me through."

The nurse let her by only when the team of emergency personnel pushed Lee into the hospital entrance. Jamison pursued, her eyes pinned on Lee's pale face. She had almost reached her side when the gurney passed through a doorway and another body moved into her path. Everyone seemed intent on keeping her from her mate's side and this was the last straw.

"Get out of the way!" Jamison grabbed hold of the white-coated figure, intending to push them aside, but had little luck against the other person's strength.

"Jamison Marie Kessler, stop it this instant."

She looked up into a familiar face. Jamison hadn't considered that she would run into her mother here, but Darlene Kessler was Harmon Medical Center's chief surgeon. "I need to see her."

"Not right now," Darlene stated succinctly. "She'll need full body x-rays and a CAT scan for starters and you cannot be in there for that. You'll just be in the way. We also need to determine if she has any internal injuries. I'm sorry, honey, but you'll have to wait until we know more."

"Mom, we...we had an argument this morning." Jamison felt tears in her eyes. "It was stupid, over nothing and I never had the chance to say I'm sorry."

Darlene took her hand and squeezed gently. "You'll tell her later. You just have to have patience and let us help her. Jamison, you know better than anyone how resilient our people are, but that's going to do her little good if you prevent us from treating some major injury because we're too busy trying to restrain you. Please, let us do what we do best."

Jamison felt miserable but nodded her understanding. She could only stand there helplessly as her mother entered the triage area and the double doors swung closed.

"There you are. What the hell was that? Are you trying to join Ms. Grayson in your own semi-private room? You could have gotten yourself killed jumping out of the car like that."

Jamison's attention swiveled to the sheriff and she noticed Macke clipping her cell phone to her belt. Rather than respond to the comments she asked, "Who were you talking to?"

"Hex. She's going to have someone check out the car to make sure it wasn't tampered with."

"I'm glad someone can get hold of her. I haven't heard from Hex in days." Jamison realized she sounded petty but couldn't seem to stop.

"It's called investigating a homicide. You might have heard of it. I'm sure you'll hear from her—*we'll* hear from her—if she finds anything pertinent."

"You have a lot of faith in someone you've never met before, Sheriff."

Sam shrugged. "I don't know about faith, but I do get the feeling that Hex is a professional and that she just might be good at her work."

"That's all well and good but we're running out of time. Her professionalism isn't going to do us a lot of good when we have another body on our hands."

"And what have you been doing all this time, Kessler?" Macke asked, her tone suddenly angry. "I don't see you finding any suspects, or is that what you brought the Park Police in for? So they could do your job for you?"

"Don't you dare turn this around on me. I've been working almost twenty-four hours a day since this whole nightmare began. Without any forensic evidence to go on—"

Macke held up her hands in surrender. "Yeah, yeah. Okay. Look, this is no one's fault. We're all frustrated and this accident with your girlfriend doesn't help matters any."

"If it is an accident," Jamison muttered.

"Exactly. Look, I know you're needed here right now. Why don't Hex and I check things out with the car and take a look around the accident site? I'll let you know if I find anything."

Curious about why Sam was in such a hurry to get out of the hospital Jamison asked, "You're not going to wait to see how Lee is?"

Macke rubbed a hand across the back of her neck, looking extremely uncomfortable. Reluctantly, she admitted, "I hate hospitals, especially this one. I'll feel better if I'm doing something proactive, but keep me informed. All right?"

"I will, and Sam? Thanks for looking into this for us. I don't really believe it was anything but a senseless accident, but I'll feel better knowing for sure."

Macke smiled and Jamison realized it was the first time she could remember her doing so in all the time she'd known her. "I think that's the first time you've ever called me Sam."

The sheriff coasted away and Jamison was alone. She had forgotten that Sheriff Macke's partner died in this hospital a few years ago. Cancer: a long, debilitating ravishment of the body. Jamison didn't know if it was worse to lose someone you loved suddenly or to watch as the person who held your soul slowly waste away before your eyes. It took real courage to put a smile on every day and pretend everything was all right when you knew that it really wasn't. Her respect for Sam Macke went up another notch.

Jamison prayed they wouldn't find anything wrong with the Mercedes. She wanted to think Lee was safe, that no one wanted to harm her partner. In fact, Jamison couldn't think of anyone with a motive. Lee had lived in Harmon for over a year and got along great with everyone. If someone was after her, it had to be related to her past. But who would wait this long to try and settle a score?

With no answers in sight, Jamison went in search of a coffee machine. It would probably be a long time before she heard anything about Lee's condition. Jamison spent the better part of two hours pacing the hospital corridors and thumbing through out of date magazines in the waiting room. Jeanie called once to find out what had sent her boss hustling out of the office. Other than the one phone call, Jamison had nothing to do but sit and fret.

The usual bustle of a busy hospital continued on around her. Orderlies, nurses and other hospital personnel moved around her without seeming to notice she was even there. Jamison began to think everyone, including her mother, had forgotten that she awaited information concerning her partner. Finally, she couldn't take it anymore. Jamison pushed out of the hard plastic chair and headed for the nurse's station.

"Excuse me." She spoke to the small brunette nurse behind the counter. The young woman turned toward her, but Jamison didn't have the opportunity to ask about Lee.

"Jamison."

She turned to see that her mother had come up soundlessly behind her. Darlene appeared exhausted and her expression hinted at suppressed strain. Jamison instantly assumed the worst. She felt the blood drain from her face.

"Mom, is she...?"

Darlene held up a hand to stop Jamison before she panicked completely. "She'll be fine." She glanced around the area and her gaze stopped on the nurse with whom Jamison had almost spoken. "Walk with me."

She led the way to her office without giving Jamison the opportunity to refuse. Her behavior had Jamison concerned but she followed without argument. That all changed as soon as Darlene closed the door and shut out any potential prying eyes or eavesdroppers.

"Spill it. I assume you're being so cryptic because Lee's condition is directly related to her Panthera abilities."

Darlene settled behind her desk and raised her eyebrow suggestively until Jamison huffed and sat in the chair placed in front of the desk. Being patient wasn't high on her list of priorities.

"Of course the two are related. You can't exactly separate her jaguar nature. You need to know that Lee will be fine in a day or two. That wouldn't be the case if she were fully human. If she wasn't one of us, she'd likely be dead."

Jamison swallowed hard and nodded.

"She took some pretty good knocks on the noggin and has a mild concussion. Something struck her at the base of the skull during the crash, probably a tree branch, and it looks like she smacked face first into the steering wheel before the airbags deployed."

"It looked like her nose was broken."

"It was," Darlene confirmed. "I reset her nose and stitched up the laceration. The sutures will need to come out next week. We didn't find any internal injuries or broken bones, thankfully. It's pretty amazing, even for our kind, that things weren't worse."

"The top was down on Lee's convertible, but she had her seatbelt on. I had to cut it off with a knife because it was jammed. If she hadn't been wearing it, Lee would have been thrown from the car. She might have died."

"Or she might have shifted when thrown and been able to walk away without any repercussions."

Jamison shook her head. "Maybe, but I'm not sure she can change that fast yet. It's not instinctive for her. Still, as much as I don't like her being hurt it's probably better that it worked out this way."

"Ah, now you're thinking like an elder."

Darlene smiled, clearly pleased, but Jamison grimaced in response. Lee was more important to her than anything or anyone and she didn't like that her mother, of all people, assumed Jamison placed the Panthera first. "I'm just being logical. Lee was lucky that she wasn't more badly hurt but if she'd escaped that crash unscathed there would be a lot of uncomfortable questions."

"You're thinking of the Park Police people that are here to help you solve those murders."

"Precisely. Hex and her team are pretty sharp."

"Do you think they pose a threat to us?"

Jamison felt her blood run cold. "No, and I don't want you assigning some hunter to follow her around. If she detected anything like that, you'd be telling her that there was something more in Harmon to investigate besides the killings."

"You're never going to let me live that down, are you?"

"What, that you had Aaron Dalton interfere with my investigation last year and almost got Lee killed?"

"It wasn't like that, Jamison."

"It was exactly like that, *Caber*," Jamison asserted angrily, deliberately calling her mother by her title as leader of the Panthera Council of Elders. "Well, I'm an elder now and I'm telling you that you will not take action against Hex."

Darlene stood up so fast that her chair rolled backward and struck the wall with a bang. "You forget your place, Jamison. You may be my daughter, but you are a junior council member and have no right to give orders."

"I don't intend to, but I know how human law enforcement officers operate and I'm telling you that it would be a big mistake. Of course, if you want to take the risk of letting Hex find out about us and reveal that information to the world at large, that's your decision."

Darlene scooted out from behind her desk and strode past Jamison, pacing across her office. In aggravation, she ran a hand through her thick dark hair. When she turned back, she had her emotions firmly under control. "Fine, for now. But if I think for one minute that Detective Hex suspects anything about our people's abilities, I will have her followed."

"And eliminated?"

Rather than answer the question, Darlene said, "Would you like to see if Lee's awake or do you want to continue to argue?"

The change in topic told Jamison all she needed to know. As leader of the Harmon Panthera, Darlene Kessler would do whatever it took to protect her community. Jamison wasn't quite as ruthless. She didn't condone the killing of an innocent just to protect their secret and knew that was exactly why she would never be *Caber*. The Panthera leader had to be more in touch with their animal instinct, attuned to and prepared to annihilate any threat. Revealing their presence to the world at large was a serious danger. Humans would exterminate anything they perceived as different and shape changers were definitely that. Jamison could see how the death of one person to protect an entire culture would be acceptable but she could never condone it. She couldn't argue against the possibility, but she could try to ensure that it never became necessary.

"Let's go see my girlfriend."

Jamison's cell phone rang as they left her mother's office. She recognized Sheriff Macke's number on the display. "Kessler."

"This is Macke. I'm at the garage."

"I take it the news isn't good?"

"You could say that. Detective Chase brought in a third party to check over the Mercedes and he's found something. The brake line on Ms. Grayson's car was cut."

Jamison stopped. "Are you sure?"

"Very. I don't know if your theory about a stalker is on the mark or if it's related to the other case, but the crash was no accident."

Chapter Six

SHERIFF MACKE CLOSED her phone and slipped it into the holster, watching Hex the entire time. She couldn't tell what the detective was thinking and that bothered her. Sam didn't like being unable to size someone up. In her line of work, it could get her killed. Sam couldn't help but wonder if it had been such a good idea to bring the Park Police into their investigation. So far, they hadn't been much help and this attack against Lee Grayson had Sam's teeth on edge.

"That was nice of you to send a deputy over to keep an eye on Grayson."

Sam shrugged. "She won't be there until tomorrow morning, but I doubt Kessler will leave her partner alone tonight anyway after what we've found. Even then, I can't provide protection for more than twenty-four hours. We just don't have the manpower for that kind of operation."

She kept it to herself that Ranger Kessler and her kind would keep an eye on Grayson after that anyway. Sam had never been one to tell someone else's secrets and this was a big one. As much as she didn't care for Panthera, they were still members of her community. She didn't know Hex very well and letting her in on the shape changers' unique gifts could be a fiasco. Sam had enough disasters on her hands lately without senselessly inviting more trouble.

Jack Chase and Leann Seaver ambled up, interrupting the conversation. Chase looked like he hadn't slept in a week and Sam noticed the dark stubble he sported on his cheeks. His normally pristine suit appeared rumpled and his shoes were scuffed. Seaver looked better. Her clothes freshly laundered and perfectly tailored, she presented the image of a consummate professional. Only the dark circles under her eyes hinted at her lack of sleep. Sam doubted she would have noticed had she not been trained in such attention to detail.

"What have you got?" Hex asked.

Chase shook his head. "Nothing much right now. We know someone cut the line with a smooth blade because there aren't any jagged edges, but leaking brake fluid contaminated any trace. Leann and I want to stay here and process the car ourselves for any fingerprints that don't belong."

"You don't trust the crime scene technicians?" Sam asked.

"It's not that we don't trust them," Seaver responded. "It's just that we have better equipment and we can run anything we find through the national databases more quickly."

"All right, I'm certainly not above taking advantage of any resources available, but you'll need elimination prints from Ranger

Kessler and Lee Grayson."

"Not a problem," Hex interjected. "Kessler is a federal employee and Ms. Grayson's been fingerprinted for a passport. They're both in the system."

"It sounds like you've got everything under control. In that case, I think I'll call it a night. You two might want to get some sleep though. You both look like hell," Sam observed.

Seaver and Chase shared a smile of commiseration, but didn't say anything. They turned away to begin work and Sam realized Deputy Gomez's shift had ended four hours ago. The man sat on a stool at the rear of the garage, but he was alert. He noticed Macke watching him and sat up straight.

"James, go home. I don't think the federal agents need you to babysit. Once they finish up, it won't matter if anyone touches the car."

It wasn't much of a threat anyway, Sam thought. Regardless of Kessler's thoughts on the subject, Sam felt pretty sure the same suspect involved in the murders was behind this attack. That individual tended to leave very little forensic evidence behind and had yet to show a penchant for returning to the scene of the crime. She didn't think this time would be any different.

"Thanks, Sheriff Macke. I'll see you tomorrow."

Sam nodded and headed for the door. It had been a long day and she was very aware that things weren't going to calm down any time soon. Already, eleven days had passed since the last murder victim and her heart twisted to think there might soon be another. Sometimes she envied the Panthera their abilities. At least then she could change into an animal form and vent some of her frustration by running through the forest, ripping into trees and turf. For the first time that she could remember, Sam actually disliked them less.

"Hang on," Hex stopped her. "Can you give me a ride to the Harmon Arms? I rode over with Chase and Seaver."

Stifling her sigh, Sam nodded. All she wanted was a shower and her bed, but she couldn't let Hex walk two miles in the dark to the bed and breakfast. Six o'clock wasn't very late, but the sun set early this time of year. She zipped her jacket and stepped out into the chilly night air, aware of Hex following close behind.

Detective Hex spoke as they drove. "Listen, would it be all right if we grab a bite to eat before you drop me off? I'd like to talk about everything that's been going on, maybe compare notes, and I'd rather not risk a hypoglycemic reaction while we do."

"What about Kessler and your team? Shouldn't we wait until everyone's together?"

"Nah, it's not like this is official." Hex bounced her knee up and down and gazed out her side window so that Sam couldn't see her face. "We don't have any real clues. There are just some things that don't make sense to me and I need a second opinion."

Sam felt the first throb of a headache behind her left eye. In a way, she felt like they were conspiring behind Kessler's back but that was just an excuse. Having dinner with Hex went beyond the scope of what Sam considered professional interaction. Something she avoided. Yet, she couldn't say no. Hex was right when she said they had nothing pointing to the killer. If a brainstorming session could generate a breakthrough then she could miss a few more hours of sleep.

Her decision made, Sam turned right onto a road leading away from Harmon Arms Bed and Breakfast and out of town. Sam drove south on Highway 30 and had passed Meacham Lake before her companion spoke.

"Where are we going?"

"Clear Lake. It's a little town about ten minutes from here."

"Clear Lake's not a town," Hex disagreed. "It's more of a hamlet."

Sam smiled at the disdain. "I see you've heard of it."

"Saw it on a map. I haven't been there, but I'm familiar with the area because of the case."

"Right, know your surroundings," Macke said. "Officer basic training survival skills. Well, don't worry. There's this little pub in Clear Lake that makes the best chili dogs you've ever had."

"Do they have steak? I could go for a nice, juicy porterhouse."

Sam's eyes darted to Hex, but couldn't really make out her features in the darkness. She over-corrected a little and had to jerk the vehicle back into the proper lane. Frowning hard, Sam tried to keep her attention on the road.

"What? Did I say something wrong?"

Unable to explain that Hex's remark sounded like one a Panthera would make, Sam kept quiet. Sometimes it felt like she held more secrets than Pandora's box and all it did was make her job even harder. Unfortunately, there was no way Hex would ever understand. Hell, most of the time Sam didn't understand. They finished the ride in silence. She sighed tiredly as they pulled into the Red Robber's parking lot. Sam parked near the rear of the lot under a streetlamp. This area wasn't crowded, but a few cars sat lined up in front of the pub's entrance. From a distance, they could hear people laughing and talking.

Hex slammed the passenger door and headed to the entrance beside Sam. "Do you come here a lot?"

"Not really." Sam opened the door for Hex and followed her inside. "Usually, I just make something at home."

A young woman showed them to a table and took their drink order before striding away. Sam was grateful for the few moments afforded to gather her wits. She hadn't meant to make such a personal comment, but it was so easy to relax around Detective Hex. Too easy. The waitress delivered iced tea for her and a mug of beer for Hex, and then disappeared with their food order. Hex took a swallow of beer and swiped at the suds on her upper lip with a thumb.

Sam watched her look around the rustic interior of the pub, but didn't see any sign of genuine curiosity. Like most rural clubs, the Red Robber boasted lowered light to hide the stains from numerous spills. Cigarette smoke hung thick in the air and patrons filled bar stools, watching hockey and football on the two televisions that occupied each corner overhead. Sam didn't come here for the ambiance. The Red Robber served good food and she could escape from Harmon's more eccentric inhabitants for a time.

Hex, on the other hand, was up to something more than just wanting to talk about their lack of progress with the investigation. Suddenly, Sam questioned the impulsive decision to bring Hex here. She lamented allowing Hex inside her defenses, even if only in a small way, and she regretted her instincts that made her suspicious of the detective's motives for asking her to dinner. Ready to push things along so that she could go home and finally have some peace, Sam placed her glass on the table with a thunk.

"Out with it, Detective."

Hex looked at her and took a slow draw from her beer. She eschewed the mug's handle, wrapping the glass in her long-fingered grip. "Call me Pat."

Irritated, Sam tried again. "You wanted a second opinion. What is it that's bothering you?"

"You're not overly friendly are you, Sam?"

"That's Sheriff Macke and my cordiality isn't in question." It stung a little that Hex thought her unfriendly. "Let's focus on business."

Hex smiled, seemingly unconcerned by Sam's brusqueness. "Okay, for now. First, I do not in any way believe all the stuff going on here is unrelated. Look me in the eye and tell me you don't think Grayson's little *accident* was caused by someone other than our killer."

"I can't." Sam shrugged. The idea had already occurred to her, but Jamison had presented a good case for the opposite point of view. "As you pointed out in the car, we don't have any evidence. Still, I can't discount the possibility of a second suspect."

Hex snorted and put aside her half-empty mug. "Come on, Sam. It's Occam's Razor. The simplest explanation is usually the correct explanation."

"Well, you've certainly simplified Occam's Razor."

"That's not the point and you know it. Once your deputy gives up on protection detail for Ms. Grayson, Detective Seaver will take over."

Sam felt her face harden. Hex was playing a dangerous game, and she didn't even know the rules. "As bodyguard for Grayson or do you intend to use her as bait?"

"Relax, Sam. It's not like we set this up deliberately, but we'd be fools not to take advantage. Our perp clearly has a hard-on for the woman. I just can't figure the change in M.O."

"I must be missing part of this conversation. What are you talking about?"

Hex frowned in confusion. "You mean you haven't noticed how much this Grayson woman resembles our two victims? It seems clear to me that our whacko has selected his next target."

"Actually, I hadn't thought about it." Sam felt startled by the idea.

The young waitress delivered the food and Hex tucked in with gusto, but Sam's appetite had disappeared.

"That's because you're too close to these people," Hex said around a bite of steak. She speared another piece of beef and pointed to Sam with the handle of her fork. "It just proves how important it is to bring in a fresh set of eyes."

"Okay, Detective Fresh-Set-of-Eyes, what do you suggest?"

"Just what I said before. We'll take turns keeping Grayson under surveillance, from a distance of course, and hope our suspect slips up."

Sam couldn't even think of all the ways that little scheme could go wrong. Unknowingly, Hex had just placed her in an awkward position. Things could get really ugly if one of the Panthera got caught changing into their animal forms by a federal investigator. An image of a mutilated federal detective played across her mind's eye. Sam didn't care for the Panthera; in her opinion, they were more beast than human. Even so, she realized that didn't apply to everyone. She would have to let Kessler know what Hex was up to or things could spiral out of control very quickly.

"What are you thinking about?"

"Nothing. I'll consider taking turns watching Grayson, but I'm not making any promises. What else is bothering you?" Sam wasn't sure she wanted to know.

"Are you going to eat that?" Hex pointed at the now cold chili dog and fries. Her own plate was empty.

Sam pushed her food across the table. "Where do you put it all?"

"I have a high metabolism." Hex took a large bite out of the hot dog and chewed for a minute before speaking. Sam ignored the chili at the corners of her mouth. "Am I the only one who thinks it's strange how Ms. Grayson avoided any major injuries?"

For the second time during their meal, Sam experienced a sinking sensation of dread. "I think she was very lucky. You should be happy about that."

"I am, but did you see her car? That Mercedes was totaled and Grayson walked away with a busted nose and a concussion."

"She hardly *walked* anywhere. You do recall there was an ambulance in the equation?" Sam couldn't believe she had to actually defend the community's shape changers. "Grayson was also, still is, unconscious."

Hex waved her remarks away. "True but there was no internal bleeding or broken bones. A tree limb fell on her that should have bashed her head in and all she has is a concussion."

"I'm sorry, Detective, but you're not going to convince me that

Grayson is some kind of Wonder Woman." Sam hoped she wasn't overdoing things. "The truth is that a woman got very lucky and survived an attempt on her life. Let it go at that."

Hex held Sam's gaze while she licked chili off her fingertips. Then she picked up the napkin and wiped her mouth. "Fine, moving on. I have another suggestion besides trailing Lee Grayson around."

"Am I going to like this?" Sam leaned back, expecting the worst.

"I think it's time to use the media. We thought an information blackout would prevent someone from accidentally releasing vital evidence to the public, but since we don't have any evidence..."

"You're hoping someone might have seen something and will come forward. The problem is that the bodies were dumped in the middle of federal lands that are notoriously short on crowds."

"Ah ha," Hex said triumphantly. "They were dumped there, not killed there. We don't know where they died."

"Okay, you have a point, but we need to bring Ranger Kessler in on this before we do anything. Once the media gets hold of this story, people are going to be flocking into the park trying to see something."

Hex nodded. "It's sad how the macabre brings out the sickos."

Sam leaned forward and took a remaining fry off her plate. She chewed without enthusiasm before draining the last of her tea. Staring down at the wooden table surface, Sam wondered how things could get so complicated. At first, living in these mountains had been like a dream. That dream became a nightmare a few years ago starting with Nicky's death and the hits just kept coming. Sam had actually thought last year was as bad as it could get with a shape changing monster slaughtering people and animals in these woods. Now, another killer haunted the park and they didn't have any idea how to stop them except by using an innocent as a lure. She felt ill.

She kept her gaze on the scarred table while Hex ordered and received another beer. Time seemed to drag as people surged around them, coming and going from the pub. When they'd arrived, Sam wanted nothing more than to turn around and head home. Now, she didn't have the strength to lift her head.

"What was her name?"

Through the din of customers, Sam barely heard the question. "Who?"

"The woman who broke your heart. I mean, I'm assuming it was a woman. If I'm wrong, let me know and I'll back off."

Sam finally looked at Hex. "What makes you think anyone broke my heart, as you so dramatically put it? Why can't I just be tired?"

"You're tired," Hex allowed, "but you wear your professionalism like a shield all the time. No one does that unless they're trying to avoid letting someone in. So what did she do, cheat on you and run off with another woman?"

Sam swallowed hard and drew a shaky breath. Hex's tone was a mixture of light teasing and compassion, like she didn't know how to broach the subject but wanted to pursue the topic just the same. Sam couldn't fathom what possible purpose there was for Hex to know this information, but she hoped that if she answered, Hex would stop.

"No, Pat. She died of bone cancer three years ago."

Hex's eyes closed and her empty mug hit the table. When she looked up, Sam could have sworn there were tears in her eyes. "God, I'm sorry. I feel like an absolute ass."

Seeing Pat's remorse touched Sam in a way that nothing else had in years. For the first time since losing Nicky, she was concerned for another woman's feelings and not in a professional capacity. Sam felt the urge to reassure Pat, but it had been so long since she reached out to another person that it proved awkward.

"You kind of sounded like one, too." She smiled to show she wasn't angry.

Pat's eyes widened in shock and then she relaxed. "I really am sorry and I promise not to tease you anymore."

"I'll believe that when I see it."

The rest of the evening passed more pleasantly. Pat insisted on picking up the tab in an effort to make amends for bringing up a painful subject. Sam drove Pat back to the bed and breakfast before things became uncomfortable again. She pulled to the curb in front of the renovated Victorian house and expected Pat to get out immediately. She didn't. Instead, Pat bounced her leg up and down again and Sam realized it was a nervous gesture. She had done the same thing on the way out to the Red Robber.

"Is something wrong?"

"Uh, no, of course not."

Watching her in the darkness, the truth hit Sam so hard that she almost flinched. Pat was attracted to her. The knowledge struck her like a sledgehammer to the forehead. Sam's heart pounded in sudden fear and she felt her scalp prickle. She did not know how to handle this situation. Life and death scenarios were one thing, but she had decided long ago that she was finished with matters of the heart. Way out of her element, Sam sputtered for a way to end this awkward moment without hurting Pat's feelings or leading her to believe there was a possibility of anything developing between them.

"Okay, I'll see you tomorrow then. When do you want to go see Kessler?"

Pat turned her head away and Sam felt some of her tension drain. When she spoke, her voice sounded husky, her tone disappointed. "How about two o'clock tomorrow? I'll meet you at Kessler's office. I'm sure I'll have something from Chase and Seaver about the car by then. Hopefully, they'll find something that our killer left behind."

"Sounds good to me, but I don't know if Kessler will be there tomorrow. I guess that all depends on how her partner is doing. I'll call

Jamison and see what she thinks."

"Fine, let me know." Pat seemed to be waiting for something more, but Sam didn't know what to say. After a second, Pat reached for the door handle. Sam thought she was upset and wanted to reach out to her in some way.

"Pat..."

"I'll see you tomorrow, Sam." Pat slammed the car door behind her and jogged up the concrete steps to the inn's entrance.

"Damn."

Sam's head flopped back against the seat and she rubbed her eyes. She didn't have the time or inclination to worry about hurting Pat's feelings because this night wasn't over yet. Sam still needed to call Jamison and let her know what Hex had planned. She decided she wasn't going to make that call from her car. Pulling away from the Harmon Arms, Sam headed across town. Most of the Panthera around town lived in the more rural locations, which was exactly why she chose to reside inside the city limits. Her only concession to privacy was in purchasing a home on a double lot toward the edge of town.

The ride home didn't take long and Sam sighed unconsciously in relief as she pulled into the driveway. She parked inside the garage and took the adjoining door into the kitchen. Usually she felt the tension of the day drain away as soon as she closed the door. Tonight that was decidedly not the case. The situation with Hex left her with a knot of tension between her shoulder blades.

After removing the gun belt and pouring a shot of scotch, Sam settled into an overstuffed chair and put her feet up on the ottoman. She took a sip of the amber liquid and allowed it to burn a trail down her throat. Images of Patricia Hex crowded behind her closed eyes and she pushed them away. To banish those impressions entirely, Sam picked up her cell phone and flipped it open. The sooner she finished this call, the sooner she could get some sleep.

Chapter Seven

JAMISON SIPPED AT the hot mocha and savored the caffeine as it hit her bloodstream. "Thank you, Dinah. This is exactly what I need."

"No problem. Has she woken up yet?"

The sisters stood in the hallway outside Lee's room. Jamison preferred to talk outside since a human nurse was currently taking Lee's vital signs.

"Not yet. Mom says it's not that unusual considering the head injury, but I'm starting to get worried."

"I'm sure it's okay. Mom wouldn't lie to you about this."

Jamison realized logically that Dinah was right, but it didn't make her feel any better. She just needed Lee to open her eyes. Darlene said Lee wasn't that badly injured, and Panthera healed at an accelerated rate as compared to humans. She was smart enough to realize that her reasoning did nothing but drive her blood pressure up. Jamison needed to change and run through the forest, feel her claws ripping into damp soil. It was the only thing, other than Lee actually opening her eyes, that would ease the pressure on her chest. Only, she couldn't do that. Jamison refused to leave Lee's side. Given no other options, she felt like she might explode.

"Jami, why don't you take a walk outside? Don't freak," Dinah interrupted when Jamison's expression hardened. "I just mean a walk around the parking lot. Stretch your legs and get some fresh air. I'll sit with Lee and I'll call you if she wakes up during the five minutes that you're actually out of the room."

She considered the idea. If Jamison didn't get away from the smell of antiseptic and the sounds of beeping hospital equipment, she was afraid she'd lose control of her beast. Even a partial shift would help her to feel more centered and she couldn't do that inside the confines of a medical center. It wouldn't be for long and she wouldn't go far away.

"All right, but you'll call."

"I promise."

"Even if you just *think* she's waking up."

"Get out of here," Dinah finally ordered.

Jamison nodded and headed outside. She exited into the parking lot to find it mostly deserted. The moon was high overhead and there was a definite chill in the air. Goosebumps rose on her forearms. Like most cats, she didn't like the cold but hadn't thought to grab a jacket earlier when the call came in about the accident. Regardless of the temperature, it still felt good to be outside. Jamison took another drink of her coffee and felt the heat flow into her, in counterpoint to the air on her skin. She headed toward a far corner of the lot to a place where the streetlights didn't reach. Jamison stood facing out into the shrubs lining the asphalt and her eyes slipped closed. She concentrated on the sounds of the night, wind in the trees and small animals in the underbrush. When she opened her eyes, her sight had expanded.

Outside of the parking lot, the hospital grounds were perfectly manicured. Benches sat under trees and a small creek wound around the south side before trailing away into the darkness. In the distance Jamison spotted a tabby striped house cat moving over the bridge just above the stream. He played in the shadows, darting and swatting at nothing. After a few seconds, he stopped and sat down before turning his head and meeting Jamison's gaze. Whether the distance between them gave the cat courage or because he was unafraid of his larger cousin, the housecat evidenced no sign of fear. Amused but impressed by his bravery, Jamison glanced away and scanned the rest of the area with her Panthera enhanced vision. Although she'd only allowed her eyes to change, Jamison felt more at peace than she had in days. Nearby she could sense Lee's heartbeat, their connection powerful. Jamison sensed her partner's strength and finally believed her mother's words. Lee's essence was strong, her sleep a healing one.

When the phone rang, Jamison growled low in her throat at the intrusion. Then she thought the call might be from Dinah and she quickly reached for the cell. She blinked and her eyes assumed their human shape. The display told her it was a call she couldn't ignore. "Kessler here."

Silence greeted her. Then the caller spoke. "What are you doing answering the phone?"

Jamison smiled and started back toward the hospital. "You called me, remember? Why shouldn't I answer?"

"Because you're in a hospital and cell phone usage is typically frowned upon."

"Then I guess it's a good thing I'm outside. What can I do for you, Sheriff?"

"I just had dinner with Detective Hex."

Jamison stopped. Somehow, she didn't think Sheriff Macke was about to confess to a lover's rendezvous. "I'm listening."

"After Deputy Harris gets off protection detail, Hex is going to assign Seaver to follow your partner around."

"Why?" Jamison asked slowly.

Sheriff Macke sighed over the connection. "She made a pretty good case, Kessler. I don't know why I never saw it, but Hex pointed out that Lee Grayson resembles the two dead victims. Detective Hex doesn't buy the separate stalker theory and thinks our killer has chosen Ms. Grayson as the next target."

Jamison mentally ran through all the ramifications of what Macke said. "I can see a small resemblance, but it doesn't track. Killers don't usually change their M.O. and whoever went after Lee cut her brake lines. Our guy uses a blitz attack, remember? The method of attack is completely divergent."

"That is the question," Macke agreed. "Even Hex questioned the change. Regardless, I thought you should know. Oh and while I'm thinking about it, we're going to need a list of anyone who might have a grudge against Grayson."

The Council would not be happy about this. Having a federal investigator following one of their people around could result in exposure of their kind to the human populace. Jamison's conversation with her mother came back to her and she realized just how out of control things could get. Already Darlene Kessler viewed Hex and her detectives as a threat.

"This isn't good. If the Council finds out about this..."

"They'll what?" Macke sounded angry.

Jamison cursed the fact that she had said too much. "Don't worry about it, Sheriff. I'll take care of everything."

"How exactly are you going to 'take care' of things? Look, Kessler, I don't really like your kind. You run around Harmon and the park like you own the place and do exactly as you please. You circumvent the law with your venerated Council, internal investigators and your own way of enforcing whatever rules you see fit."

"You make us sound like the mob."

"In my eyes, you aren't much different."

"Then why do you stay if you hate us so much?" Jamison asked sharply.

"Because I made a promise to someone I loved to try and protect you people as much as possible. And because, as much as I don't like it, you all have the right to live just the same as anyone else. But make no mistake. If anything happens to Detective Hex or her people, I'll know where to start and I'll cage the guilty party the same as I would any other animal. Are we clear on this?"

"You don't have to preach to me, Sheriff. I'm in full agreement." Unfortunately, that didn't mean the Council would feel the same way.

"Glad to hear it. There's more."

"You mean that wasn't enough?"

Macke continued on without responding to the comment. "Hex suggested meeting with you in your office around two tomorrow afternoon. She wants us to consider bringing the media in on this. She's hoping someone saw something that might help us solve these murders."

Jamison was startled by the idea of bringing in the press. Panthera did not seek media attention for any reason. Nevertheless, she couldn't see the harm. Harmon might experience a few more tourists than usual from the curious and thrill seekers once the media weighed in, but the Panthera were accustomed to hiding in plain sight. What with the Adirondack National Park visitors they typically encountered, she didn't see that a few more people would make any difference.

"I don't have a problem with bringing the press in to help us, but I'm not sure I'll be in my office tomorrow. Lee still hasn't regained consciousness and I'm not comfortable leaving her until I know she'll be okay. Why don't you go ahead and set something up with the local news, that's sort of your bailiwick anyway."

Sam hesitated a moment before speaking. "You trust me to do this on my own? Won't your venerated Council have a problem?"

"Please, Sheriff. We both know you don't give a damn about what the Council thinks and you wouldn't listen to them anyway. Besides, since when do I tell you how to do your job?"

"Since never," Sam acknowledged. "I just expected you to throw a fit about the media."

"Would it have done any good?"

"Not really. We don't have any answers and we can use help anywhere we can find it, and not to put too fine a point on it, but from where I sit things are getting worse."

"I wish I could argue the issue with you, Sheriff, but I just can't. Do what you think is best. I'll soothe any ruffled feathers with the Council."

"Glad to hear it. Now go take care of your partner and make sure she knows to act natural until we get things sorted."

"Sheriff Macke, I might point out that the Panthera are probably more natural than any full human."

"Don't give me that transcendental crap, you know what I mean. Make sure Grayson remembers to act like a person."

Jamison wanted to pursue the point but let it go. They'd be there all night arguing semantics over feline versus human nature when both states were equally a part of the Panthera psyche. "I'll make sure she knows, and I'll also make sure that the Council doesn't take any action on the feds. To be honest, I'm not sure there's any reason for them to know about this anyway. As long as Hex and her people don't suspect anything unusual about Lee, there shouldn't be any problems. Anyway, thanks for warning me. You didn't have to do that."

"I didn't do it for you."

Jamison wondered why Macke couldn't just be gracious.

"I've seen a mountain lion's idea of justice before and I'm willing to bet the Panthera aren't that different while in a regressed state. If anything happened to one of these detectives we'd have every alphabet agency in the country descend on our mountains. That's something I'd prefer to avoid."

"All the same, I appreciate the heads up."

"Sure, whatever. Oh and Kessler, I really am happy Grayson will be okay. No one should have to survive the loss of a partner."

Jamison heard the connection terminate and shook her head. Samantha Macke was such a strange combination of contemptuous and compassionate. She turned and reentered the hospital. Striding with purpose, she returned to Lee's room. Unfortunately, nothing seemed to have changed while she was out. Dinah still stood gazing out the hospital window into the night and Lee lay unmoving. The machines continued to beep.

Disappointed and concerned to find Lee still sleeping, Jamison settled onto the chair beside the hospital bed. She clasped Lee's cold hand between her own and studiously ignored the worried expression on Dinah's face. Jamison tried to stay positive. Maybe Lee hadn't slept well before the accident and this was her body's way of making up for it. Despite her determination to strive for optimism, Dinah voiced Jamison's fears.

"Why doesn't she wake up? I can sense that her injuries are healing."

"I don't know," Jamison admitted softly. "Mom said that sometimes people just need to sleep."

"Who can sleep with all the chit chat?"

Startled, Jamison looked up at Dinah to see if her mind was playing tricks. She discovered her own shock mirrored in her sister's expression.

"Lee?" Jamison squeezed Lee's fingers and choked back a sob of relief when blue eyes opened.

Dinah scooted up on the bed's opposite side and grinned down at Lee. "Hey there, how are you feeling?"

"Fuzzy." Lee attempted to raise a hand to her forehead but the various medical feeds prevented the movement. Confusion clouded her eyes. "What happened?"

"You had a wreck while driving home from Harmon," Jamison said. "Can you remember anything?"

Lee's brows furrowed. "That's right, the brakes quit working. I think my car bounced off a guard rail."

"It did more than that," Dinah grinned. "You went airborne across a ditch and slammed into a tree. I'm pretty sure the car is totaled."

Jamison growled and directed an angry mental shout to Dinah when Lee flinched.

Stop! What's wrong with you?

Aggravated but trying to contain her ire for Lee's sake, Jamison schooled her voice. "It wasn't an accident, honey." She brushed blonde hair back from Lee's forehead. Jamison hesitated to say the words but finally decided Lee deserved to know the truth. "Someone cut the brake line."

"I had considered the possibility. It just seemed too strange after everything else that has happened."

"You're not surprised?" Dinah asked.

"Hardly." Lee stifled a yawn. "When you've had a box of snakes and bugs delivered to your front door, this seems like the next logical step. I just can't imagine who I could have hurt enough for them to try and kill me."

"Snakes and bugs?" Dinah looked to Jamison for an explanation.

"I'll tell you later. Lee, there's more."

"Oh great, like a stalker isn't bad enough."

Jamison kept her doubts about the perpetrator to herself. She couldn't admit to the sheriff that the serial killer might have his sights set on Lee and she wasn't going to share that belief with Lee either. Instead, she changed her approach to deliver the next bit of information in a more positive light, hoping some good news would help speed Lee's recovery.

"Actually, this is a good thing. Mom said that as soon as you woke up they could move you out of ICU. And don't worry about a stalker. Sheriff Macke is going to have a deputy posted outside your door."

"My own private bodyguard?" Lee smiled. "I feel special, but is the deputy going to follow me around until this psycho is caught?"

"Um, no," Jamison hedged, glancing between Lee and Dinah. "Detective Hex plans to give that particular honor to Detective Seaver."

The room went still, but Jamison felt Lee's wariness in her mind. *Why?*

Their eyes locked and Jamison attempted to communicate Hex's human concerns. Dinah kept silent throughout the exchange, nothing less than Jamison expected of her. This conversation was for Jamison and her mate.

Think you are killer's target. No stalker.

Why?

You look like other prey.

So do others.

No others get warnings.

Frustrated, Lee turned away. "It doesn't matter what I want, does it? You've already decided."

"No, you don't get a say in this. This is how it has to be. And it would make me feel better to know Seaver is there."

"You don't trust my instincts to know if someone is about to attack?" Lee sounded angry. "I couldn't have known about the other events because I wasn't there when they happened. Someone left the box on the porch before I got home and whoever did this could have cut the brakes anytime. But I will know if someone comes after me."

"You're going to allow this?" Dinah finally asked.

Jamison stood up slowly, pinning Dinah with her gaze until her sister looked away. "I am still an elder and I have to weigh all our options, not just for Lee's sake but for our people." She looked down at Lee. "Yes, I trust your instincts, but I'm not adverse to someone providing backup. As for the Panthera, if I resist Hex on this I run the risk of making her suspicious. Whenever I talk to her, I get the feeling that somehow she already knows something. I won't take that chance."

Lee still radiated irritation, but the challenge had faded from her gaze. "Fine, I'll have a chaperone. At least I'll know she's there."

"Jamison, the Council isn't going to like this."

"Noted, but at this point they don't need to know anything."

Dinah looked at Jamison as if she'd never seen her before. "They're going to be really pissed when they find out. It's not like you to keep the Council in the dark."

Jamison considered that truth. The stakes had never been this high before. Jamison wasn't comfortable with the idea of sacrificing a human life for any reason. She was already at odds with her mother over the incident with Aaron Dalton last year and Marie Tristan, second in command of the Panthera Council, would be thrilled if Jamison didn't make it through her probationary period as an elder. Marie had never approved the idea of two elders on the Council from the same family. This would be just the excuse she needed to question Jamison's loyalty to the community. Regardless Jamison stood firm.

"I don't care. The Council would willingly eliminate Hex just because she's human if they thought it would help keep the Panthera a secret from the world."

"Is that so wrong?" Dinah asked. "You know what would happen if we were discovered. It may be a tired cliché, but you've seen the black and white creature features where the villagers show up with torches and sharp sticks to kill the monster. In reality, discovering shape changers will cause riots and mass casualties as every human in the world attempts to exterminate us."

"You don't know that. Maybe the humans will surprise us."

"Are you saying you want the world to know about the Panthera?"

Lee interrupted the sisters. "As much as I like the sound of being welcomed with open arms, I'm afraid I have to agree with Dinah. The world isn't ready to know that werewolves, or were*cats*, are real."

Jamison turned to her partner in complete surprise.

"Don't get me wrong," Lee held up a hand. "I do not agree with putting Detective Hex in danger. Killing people to save your own ass is not honorable. But I do think the Council needs to know about her putting a bodyguard on me. If they find out later you'll be in a lot of trouble and this is such a minor thing I don't think it will matter."

"All right." Jamison nodded. "I'll tell them, but only about the bodyguard. I won't tell them about my suspicions. Neither will you." She directed the comment to Dinah. "It's not like I can prove anything at this point anyway. This is all conjecture."

"I understand, elder. For the record, I don't agree but I will follow your orders."

"Your opinion is noted. Now please go let Mother know that Lee is awake."

Dinah left without another word and Jamison settled into the chair next to Lee. She let the tension drain from her shoulders as she reached out to stroke her cheek. Seeing her partner's open eyes and clear expression made Jamison feel better than she had since hearing about the accident.

"I'm sorry about what I said before you left the house. I was frustrated over this case and I took it out on you. Please forgive me."

Lee leaned into the touch and Jamison wanted to purr at the contact. Sometimes it was truly unfortunate that big cats were incapable of such a reaction. A physiological trade-off for the ability to roar was that jaguar did not purr. Unable to make that simple contented sound, Jamison sought another way to express her feelings. She leaned forward and captured Lee's lips with her own in a sweet caress. After a few moments Lee pulled away.

"There is nothing to forgive. I should have been more patient. I know how much pressure you're under and it was selfish of me to demand your attention. Catching this killer is more important. I bought you a piece of Andy's cheesecake as a peace offering, but I guess it's gone now."

"Probably flipped right out of the car and into the woods." Jamison said, her eyes pinned on Lee's and not really conscious of what she said.

"Probably." Lee sounded a little breathless.

"Right now some raccoon or possum is eating my cheesecake."

"Shut up and kiss me."

Jamison did as Lee instructed. She took her time, slowly stroking Lee's lips with the tip of her tongue before kissing her gently.

"I see you're feeling better."

Jamison ignored her mother's voice and slowly completed the kiss. She wouldn't rush away from showing her mate how much she cherished her. Finally, Jamison eased back and faced Darlene. Dinah stood beside their mother. As soon as Jamison looked at Darlene she realized her decision to keep the Council out of the loop had created even more distance between them. Jamison felt coldness settle into her heart and watched confusion grow in her mother's gaze. Darlene might not know of the reasons for Jamison's withdrawal, but she clearly felt it all the same.

Lee seemed unaware of the sudden tension, or perhaps she was simply more concerned with other things. "Yes, thanks. When can I go home?"

Darlene shook herself slightly and stepped toward her patient. When Jamison didn't relinquish her seat, Darlene raised an eyebrow and changed direction to walk around to the far side. She kept silent while she checked Lee's vitals and shone a penlight in her eyes.

"Everything looks good but you might have a headache for a few days. You broke your nose in the crash and even with your metabolism that's going to take some time to heal fully. I'd like to run a few more tests, but if everything checks out I don't see why you can't go home tomorrow."

"So soon?" Jamison asked before Lee could respond. "Are you sure she doesn't need to stay for a few more days? That was a pretty bad accident."

"I'm fine."

"I wouldn't say it if I didn't mean it," Darlene said a little sharply. When Jamison refused to drop her gaze, Darlene's tone dropped a few octaves. "Stand down, Jamison. I wouldn't release her if I thought for one second there was any problem."

Jamison felt Lee take her hand. "Honey, please. Don't."

That simple plea was the only thing that got through to her. For Lee's sake, Jamison dropped her gaze. Still, she made it clear that she didn't lower her gaze in deference to the *Caber,* but so that she could gaze into her partner's eyes.

"You sure you're okay?"

"Would I lie to you? Besides, I'm starving and I have a date to go up onto Wolverine Summit with Dinah soon. Are you really going to deny me a helicopter ride?"

Jamison smiled at the strength Lee displayed. "I wouldn't dream of it. Just do me a favor and wait until the day after tomorrow. It'll make me feel better if you get some rest before you start running all over the country again."

"Only if I can get something to eat."

Typical Panthera. The response was just the thing to bring a laugh to Jamison's lips. "Deal."

Chapter Eight

LEE COULDN'T HEAR anything over the noise of the helicopter rotors, but the view was breathtaking. Snow had yet to fall on Wolverine Summit. The air was so clean without the smog of civilization that Lee could see for miles, and the crisp breeze chilled her cheeks. Up so high, trees were noticeably absent. Boulders, crags, hearty scrub and mountain predators were the dominant occupants. At the moment, the animals had vacated the area, startled by the helicopter's approach.

She still felt bad for leaving Detective Seaver lurking behind the hangar, but not bad enough to miss this trip. Lee had felt Seaver's presence since leaving the hospital, vindicating her assertion that she'd know if anyone tried to attack her. Yet, she couldn't regret making her promise to Jamison. Allowing the young detective to follow her around was a small price to pay if it allowed Jamison to focus on finding a killer. After a few days, Lee expected Seaver to give up from sheer boredom.

"I'll set down over there."

She pressed the headset against her ear with one hand, trying to hear Dinah over the roar. Looking ahead to where the pilot pointed gave Lee more information than the few spoken words. Rather than attempt to respond, Lee nodded. She felt a small throb between her eyes from the persistent headache. Lee looked forward to this excursion, needing a break from all the stress of the last few days.

The helicopter settled with a bump and Lee waited until the rotor blades stopped and the engine died before removing her harness. The thick tread on her hiking boots grabbed the top of a boulder jutting from the mountaintop as she stepped from the conveyance. Lee stepped away from the helicopter toward the edge of the summit, greedily taking in the view before closing her eyes to take a deep breath. After years of shooting scenes in some of the most remote locales, this was still her favorite thing to do. Drawing the clean air deeply into her lungs was always exhilarating.

"Are you all right?" Dinah asked after a few minutes of respectful silence.

Lee opened her eyes and met her concerned gaze. She offered a half-hearted smile. Even the beauty of the area couldn't completely dispel her trepidation. "I'm fine."

"Uh huh, that's why you haven't said two words since I picked you up."

"I appreciate you taking a day off from flying tourists around the area, but it's hard to engage in small talk inside the confines of a helicopter," Lee prevaricated and turned away to retrieve her equipment.

"Okay, I'll let that go for now in the interest of family relations."

"Good, now tell me about Andy. How are things going with you two?"

Lee thought the heavyset woman who liked to laugh couldn't have been more opposite than Dinah, but couldn't deny that they seemed like the perfect couple. Dinah accepted the bag of equipment Lee passed to her. Lee reached back into the helicopter for her tripod as she waited for a response.

"Never better. Why do you ask?"

Lee shrugged. "Just curious. You hardly mention her name anymore. I saw her the other day and she seemed upset about something."

Closing the door, Lee stepped back and looked at Dinah. She couldn't quite describe the expression on her face, but it wasn't one of unmitigated happiness. The sense of something not quite right she'd experienced after seeing Andy at the café a few days ago returned.

"What is it? What's wrong?"

Dinah's gaze slipped away from her face and she looked everywhere but directly at Lee. "Nothing's wrong."

"Now who's not being truthful? Spill it."

"Seriously, Andy hasn't done anything wrong. It's me. I guess I'm just a little worried that things are getting too serious between us."

Slightly reassured, Lee started across the summit with Dinah beside her. "You mean you're getting cold feet."

Lee didn't feel it was her place to criticize anyone. Until she met Jamison, Lee had never known what it meant to truly love someone. She had experienced the fear of becoming too involved too quickly herself. All she could do was offer Dinah moral support and understanding. The lack of judgment in her tone must have been just what Dinah needed to feel comfortable enough to confide in her.

"I think about her all the time and it's a little scary."

Lee set the tripod near the edge of the north face. She didn't look at Dinah while she worked. "You do know that you've been dating for over a year. If you still think about her all the time, maybe it was meant to be."

"Yeah, but what if it isn't? I've dated other people before and thought it was the real thing. What if I'm wrong?"

What if she was? Lee thought that was a very good question. She certainly didn't consider herself an authority on the subject, just extremely fortunate to have found Jamison. Lee weighed her response while screwing the Nikon onto the tripod.

"Dinah, I can't tell you what to do, but before you do anything crazy like breaking things off I think you should consider the consequences."

"I didn't say I was going to break up with her."

Dinah sounded a little defensive and Lee wondered if she'd misread the situation. "Sorry, you're right. Butting out now."

Staring out over the canyon below, Lee searched for the perfect shot. She'd have to wait for the light to be just right and for that one moment that spoke to her. Photography was as much about patience as it was luck in capturing just the right image.

"Let's say I was thinking about breaking up with Andy, just for argument's sake. What do you think I should do?"

Lee suppressed her smile, relieved that she hadn't offended Dinah. "I think you're the only one who can answer that, but how are you going to feel if you do? Do you love her? You need to think about this, Dinah, because once you make that move there's no going back."

Silence reigned on the mountaintop after that. Dinah seemed to need time to think and Lee lost herself in doing what she loved best. The sun moved steadily across the horizon and Lee managed a great shot of a bald eagle taking off from a nest on the opposite side of the canyon's rim. When nothing else happened for a while, she took another camera from her bag and looked around for her companion. Dinah sat inside the helicopter with her eyes closed. Lee didn't know if she was sleeping or merely relaxing, but she couldn't resist snapping a couple of pictures.

Hours passed and they shared a quiet lunch on the mountaintop. Lee wasn't in any hurry to return to civilization and deal with insurance agents over the loss of her car. After lunch, Dinah returned to napping in the cockpit while Lee set up her Nikon with a zoom lens. She planned to scout the area away from the cliff in search of wildlife but she couldn't tear the plastic zip tie holding the price tag on her new lens with her human fingers. She lacked the control Jamison had and couldn't change just one part of her body so transforming her fingers into claws was out of the question. She needed something to cut the hard plastic.

"Hey, loan me your pocketknife," Lee said, standing outside the open helicopter door. Instead of jumping in surprise, Dinah reached into her pocket with her eyes closed.

Lee cut the zip tie, folded the knife and held it out. "Here you go."

"Keep it."

Dinah folded her arms, clearly intent on a catnap so Lee stuffed the knife in her jean pocket and walked away. She'd return the blade once Dinah was fully awake. Cats didn't like being interrupted while trying to sleep and Lee wasn't about to press her luck. She set off on foot away from the cliff's edge, but had only taken a dozen steps when she heard the helicopter radio sputter to life.

"Skyhawk eight Charlie Papa, come in."

Lee frowned and started back to the chopper when she recognized Sheriff Samantha Macke's voice. Somehow she knew this wasn't good news. There was no reason for local law enforcement to contact a civilian helicopter pilot unless someone was in trouble. Instantly, Lee thought of Jamison and the recent killings and her blood ran cold.

Dinah met her eyes through the cockpit window, easily communicating her own dread as she sat up and reached for the mic. "Skyhawk eight Charlie Papa on the air. What can I do for you, Sheriff?"

"Sorry to intrude on whatever you're doing Ms. Kessler, but it seems we have a couple of missing kids. I'm calling in all the help I can get to find them."

Lee glanced toward the horizon at the setting sun. In the valley, it would already be dark.

"Okay, do you need the helicopter or are you just putting together a search party?"

Lee thought that a valid question. The Panthera had senses that would be useful in a ground search, but Lee couldn't imagine the human sheriff being comfortable enough with shape changers to ask for that kind of help unless the situation was dire.

"Rendezvous with us at my office. You'll get all the information you need once you arrive."

"Understood, Kessler out." Darlene looked at Lee through the safety shield. "Let's go. I still need to drop you off before I meet with Macke."

"I'm going with you." Lee settled into the passenger seat and snapped her harness in place, silently daring Dinah to refuse.

"No way. Not a chance. Jamison would have my hide if I brought you with me."

"Are you afraid of her or something?"

Dinah shot her an amused look. "As a matter of fact, yes."

The helicopter roared to life, preventing any further discussion.

LINDSAY LOOKED OUT past the curtain when she heard the car horn blow. Her smile was automatic as she spotted Mira behind the wheel of her dad's old Buick. Yanking open the front door, Lindsay stepped onto the porch. Across the street and directly behind the Buick, she couldn't help but notice a battered, white panel van. It stood out because of the copious amount of rust that was probably all that held the vehicle together, and the fact that it stood parked directly under the streetlamp. No one occupied the driver's seat and she easily ignored it.

"Hey, I need to finish drying my hair. Come in for a minute."

Lindsay heard Mira sigh from a distance of thirty feet. "We're going to miss the start of the movie."

"It's only six thirty. The movie doesn't start until eight. Besides, I thought we were going to get something to eat at the mall first."

"Fine," Mira groused and got out of the car. "Have we even

decided on a movie yet? I want to see a romantic comedy."

Mira shook her head and dark hair caught the artificial glow from the street lamp behind her. Lindsay felt breathless from the sight, but didn't say anything. As her best friend, Mira wouldn't be receptive to any signs of attraction. The fact that Mira had a crush on some boy motivated Lindsay to keep silent about her feelings.

"I thought we were going to watch that new action thriller. Grab something to drink out of the fridge. I'll be down in five minutes."

Lindsay turned and ran up the stairs to the bathroom. She heard Mira's cell ring and knew the other girl would be on the phone the whole time it took her to finish getting ready. It was probably Dylan anyway. Lindsay grimaced in distaste and switched on the blow dryer. True to her word, it only took a few minutes to finish drying her hair. She borrowed a little of her mom's perfume hoping to make an impression on Mira and ran back down the stairs. Mira closed the phone just as Lindsay snatched up a small purse and grabbed a jacket off the peg by the door. She let Mira close the door while she buttoned her coat.

"I wish it wasn't so dark already," Mira said, following her to the car.

"It's winter time." Lindsay didn't care one way or the other. Her natural abilities allowed her to see fine in either condition.

"Yeah, but it's just that there aren't any street lights between Harmon and Lake Placid on these little roads." Mira started the Buick and pulled away from the curb.

"Oh, you're worried about driving in the dark. Can't you see the road?"

"Well, yeah, I've got the headlights. I'm just not used to it yet, that's all."

"At least you have a car. My mom won't let me have one yet."

Mira smiled and glanced at Lindsay sideways. "You're only sixteen."

"Like you're so much older. One year isn't that big of a difference."

"You're the lucky one," Mira rejoined. "My parents wouldn't let me go anywhere on my own when I was your age."

"What can I say? I'm very mature."

Mira didn't respond. Lindsay watched the scenery out the passenger window and wondered why Mira had to act so stuck up sometimes. She really liked Mira, but she could be annoying. She decided to ignore it and just try to have fun.

"Was that Dylan that called you earlier?"

"Yeah." Mira bounced a little in her seat. "His parents are going to let him have a keg for his twenty-first birthday. Isn't that so cool?"

"He's too old for you," Lindsay responded, not considering the question. "Why do you hang out with him anyway? What kind of loser still lives with their parents at his age?"

"What's the matter, jealous?" Mira teased.

"No, of course not. Why would you say that?"

"Because I have a boyfriend and you don't."

Lindsay rolled her eyes and turned back to the scenery. "Whatever." She was jealous, just not the way Mira thought. They weren't even out of town yet and already fighting. Mira turned onto a dirt road that would lead to the highway and Lindsay spotted the warning sign for the railroad tracks.

"Wow, it's really dark over here."

"The streetlights are out. Why'd you come this way anyway?"

"It's a shortcut."

Mira slowed and drove over the railroad tracks but just as she crossed the top of the trestle, there was a loud bang and the Buick lurched to the right.

Lindsay felt her heart jump. "What was that?"

"Crap, I think we had a blowout."

She could hear the nervousness in Mira's voice as she stopped in the middle of the road. "Are you going to stop right here? What if someone comes flying along and hits us?"

"Would you relax," Mira said. "No one comes out here anymore. Everyone likes to stay on the highway."

"Yeah, I can see why."

Mira tapped the steering wheel with a fingernail. "There has to be a spare in the back, right?"

"I guess so. Do you know how to change a tire?"

"How hard can it be? Come on, you can help me." Mira took the keys from the ignition and climbed out of the car without waiting for an answer, leaving Lindsay no choice but to follow.

When the trunk opened, Lindsay knew they weren't going anywhere. "That's great. Have you ever put air in that thing?"

"It's not my fault the tire's flat," Mira said sharply. "I've only had the car a few months."

Lindsay could see a large gash along the sidewall and doubted the tire would have even held air. On top of that, there wasn't a jack in sight. She'd never changed a flat herself, but she'd seen her dad do it and had no doubt that they lacked the proper equipment. A prickling sensation along the back of her neck made her turn away from the trunk and look around. She didn't see anything, but she had the feeling that they were no longer alone.

"Um, why don't you call your dad and see if he can come and get us," Lindsay suggested.

Mira perked up at the suggestion. "I could call Dylan. I bet he'd love to give us a ride."

"He'd love to give *you* a ride, maybe. That's fine, I don't really care who you call as long as it gets us out of here."

"You really are a little scaredy cat."

Lindsay flinched and clamped down on the urge to deny being a feline shape changer. Then she realized that Mira hadn't a clue to the Panthera and was only teasing her again. Mira pulled out her cell and turned away to have a little privacy, Lindsay thought. Fat chance of that. Lindsay wasn't about to slog off into the darkness just to give Mira a chance to exchange kissy noises with Dylan. She didn't know for sure that someone lurked out in the weeds but she thought they did and that was enough. She wished she had Lee's abilities and instincts, but Lindsay was only a teenager. The *Kadin* hadn't even known about the Panthera a year ago, yet seemed to have an amount of control that Lindsay could only envy. Lee told her it would come with age and experience.

"Damn, I don't have any reception. Let's walk over to the train station," Mira suggested. "Maybe we'll get a better signal."

Lindsay's scalp prickled and she tried to scan all around as they moved toward the now-defunct transit station. She pushed aside weeds as tall as her thighs and tried not to run like a frightened rabbit every time she heard a noise. Lindsay gritted her teeth and wished she really had eyes in the back of her head. Not wanting to appear over-reactive or immature in front of her friend, Lindsay kept quiet. She tried to believe it was just the unusual situation that had her on edge.

Still twenty yards from the station Lindsay asked, "Do you have a signal yet?" The screen lit up.

"Two bars."

Distantly, Lindsay heard the phone ringing. A squeak from up ahead caused her to stumble over an uneven patch on the ground. At the same time she could have sworn she heard a brief metallic snick from somewhere behind. Lindsay grasped Mira by the upper arm and urged her to move faster. Mira shot her an irritated glance and pulled free.

"It's going to voicemail. Hey, Dylan, it's Mira. Me and Lindsay have a flat tire out by the old train station. Call me when you get this message. Bye."

Lindsay approached the old station. In the darkness, the structure resembled a hulking beast with a gaping mouth that invited them to enter at their own peril. Lindsay was smart enough to know that her imagination supplied those helpful images. In reality, it was just a rundown wooden structure that had lost all hint of paint. Windows were smashed out long ago by vandals, and the door hung by a single rusty hinge. The hinge caused the squeak Lindsay heard earlier as the door blew in the evening breeze.

Stepping onto the platform provided them with some concealment, giving Lindsay a sense of security. Mira's concerns seemed to focus on more tangible things than the inexplicable noises in the night. Lindsay worried about an entirely different type of predator.

"Look out for snakes."

"There aren't any," Lindsay said. "Snakes are cold-blooded and most likely holed up somewhere staying warm."

Lindsay heard gravel crunch under a booted foot and turned toward the sound. With her back to Mira, she tried to control the shift to adjust only her eyes. Remembering all the warnings drilled into her by her parents and other Panthera over the years, she couldn't allow Mira to see anything unusual, though she doubted Mira would notice if she sprouted wings. Lindsay could hear her loud footsteps as Mira endeavored to explore the platform through the weak glow of the Buick's headlights.

She felt a shiver travel throughout her body as she strained to contain the transformation. Bursting into a fully formed jaguar adolescent was easier, barely requiring a thought. Controlling her body to alter a single feature required tremendous concentration, something hard to attain considering the situation. While she had to hide her nature from Mira, Lindsay's instincts were screaming that danger approached and she needed to *see*.

"Oh man, I just remembered that Dylan went to New York this weekend to watch the Jets play. Let me try to call my dad."

Lindsay barely heard her. Her eyes narrowed, the pupils elongating as her vision expanded outward. She quickly scanned their immediate area but didn't see anyone approaching the station. Belatedly, she realized the platform and old building actually prevented her from fully assessing any threat. If there was a predator, they could hide anywhere. Something caught her eye and Lindsay squinted back down the dirt road leading back toward town. Surprise caused her breath to hitch in her chest, but there was no mistake. Almost a quarter of a mile away and concealed beneath a tree sat the same white panel truck she'd noticed sitting in front of her house.

"I think you should call the sheriff's department."

Mira snapped her phone closed and drifted over to stand beside Lindsay. She glanced around trying to see what had garnered Lindsay's attention. "My dad's not picking up either. Why should I call Sheriff Macke?"

"Because I think there's someone out there."

"Really, that's great. Maybe they'll give us a ride." Before Lindsay could stop her, Mira shouted, "Hey, is someone there? We have a flat."

"Stop," Lindsay hissed, making a chopping motion with her hand. Her eyes converted back to human as she whirled toward Mira. "Don't you think whoever that is would have already said something if they were in the mood to help us?"

"You're being paranoid. There's probably not anyone there anyway. Let's just walk back to town."

"It's two miles away," Lindsay shot back, stung by the paranoid comment.

"Well, I'm not going to stand here all night. I'm going. You can come with me or you can stay here. It's your choice."

Mira stepped off the platform and into the high weeds without a backward glance. Lindsay couldn't let her go alone, but hesitated to follow. Finally she decided that if someone did attack them, she would shift and defend Mira regardless of the Panthera Council and her parents. She'd be grounded for the rest of her life, but at least they'd still be alive. Lindsay hopped off the station steps and hurried after Mira. She caught up to her as they passed the Buick.

Even as a bead of fear-induced sweat trickled from her hairline, Lindsay hugged her heavy coat closer. Mira wasn't completely wrong in accusing her of being overly suspicious. Lindsay hadn't any proof that someone lurked behind them with nefarious intent, only her instincts. For several minutes nothing unusual happened. They tramped down the road, their feet sinking into the dirt slightly with each step. Lindsay spotted the turn up ahead that would lead them back into town and felt the tension in her shoulders ease.

A metallic thump sounded from behind them, back toward the abandoned train station. Lindsay recognized the noise as metal striking metal. She thought something had struck the side of Mira's car. The fact that Mira's eyes widened and she twisted her head around to look back the way they'd come told her Mira heard the noise, too.

"Maybe you should call Sheriff Macke now."

Mira's iPhone display glowed brightly in the darkness as she complied without discussion. "I only have one bar."

"Try it," Lindsay hissed. She looked back over her shoulder, but still didn't see anyone. Her augmented abilities allowed her to hear a woman on the other end of the connection answer.

"Nine-one-one, what is the nature of your emergency?"

"This is Mira Pye. I'm on Old Mill Road with Lindsay Drake. We had a flat and someone's following us."

Lindsay turned again and forgot to listen to the ongoing attempts of the emergency services operator trying to calm Mira when she finally saw movement. The Buick's headlights backlit a figure creeping toward them. Lindsay had the impression of bushy hair, but her attention centered on the large rifle aimed in their direction.

"Mira, he's going to shoot us. Run!"

Heeding her own advice, Lindsay sprinted down the road. Mira took off beside her but they hadn't taken half a dozen steps before Lindsay heard a hissing sound followed closely by a sharp sting in the back of her neck. She gasped and slapped a hand to the wound, surprised to discover a barb sticking out of her skin. Lindsay stumbled a few more steps before stopping to stare dumbly at the needle. Orange feathers decorated the end of the dart. Lindsay's vision swam and she shook her head.

"Come on, what are you stopping for?" Mira ran back and Lindsay felt her arms grasped and shaken. "We need to go."

Lindsay heard another zipping sound and watched numbly as an identical needle struck Mira in the left shoulder. Unlike Lindsay, Mira's eyes rolled back in her head and she crumpled into the dirt. Lindsay's tongue felt thick and she wondered why Mira was sleeping in the road. She must really be tired. A nap sounded like a really good idea. She sank to one knee, aware that she needed to stay awake. Something bad was happening, but her head felt like it was stuffed with cotton and she couldn't remember what.

A foot in her back shoved her to the ground. Lindsay felt the coolness of dirt against her fevered cheek. Still, she fought to keep her eyes open. The only thing she could focus on was a pair of dark, thick trousers and heavy black boots. Their attacker didn't speak, which seemed like the most eerie thing of all.

When next she opened her eyes, Lindsay thought she must have lost consciousness for a few minutes. She was lying in the back of a vehicle with her arms immobilized behind her back. She thought they were moving, but not very fast. A warm body bumped into her when the vehicle turned.

Mira.

Where were they and why were they in the back of a vehicle? Weren't they supposed to go see a movie? She should remember the answers to these questions, but it was too hard to think. Her head was pounding.

The vehicle stopped suddenly and Lindsay slid forward a few inches. Mira's head butted into her chin. She heard a muffled curse from the front and then a phone rang. For a second she thought Mira managed to hang onto her phone, but then realized their abductor was getting a call. Lindsay tried to shout that they were being kidnapped. Her mouth wouldn't obey her commands and all she managed to do was mumble incoherently. The effort proved too much and her head swam.

Minutes later, Lindsay realized the truck wasn't moving anymore. She heard a panel slide open and strong arms lifted her from the vehicle. Then she was sitting upright in a hard-backed chair. Cruel hands tied her in place. Lindsay smelled dirt and old, crusty oil, but couldn't see. No lights burned and her vision still blurred. Her thoughts had cleared slightly and she tried to keep calm. Lee had once advised her that in a crisis Lindsay needed to take note of details. She remembered the sight of trousers and heavy boots, what else?

Sniffing carefully, she couldn't detect cologne or perfume. The kidnapper had never spoken. Sweat. She smelled sour sweat. She heard a snarl of frustration and an object flew through the air toward her. Lindsay felt the air displacement as whatever it was narrowly missed her face and ricocheted off the wall behind her. Lindsay flinched, expecting an attack. It never came. A door slammed and her senses informed her she was alone.

Where was Mira?

Lindsay struggled to pull her hands free but the bonds were too strong. With every effort her headache pounded more. With the assailant gone, Lindsay no longer felt an imminent threat. Her chin sank toward her chest and she slept.

Chapter Nine

"COME ON, PICK up," Jamison muttered.

Just as she thought the call would go to voicemail, Ranger Thomas answered. She sounded out of breath but Jamison was far too angry to worry that she might have interrupted something.

"This is Kessler. Where are you?"

"Uh..."

"Never mind, it isn't important. I need you to get over to Old Mill Road ASAP."

A startled pause ensued before Brenda said, "Okay, but I'm not exactly dressed for work."

So she had interrupted. Jamison couldn't help that. "I don't care. We have a situation. Two kids are missing and we need people to help us search."

"I understand, Chief. I can be there in about ten minutes."

Jamison wanted to throw her phone into the windshield. Ten minutes could mean the difference between finding the girls alive or dead. "Get there as fast as you can."

She hung up without waiting for an answer. A few minutes later she turned onto a dirt lane. Squad car light bars and headlights made the area almost as bright as midday. From the crowd assembled down by the train tracks, Jamison figured any evidence was already obliterated by trampling feet. Even more aggravated, Jamison pulled her truck to the side of the road and headed toward the horde of well-intentioned volunteers and law enforcement officials on foot.

Jamison smelled snow on the wind. She tucked her chin into the collar of her fur lined jacket, trying to ignore the chill seeping into her bones. The cold she felt was caused by more than just the weather. Two girls were missing, one of whom shared a close relationship with Jamison's partner. No less disturbing was the fact that Lindsay also shared Lee's general physical characteristics, the same as the two dead women who'd most recently occupied the local morgue. Determined the teenagers wouldn't share the same fate, Jamison strode up to the troop of law enforcement officials standing near a late model Buick. Sheriff Macke held court there, apparently accompanied by Detectives Hex and Chase. Deputies milled around the area, boasting suitably somber expressions. Detective Seaver hovered near the back, trying to remain inconspicuous while taking pictures of those in attendance. Jamison remembered that suspects often tried to interject themselves into any investigation, sometimes just to see how much the police really knew.

She noticed several prominent Panthera present, most notably elder Marie Tristan. Tristan stood near the sheriff and Jamison felt her hackles rise. The elder was far too ambitious as far as Jamison was concerned. As second to the Council of Elders, Tristan continuously challenged Darlene Kessler's authority. Jamison tried to forget all that for now. Lindsay and Mira were the priorities. At least Tristan brought others to help search. A small crowd of volunteers stood a short distance away including Marie's brother-in-law, Tim North. Jamison wondered if Marie would prove so helpful if one of the missing weren't a Panthera cub.

Sheriff Macke noticed Jamison's arrival and that appeared to be the cue she was waiting for. "All right people, gather around. We've got two missing teenagers. Right now we're not ruling out foul play so I want everyone to be careful. All search teams will have a minimum of two people. No one goes out alone and no one tries to be a hero. Each team will have a radio. Make sure you're on channel two."

"Who are the kids, Sheriff?" A young woman asked.

"Lindsay Drake and Mira Pye. Deputy Gomez will distribute pictures of the girls. If anyone sees them, radio me. If you see anything suspicious or out of the ordinary, radio me."

Jamison lost patience with the sheriff, tired of the posturing. "How do you want us to break up?"

Macke shot her an exasperated look. "Detective Hex, since your people don't really know the town I'd like for you to search the train station and surrounding area for anything that might tell us where the girls are."

The sheriff went on to say that all major arteries in and out of Harmon had already been shut down with roadblocks. She assigned deputies to the search teams and sent them to scour the surrounding woods. Jamison didn't miss the scent of fear emanating off the stalwart woman, which troubled her even more. Macke turned to Jamison as soon as the searchers headed off on their various assignments.

"What?" Jamison demanded.

"Don't start with me, Kessler. I'm having a pretty bad night as it is."

"Tell me what you know."

Macke rolled her eyes. "I plan to do just that. Hex and her team already know, but I didn't want this made public knowledge."

"Fair enough."

"My office received a nine-one-one call from Mira Pye. She said someone was following them. Then the dispatcher heard another girl's voice saying someone was about to shoot them."

"Lindsay."

Sam nodded. "That's the assumption. Their parents said the girls were headed into Lake Placid, but I guess they had a flat."

"So they really are in trouble."

"Now we don't know that," Sam argued. "They could have just gotten spooked and walked back toward town. Maybe they got turned around in the dark. I'm sure you noticed the street lights aren't working."

Jamison knew that wasn't what happened. Mira might get confused in the dark since she was fully human, but not Lindsay. She didn't feel the need to point that out. "I'll take some of the Panthera and head into the park."

"Then you think this is related to our killer?" Sam asked in a low voice so others wouldn't overhear.

"The timeline is right," Jamison said, shaking her head sadly. "And Lindsay is a young blonde. Not only that but she's Lee's apprentice."

"Apprentice for what?" Sam quickly raised a hand. "Belay that. I don't want to know, but I should point out that's another link back to Grayson. Even you can't deny the obvious anymore, Kessler."

"Trust me, I wish I could. Unfortunately, burying my head in the sand isn't going to change the facts."

Macke nodded. "Turn your radio to channel two."

Jamison turned to walk away from Macke and felt something twist under the sole of her boot. At first she thought it was a rock, but the object rolled too precisely. Frowning, Jamison knelt down. Although covered with sand, she could clearly make out the feathered end of a tranquilizer dart. A shiver raced down her spine.

She felt Sheriff Macke step up behind her. "What did you find?"

"Do you have any latex gloves?"

Sam stepped away and returned a few moments later. She passed the gloves over Jamison's shoulder. Rather than don the latex, Jamison dropped a glove over the dart and picked it up. The feathers were attached to a one c.c. syringe. She held it up for the sheriff to see.

"Damn. Who the hell carries a tranquilizer gun around?"

"Someone hunting specific prey."

Sheriff Macke held out an open evidence bag and Jamison dropped the dart inside. "I'll get this over to the lab. Maybe we'll get lucky and find a print."

"I hope so. We need a break in this case."

"We may have just gotten one. Mira was on the phone with us when all this happened. I seriously doubt whoever took them planned for such a quick response."

Jamison stood up. "Regardless, he still has them. As far as I'm concerned, this just proves it's our guy."

"Should I call off the search here and send the other teams into the Park? That is where we found the other victims."

"No, we still don't know where those women were killed, even though we know their deaths were almost instantaneous. That didn't happen where they were found so there has to be another explanation. If our killer did make a mistake, you'll find the signs of it here."

"Because he didn't have time to clean up after himself?"

Jamison nodded, glancing at the dart Macke held. "That's the theory."

"From your lips to God's ears."

"There's something else, Sheriff. The killer has always taken his victims when they were alone, with no witnesses. Why the change? Was Mira an accident?"

"Or has our psycho escalated to taking two victims now?"

"It's happened before, but I just don't know. Too many things aren't adding up. The first two crimes were well executed and there wasn't any evidence left behind. Why would he suddenly do something like cutting Lee's brakes or taking two victims in such a sloppy way? It's almost like he's becoming unhinged."

"I hate to say it, Kessler, but if he is devolving, this could be the start of a spree."

The throb of a helicopter sounded overhead and they both looked upward. Dinah's craft came into view and her searchlight winked on, scouring the ground. Jamison felt the heat generated by the strong light as it passed over her skin. More optimistic with the air support, she decided to leave Sheriff Macke to her work.

"For what it's worth, I don't think that's it. We just don't have enough answers yet. I'd better get moving, but please let me know if you find something with the dart." Jamison glanced away from the helicopter and caught Marie's eye. She gestured for Marie, Tim and the others to follow her.

She saw Marie shoulder her way to the front of the group and didn't look forward to what would happen next. Assigning the elder to search the woods along with the rest of the volunteers was liable to backfire in her face. No doubt Marie would deem such a task beneath her and take over the operation. Jamison waited near her pickup, sizing up the group of about fifteen as they approached. If they'd been human, she'd have worried the force wasn't large enough. However, more than a dozen Panthera were a formidable force. Too bad the Adirondack Park was so huge. Still, Jamison realized she needed to utilize her resources to the best advantage.

Jamison had already triangulated the area where they'd discovered the previous victims. She thought it important to concentrate on that remote section. If caught unprepared by Mira's timely call to the local constabulary, the killer would be inclined to dump the girls quickly. At least that would be the smart thing to do, as disturbing as Jamison found the possibility. Altogether, the area equaled about sixty-five square miles, certainly not insurmountable considering their jaguar abilities.

"Kessler, tell us what's going on. Sheriff Macke won't say anything."

Jamison wasn't surprised that Marie made the demand. The others looked to her for guidance and as much as Jamison didn't care for the woman, there had to be a chain of command. Marie Tristan represented the Council here and everyone knew it. "You all know we're looking for

Lindsay Drake and Mira Pye. You are our best chance of finding these kids unharmed. Macke and her people mean well, but they would literally stumble on top of a clue and never know it. If there's something to be found, we are their best hope."

"They shouldn't even be here," Marie snapped. "Did you see how they've been tromping all over the place? You can't even get a decent scent."

"Yeah," a faceless voice agreed.

Jamison heard murmurings among the group and quickly silenced them. "Which is why some of us are staying here to help out. The rest of us are moving to search the park. Elder Tristan, if you could take a group in from River Road just north of Stark Falls and move south I would appreciate it."

She deliberately couched her order in the form of a request, but it still took a moment for Marie to nod in agreement. Jamison assigned other groups to move in from the east and west to converge in the center of Carry Falls Reservoir, the Massawepie Area and Grass River Waterfalls. She assigned three cats to each group for a total of five search teams.

"Elder Kessler," Tim North began. "I noticed you have a specific area in mind. Is there something else you're not saying?"

Jamison couldn't divulge information concerning an ongoing murder investigation or how she knew this particular region was most critical. Instead, she focused on the seriousness of the situation. "The sheriff's office received a nine-one-one call from Mira. The dispatcher heard Lindsay say someone was after them."

Low, ominous growls rumbled around her and Jamison quickly checked to see that no humans stood nearby. She felt the same way, but needed to get her Panthera back under control before someone decided to lash out. Before she could, Marie spoke up again.

"They were kidnapped?"

The hardness in her gaze prevented Jamison from prevaricating. "Yes."

For once, the obdurate elder didn't continue to posture. "Let's get started. The more we wait, the longer this animal has our children."

"I think it best if we park near the entrances and search the park in pelt," Jamison suggested.

"I concur. We can cover more ground faster and will be less likely to miss anything. Let's all meet toward the center of the open field near Bog Road."

"No," Jamison interrupted, unwilling to allow Marie to usurp her authority. Jamison was still a jungle cat and the park was her territory. "We'll meet behind the camp area near Roman Falls. It's closer to the center of the park and off a main roadway where a human might see us."

"Makes sense," Tim offered, clearly trying to appease the two dominant jaguars.

Marie's nostrils flared and Jamison thought she would dispute the decision. "Fine, but let's move. I feel like time is racing by and we do not have that luxury."

Jamison agreed. She nodded and turned away, trusting the Panthera to comply with their instructions. Vehicles started and pulled out in a semi-orderly fashion. Jamison opened the door of her truck but had yet to slide inside when a beat up station wagon drove up beside her. She caught sight of Brenda's frizzy hair, looking even more untidy than usual.

Walking up to the driver's window, Jamison waited until Brenda lowered the glass. A slightly acrid scent wafted out of the interior. Wrinkling her nose, Jamison leaned down slightly. "I'm glad you could make it. Head down to the train station and help Detective Hex and her team out. They're concentrating on the tracks and the old platform."

It would have been nice to have Brenda's help searching the park since she definitely knew the region, but couldn't have her in the national park area with a prowl of jaguars searching the woods.

"What about Mira's car?"

"Yeah, they have the Buick, too. They're looking for anything right around the immediate area that might indicate the girls headed into the woods."

Brenda nodded. "What if they didn't?"

Jamison thought it pretty sad that Brenda was hardened to the point of assuming this wasn't just a case of a couple of lost kids. "Then we need to find evidence that would point to a suspect."

"I'll park and head right up there."

"Good, and watch your step. You never know when you might mess up something important."

Jamison moved away and climbed into her vehicle. She reached for the cell phone to call Lee while starting the engine. She had healed and deserved to be involved in the search for her apprentice. Lee picked up on the first ring and Jamison smiled, knowing her partner had been with Dinah when the sheriff called. Jamison was just surprised Dinah had talked Lee into getting out of the helicopter.

"Have you found them?"

"No, not yet. How would you like to help out with the search?"

"Where should I meet you?"

"Some of the Panthera are heading into the park to search. Can you meet me at the Deerlick Falls campsite?"

"Of course," Lee said. "I'll get there as fast as I can."

Jamison told Lee which park road to take that led straight to the campsite and quickly hung up. She fastened the seatbelt and pulled out onto the dirt lane, her mind already occupied. She didn't intend to join the main hunting teams. While it was important to search those areas, she had a feeling the Panthera would come up empty. Before long, she drove into the park. Jamison bounced along on the dirt lane, but refused to slow down. She stopped in the high grass on the shoulder about a quarter of a mile from the campground.

Headlights appeared in the distance and Lee arrived a few moments later in her dark blue rental car. The lights shut off and she had already stripped off her shirt when she slammed the door. "Where are the others?" Lee asked, hurrying over to Jamison's side.

Jamison surprised Lee by embracing her. She pulled Lee against her and briefly closed her eyes, needing the feel of her mate. Lee's strong form provided a sense of comfort Jamison couldn't find anywhere else. The anger she'd experienced all night, generated by the fact that someone had the gall to kidnap two of Harmon's children, slowly dissipated. Long fingers threaded through her hair, further cooling her ire and helping Jamison center her focus.

"They're searching other parts of the park."

Lee squeezed her and stepped back a pace. "Then what are we doing here?"

Jamison dropped her arms. "Playing a hunch." She gestured toward the tree line. "About a hundred yards through the trees is the campground used by our first murder victim. It's been closed to the public since we found the body."

"You're not expecting whoever grabbed Lindsay and Mira to bring them here are you?"

"No." Jamison shook her head. "I think our murder victims were ambushed in the woods, possibly along one of the hiking trails. They were killed in the forest, placed inside some kind of four-wheel drive vehicle and transported over near Cherry Falls. Detective Hex had Seaver and Chase check out this road and the nearby hiking trails, but they didn't find anything."

Lee frowned in frustration. "Jamison, I appreciate that you still have a murderer to catch, but shouldn't we concentrate on finding the girls."

Jamison almost snapped that finding Lindsay and Mira was exactly what she had in mind. She caught herself at the last minute and realized they were right back where they'd been before Lee's car wreck. Jamison let go of her impatience with difficulty. Sometimes being a dominant Panthera made her lash out without thought.

"I am," she said as calmly as she could. "Look, Lee, all of this is connected. I don't know how, but I know it is. The person who has the girls is the same one who killed Lauren Reid and Pauline Nielsen and the best way to find them is to figure this out."

Lee slipped her t-shirt back over her head and ambled over to the tree line in question where she turned back to face Jamison. "All right, we need to find something, some kind of trail that Chase and Seaver couldn't. You said before that both women died by bleeding out from severed arteries. That would make quite a mess. No one has reported anything like that on the hiking trails?"

"No, but it's the off-season. We have few campers this time of year and even fewer bird watchers or hikers. The detectives only searched the immediate area, but really, the killings could have happened anywhere."

"Not anywhere," Lee disagreed. "I think you can rule out any areas where a vehicle can't travel. I don't care how strong someone is, you can't carry dead weight for long over rugged terrain."

"That's true and the hiking trails aren't wide enough for that, but they all merge with a main road. I'd like to change into pelt and scour this area for ourselves. If we can find a blood trail, we might be able to trace it back to the source. We'll probably only end up with tire tracks..."

"But we could follow those tracks."

"A human couldn't do it, but we haven't had any rain since the last death."

"And like you said before, there aren't a lot of tourists this time of year so there should be few tire tracks other than the park vehicles."

"Right," Jamison agreed, "and those tracks would be easily ruled out."

"Then what are we waiting for? Let's go get my girl."

Chapter Ten

"DID YOU FIND them?"

The sound of her mom's worried voice caught Casey North's attention because it was so unusual. Sitting on her knees in the living room, Casey had been watching Scooby Doo chasing the Boo Brothers, but she forgot about them when she heard her parents talking. Even her dad sounded scared. Daddy wasn't scared of anything. Casey saw him bury his face in her mother's shoulder. He spoke in a low voice, but she heard him anyway.

"No, nothing. It's been hours now."

Casey smelled his sweat; it carried a tinge of fear. Something bad had happened and they were trying to talk about it without letting her hear. Of course that only made her more curious. She cocked her head to the side, focusing her directional hearing.

"We found Mira's car on Old Mill Road. It looks like they had a flat, but there's no sign of the girls. Some people searched the woods around the car and the train station while the rest of us went into the park. It's like they just vanished."

"Surely they haven't given up looking?"

"No and I don't think they will until they drop over from exhaustion or find something. I just wanted to come home and check on you two."

They continued whispering until her father realized Casey was eavesdropping. Abruptly he released his wife and turned toward his daughter with a strained smile. "Hey, Snow White, what are you still doing up? It's late."

Daddy always called her Snow White because she had such dark hair and pale skin. She giggled and then answered. "Mom said I could watch Scooby Doo until you got home."

"Is that right? Well then, it looks like it's time for you to turn in." Her father squatted down beside her and lifted Casey sideways into his arms.

"Five more minutes?" she pleaded. "It's almost over."

"You've seen this one a hundred times."

"I know, but it's so funny when Shaggy gets flour on his head. Please?" Casey batted her eyelashes at her dad and allowed her lower lip to tremble.

"Okay, okay," Tim chuckled. "Don't go into the act."

He sat her back on the floor and headed for the kitchen. The house phone rang and he adjusted his course toward the study.

"I'm going to make your father something to eat. When that's over go upstairs and brush your teeth."

"Okay, Momma." Casey said absently, looking at the television but no longer seeing the cartoon.

She'd never heard her dad so upset and even Mom sounded frightened. Two kids were lost in the woods. Casey thought that was silly. The old hilly road was only a few blocks away from their house. How could someone get lost when they were practically in town? Casey watched Scooby and his pals solve mysteries all the time and finding the girls didn't sound all that hard. Even Shaggy helped and he was even sillier than Scooby. If Shaggy could help Fred, Daphne and Velma find clues, how hard could it be?

Casey jumped up and headed for the coat closet beside the front door. She shoved her feet into her battered sneakers, disregarding the hole in the toe on her left shoe. Casey could smell the cold air seeping under the threshold so she pulled on her warmest coat and tugged on her fuzzy pink mittens. She had great night vision, everyone said so, but it was nighttime and she was still a little afraid of the dark. Hesitating only an instant, Casey grabbed her father's Maglite off the closet floor, turned and left the house. She was careful to close the door tightly behind her.

The heavy-duty flashlight wobbled unsteadily from side to side. Her fingers weren't long enough to wrap all the way around the handle and her mittens made her grasp slippery so she held it with both hands. Staring at the illuminated patch on the ground did little to relieve the movement-induced nausea, but Casey refused to give in. Daddy would be so proud of her when she came home with the girls. Just the thought of success made her grin as she pushed her unruly black curls back from her forehead with one hand and then quickly returned it to the handle.

Her hair was getting too long and her mom wanted her to get it cut when they went shopping that afternoon but Casey escaped the ordeal of the Beauty Shop by faking that she had a tummy ache.

Grownups all thought she was a little kid, but Casey intended to show them. They'd all see how smart she was when she found Lindsay and Mi...Mi...Lindsay's friend.

Their house was four blocks from downtown and the Adirondack forest started not far from the old lumberyard. All she had to do was look over near the woods there and she'd find the girls. They'd all be back before bedtime. Easy peasy. So why couldn't adults think the same way? Harmon couldn't be that big.

Before she reached the edge of town Casey started to shiver. It was cold tonight and already she wished she'd gone upstairs like her mother told her. She could be in her bed right now, with Daddy reading a bedtime story. Casey could almost feel the warmth of the covers. On top of being cold, she suddenly had the feeling that eyes were everywhere, watching her every move. She imagined one of those creepy old paintings from a Scooby Doo cartoon. The bad guy was always inside the painting and their eyes followed when you moved.

Swallowing hard, Casey thought of their lost girls. If she went home now, what would happen to them? Casey would want someone to come find her if she was lost. With that in mind, she took a deep breath and kept walking. Maybe she could shift into her cat form and then she'd know for sure if anyone followed. Immediately, she rejected that idea. To transform, she'd have to take her clothes off. Momma didn't like it when she changed without getting naked because it ruined her things and Casey wasn't about to strip down outside in this weather. Not only that, she wouldn't be able to hold the flashlight. If she lost the light, she couldn't see if any monsters decided to attack.

Just the thought of monsters almost did the trick. Casey stopped walking and turned around. Standing on the far side of Harmon's square, she looked back toward her house. She couldn't see it in the dark, but she did see an approaching car. Casey's heart pounded in her thin chest and she ducked behind a mailbox. The vehicle passed slowly and Casey peered around the edge of the metal box to see a police car. Deputy Gomez looked all around the deserted streets but never looked her way. Silly human, Casey thought.

As soon as he disappeared around the corner, Casey scooted out from behind the mailbox. Seeing the deputy still searching solidified her resolve. She wouldn't give up. Casey started off in the direction of the old hilly road. The hilliest road into Harmon that she knew of was where State Highway 86 came into town. The rest of the town was pretty flat.

Casey stopped at the edge of the square and carefully checked for traffic before crossing the highway. There wasn't much on this side of town except for the old police station that was now a dog grooming shop, a couple of antique stores, and a fenced off area that held the city workers' heavy equipment. The dirt here stank like old oil-soaked soil. Weeds and red dirt thrived. Casey thought it was kind of scary because no one was around this time of night. A chilly wind gusted, lifting her dark hair and she shivered. The heavy flashlight wavered.

Passing the closed shops, Casey passed out of the glow from streetlights. With no clouds overhead, the moon and stars seemed particularly bright. She jumped when the sound of a cargo train shrieked in the night. A few moments later she heard the chug of the wheels and then the enormous monolith raced into view. She watched the train for a while thinking how cool it sounded. Sometimes when she couldn't sleep, she'd lie in bed and hear the train from her bedroom window. The train never stopped in Harmon anymore, but she really liked the sound it made.

After the train disappeared from view, but not from her acute hearing, Casey started looking around the old out buildings. The nearest structure resembled a squatty concrete box with high windows. Casey considered setting the flashlight on the ground so she could jump up and grab the sill to peer inside. She rejected that idea. Being without the light was scarier than being on this side of town alone in the middle of the night. She sauntered boldly to the front of the structure and discovered that it was unlocked.

Casey grinned and leaned around the doorframe, shining her beam everywhere. Just a bunch of old machines and junk. She frowned and checked out the other small storage structures but didn't find anything except more stinky equipment. It didn't take long for the excitement of attempting to solve a mystery to wear off. Casey sniffed as her nose ran from the chill. Her ears felt numb and she had to stifle a yawn. When she turned to head for home, Casey realized she was near the dirt road that looped around the back side of the business district. It ran across a small bridge that traversed the river. There weren't any houses back here, but there was one final construct that caught her eye. She'd almost missed the deserted lumber mill because it sat in darkness beneath a couple of ancient maple trees.

"It's the last one," she said and then quickly stopped talking. The sound of her own voice frightened her.

Casey wanted to go home and go to sleep, but she couldn't say she looked everywhere if she didn't check the mill. Determined to check this last edifice as quickly as possible, Casey hurried across the city lot with her light pointed toward her destination. Twenty yards away she heard a furtive, shifting sound and stopped dead in her tracks. Her heart raced and her eyes went wide.

A possum knocked over an aluminum can and scaled the chain link fence. Beady eyes turned in her direction and the little beast hissed. Casey growled back at the creature and it scurried away.

"Yeah, you better run." Suddenly reassured that a hatchet murderer wasn't about to charge, Casey felt brave.

Expecting to find more of the same that she'd discovered in the other buildings, which was exactly nothing, Casey hustled up to a window. The sound of water rushing behind the building was loud. She shone the light through the glass, but couldn't see anything with it covered in spider webs and gunk. Casey went to the front door and found a shiny new padlock holding it closed.

Casey jumped when she heard a thump from inside the building. She wondered who would be inside a locked building and decided it was probably another possum. Regardless, until she checked inside she couldn't go home. Casey would just have to find another way in. She climbed onto the mill's porch and then noticed that one corner of the building was raised on pillars. Casey hopped down from the platform and crouched down to walk under the building. The river ran close beside the mill and Casey had to be careful not to fall over the bank and into the water. She could hear it lapping gently. Her nose wrinkled in disgust when she ran face first into a spider web.

She wiped at the sticky strands and then noticed it was really dark under the lumber mill. Feeling strangely exposed despite being under a heavy structure, Casey thought again of changing into pelt. She almost didn't care that she'd destroy her clothes. At least she'd have fangs and claws to fight with. But the fear of her mother's anger outweighed her fear of the dark. Casey heard another thud and remembered why she was there.

Looking around carefully with the flashlight, Casey saw a small wooden ladder. The ladder led up to the bottom of the building. Curious, she stepped onto the bottom rung and peered upward. She smiled when her sharp eyes noticed the seam around the edge of a trapdoor. She climbed up the stairs and put a small hand against the hatch. It didn't budge. Casey put the flashlight sideways under her chin, attempting to hold the torch while pushing on the trapdoor with both hands. The angle was impossible.

She sighed in frustration. Casey didn't see how she had enough strength to open the door without putting down her only light source. Suddenly, she realized how she could have her light without holding onto it. She stepped off the ladder and set the base of the torch against a pillar before shoving a rock under the face cap. Perfect, the beam shone directly where she needed it.

Casey climbed back up the ladder and put both hands against the trapdoor. It moved about a half inch before banging back into place. "Crud."

She took another step up until she was crammed with her back up against the door. Casey braced her feet, grabbed the side braces and shoved as hard as she could. Her stomach muscles burned and Casey felt the veins on her neck stand out. The hatch moved again, but it still wasn't enough. More discouraged than ever, Casey became angry. Her lips parted as her canines erupted into long fangs. Her vision expanded until she could see every dirty corner under the lumber mill as clearly as she could have in the day. Muscles strained against the fabric of her shirt and she suddenly felt hot.

Dirt and old cobwebs rained down upon her. Boards creaked in protest. A chunk of wood let go from directly overhead and a rusty nail caught her just below the right eye. She was so focused on the trapdoor that Casey barely felt the sting. The trapdoor lifted abruptly and shot upward, crashing onto the floor inside the lumber mill.

Casey panted for several seconds to get her thudding heart back under control. Her thighs ached and her hands trembled, but she finally had a way inside. She wiped absently at the moisture on her face and then grimaced at the sudden pain. Only then did Casey realize she'd been injured. For a moment her lower lip quivered and tears filled her eyes. The pain wasn't that bad but she was worried about having a yucky scar. Panthera healed fast, but she was a cub. Cubs had to grow into their abilities.

A soft noise overhead distracted her and Casey blinked into the dark interior. Mounting the remaining rungs, Casey climbed high enough that she could look around. This space wasn't as cluttered as the others, but there was still a large machine blocking her sight. Moonlight cast a limited glow through dirty windows, illuminating part of the room but leaving the rest in shadows. Nothing moved.

Disappointment caused her to slump slightly. After all the work she'd done to get into the building, there was nothing here. Casey shook her head like she'd seen her father do when he was upset about something. She bent over and started back down the steps when she heard a whimper. Standing up quickly, Casey took another slow look around. She still couldn't see much so she climbed up higher until she stood on the main floor. Sawdust drifted upward and tickled her nose.

Standing up on tiptoe, Casey strained to see all the way to the back of the large room. Her eyes still arrested in partial shift, she clearly saw an older blonde girl against the rear wall. Gooseflesh erupted over her scalp and Casey thought she might jump out of her skin when she realized she had found Lindsay Drake. No longer worried about monsters or bad guys, Casey ran across the dilapidated boards. She leapt over a bad place on the floor and crouched down beside Lindsay.

"Hey, what are you doing here? Everybody's looking for you."

Lindsay's long hair looked dank and greasy in the darkness and when she lifted her head her eyes looked like glass. Pupils wide and dilated, Lindsay seemed confused. "Wh...who's there?"

"It's me, Casey. What's wrong with you?"

Lindsay shook her head and frowned. "I can't move."

Casey cocked her head to the side, trying to figure out why Lindsay couldn't move. Then she saw why. "Hey, you have a chain around your waist."

The comment made Lindsay jump. She started struggling from side to side, accomplishing very little that Casey could see. Her eyes opened wide, but still looked shiny. "Get me out of here before he comes back." Her words slurred a little.

Suddenly realizing the urgency of the situation and that Lindsay hadn't been "lost" at all Casey leaned behind her looking for a way to loosen the chain. The rusty links were looped around a corner pipe and tied into a heavy knot, like someone was in a tremendous hurry. Casey pulled off her mittens and shoved them into a pocket. She wrestled with the heavy iron that was almost as wide as her hand.

"Be still. Every time I get it loose you yank it tight again."

"Just hurry."

"Why can't you just bust out of it?" Casey asked. "All you have to do is shift."

"I can't. He shot me with something."

"Whatever," Casey mumbled, not quite understanding. The links gave way under her persistence and Casey freed Lindsay from the pipe. It was only when Lindsay leaned forward that Casey saw a piece of old wire restraining her wrists. "Here, hold on a sec."

As soon as she was loose, Lindsay struggled to her feet. She lurched drunkenly to the side and Casey grabbed hold of her. She helped Lindsay toward the trapdoor and they had just made it to the bottom of the ladder when Casey remembered there was supposed to be a second girl.

"Where's your friend?" Casey asked as she bent over to retrieve her flashlight.

Lindsay whimpered again. "I don't know. She wasn't there when I woke up."

"Duh, I know that. I was there when you woke up, remember?"

"No, earlier. I haven't seen her since someone shot us."

Casey thought that was really cool, but she didn't see any holes in Lindsay and didn't smell any blood. All she could smell was the bitter scent of oil and iron. "You were shot?"

"Tranquilizer, I think."

Lindsay crouched down to slip out from under the lumber mill and hit her head on a support joist. Casey smelled blood now. She took Lindsay's hand and assisted her out from under the building. In the attempt to get Lindsay out into the open, Casey wasn't paying attention and stepped off the edge of the embankment. Her foot went into the river and she jerked it back in aggravation. When she did, Casey dropped the flashlight and it rolled a few feet away.

"I'm fine. Get your light."

Lindsay bent over with her hands on her knees. Casey gave Lindsay a minute to catch her breath while she went after the Maglite. If she lost it, her father would be mad. Later, when asked, Casey couldn't have said what caught her attention. She looked up and saw something white against the river's edge. Whatever it was, it seemed out of place. As she stared at the object, she slowly realized she was seeing Mira. She rested in the water, her arms floating with the small current. Mira's head lay in the mud near the bank.

"Oh man, I wish I had some Scooby Snacks." Casey had a feeling she would need some to get her courage up. She knew Lindsay wasn't in any shape to help her friend so she would have to.

Swallowing hard, Casey wended her way along the grassy riverbank. She leaned down and put her hand into the icy water to grab the back of Mira's jacket. Casey tried to pull the dark-haired girl farther up onto dry land but her limited human strength wouldn't cooperate.

"Help me." She glanced back and saw that Lindsay was only just coming to understand what was happening.

Even in the darkness, Casey noticed how green Lindsay's face appeared. Still, Lindsay staggered toward her and dropped to her knees. Together they managed to pull Mira out of the water. The girl remained unconscious. Lindsay held Mira against her chest, unmindful of the wetness.

"Go get help."

"Why me?"

"Because I still can't see straight and I'm not leaving her."

Casey wanted to argue the point. Now that she knew there was a bad guy out there and it wasn't just a cartoon fantasy, she just wanted to go home. Unfortunately, she knew Lindsay was right. There wasn't any point in replying so she jumped up and grabbed the flashlight. She handed it to Lindsay and then took off at a jog toward the main road. Casey could see her breath in the air and her sneakers crunched against the gravel. It seemed like it took forever to get back to the square, but she knew it wasn't that far. She forgot to check for traffic and lunged right across the road and into the path of an oncoming car. The headlights made her freeze and she turned in disbelief to look at the approaching vehicle.

The driver slammed the brakes on and Casey heard the squeal of rubber against pavement. Casey thought she heard a muffled curse. Her fingertips stung with the surge of adrenaline and she thought she'd just run right out in front of Lindsay's kidnapper. The car door opened and still she stood rooted in place. Casey snapped out of her daze when the car's suspension squeaked as the driver exited the vehicle. She took a single running step before a familiar voice stopped her.

"Casey North, what are you doing out at this time of night?"

Casey spun around and ran toward Deputy Gomez. She flung her arms around his waist. "I found Lindsay and her friend. They need help."

Gomez crushed his cigarette under his boot and then grasped Casey by the upper arms. He pushed her away enough to kneel down. "Are you sure it's them?"

Who else would it be? Casey frowned. "Of course I'm sure."

"Where are they?"

"At the river beside the lumber mill."

Gomez glanced worriedly in the direction of the river before standing up. "Get in."

He flipped on the light bar and stepped on the accelerator as he settled into the driver's seat. When the headlights illuminated the girls, Gomez reached for his radio. "Gomez to dispatch, I have the girls. They're next to the river beside the lumber mill. Notify the sheriff and send an ambulance."

Casey felt insulted that the deputy waited until he saw the girls for himself before calling anyone. Why couldn't adults ever believe her without seeing it with their own eyes?

Chapter Eleven

LEE GROWLED LOW, the sound barely disturbing the night. Still, Jamison heard and loped over to where her mate's white coat stood out against the inky blackness of shadows. The sound carried a mixture of feline fascination with a hint of disgust. She'd never heard Lee make that particular vocalization before and it understandably roused Jamison's curiosity. Padding across the hiking trail, Jamison's black pelt all but disappeared beneath the darkness cast by the huge tree. She scented blood on the back of her tongue before arriving next to Lee. As a jungle cat, she could discern that the blood belonged to a human. Judging from the sheer volume, the human would not have survived the loss.

The prey?

Jamison captured the impression from Lee's mental projection that she asked if the blood belonged to the two murder victims. In their animal forms, Lee would instinctively phrase any inquiries from that mindset. Prey naturally referred to any creature hunted and killed. Jamison wrinkled her nose and then sneezed in disgust.

Yes, one of them.

Sniffing around, Jamison found a cigarette butt. She coughed when she detected the stench of burnt tobacco, nicotine and saliva. The smoke stick lay atop the blood, dried into the pool. The positioning of the cigarette told Jamison it was deposited there while the blood was fresh. Their predator had made a mistake. Not quite the skilled killer they had assumed.

Something crashed through the underbrush and Jamison swung around with her tail toward the tree trunk. She felt Lee take up a similar stance with their rumps together so that they faced outward. Jamison raised her head and scented the air, but couldn't detect whoever approached. There wasn't enough wind to carry the information she needed. Crouching low so that her chest brushed the grass, she peered into the night.

Long moments later, a lean, tawny jaguar with a white muzzle sauntered down the trail. Jamison spotted the gleam of metal from his left ear. Travis Rooker, Andy's younger brother. Jamison chuffed from her place of concealment and his head turned sharply. Instinctively, Travis tucked his body in and hissed a warning. Jamison growled, but only to announce her presence. Travis immediately relaxed, but dropped his eyes to the turf to show deference.

The cubs are found, he informed her without preamble. *Healer treating.*

Jamison felt triumphant at the news and roared, uncaring of the fright she might cause in any park visitors. The sound carried joy that the cubs lived, but also a warning to anyone who might injure Panthera young. Jamison felt Lee urge caution, yet her mate couldn't refrain from growling her support. Travis added his own deep rumble. Jamison's roar would carry or a mile or two in the darkness, but the growls would not. Had she been in her alternate form, Jamison might have cared.

Others?

Elder released.

Annoyed, Jamison's ears flattened against her skull. That she would have sent the hunters home herself made little difference. Jamison didn't like it that Elder Tristan had made that decision in her absence. Higher reasoning held little sway at this juncture. This was Jamison's territory.

Issuing a threatening growl, Jamison turned and loped back toward her vehicle. Lee followed closely and Jamison felt the panting breath on her tail. She heard Travis depart in the opposite direction and assumed he intended to engage in a more satisfying pursuit while darkness remained. He'd earned it.

By the time they reached the Chevy, Jamison had all but forgotten Marie's transgression. She felt good running free under the night sky, full of hope for the future that their young were safe. Threats would always exist, that was the way of the world. But right now, life was good. Reluctant to convert back to her human form, Jamison nevertheless felt the overwhelming desire to see the children. She couldn't wander into a hospital in her current state.

Jamison lay in front of the pickup, feeling Lee hover protectively over her. Green eyes closed and she willed the transition. Bones realigned quickly, sliding and reforming. Her thick tail shrank until it disappeared into her spine. Jamison's teeth and claws retracted. While painless, the transformation back to her humanoid form brought none of the joy she felt when shifting into a jaguar. The world seemed to shrink in on itself, narrowing down to only what she could see with her reduced visual acuity. Scents faded until all she could smell was the cold night air and the dirt on which she lay.

Shivering, Jamison stood up and slid her fingers into the fur on Lee's head. "I'll be right with you, baby. I'm freezing."

She ran around to the side of the truck and grabbed her clothes off the seat. Jamison dressed quickly, finishing up just as the first snowflake drifted onto her cheek. Rather than allow Lee to lie in the cold while she changed shape, Jamison threw open the passenger side door.

Lee didn't wait for an invitation. She leapt onto the seat to initiate her own alteration. Jamison knew it would take Lee a few minutes since she wasn't quite as practiced, having grown up in a full human home knowing nothing of the Panthera. Giving Lee some privacy, Jamison went to retrieve Lee's things from the rental car. She felt like skipping, happy that the girls were at the medical center.

She returned to the Silverado to discover Lee lying shivering on the bench seat. "Hey, you're getting pretty good at that."

"Practice makes perfect," Lee quipped, reaching for her clothes. "Was it this cold when we got here?"

Jamison shook her head and looked up. "The temperature has dropped in the last few hours. It's snowing."

"Yeah, I noticed." Lee sat up, pulling on her hiking shoes. "What are we going to do now?"

Jamison could see the hopeful look in Lee's blue eyes and felt torn between responsibility and desire. She wanted to go see the girls, but needed to collect the evidence they'd discovered. The crime scene needed to be isolated and searched for any other clues. Finally, she decided on a compromise. "I'll go collect the cigarette butt. It's been immersed in blood and exposed to the elements for weeks but I can't just leave it here. I'll radio for a forensic team while I head to the hospital. Why don't you go ahead? I'll be right behind you."

"No," Lee said slowly. "It shouldn't take but a few minutes and I'd rather not leave you out here alone."

"I am a big, bad jaguar, you know," Jamison teased with a slight smile.

"I know, but with all the crazy stuff that's been happening I'd just feel better if we stay together."

Warmed by Lee's concern, Jamison promised to hurry. They took the pickup back and Jamison used a pair of latex gloves from the first aid kit to collect the butt. Without a handy evidence bag, she could only wrap the cigarette in the glove and place it in a compartment on the console. Then she drove Lee back to the rental car. Turning around on the narrow trail required that they drive off into the scrub. The task wasn't difficult for the pickup, but Lee had to employ more care in turning the sedan around. Finally, they headed back in the right direction and Jamison followed Lee out of the park.

Ten minutes later, Jamison shut off her headlights as she pulled into the parking space, navigating easily by the scattered light poles. Lee parked in the space beside her and they headed for the nearest hospital entrance. Neither spoke, each lost in her own thoughts. Jamison had the nagging sensation that she'd missed something vital tonight, and it had nothing to do with abandoning the killing field in the park. Technically, it wasn't a field, but Jamison thought the description accurate.

No, it was something else that she couldn't place. Jamison thought she'd focused so extensively on finding the missing girls that she'd been blind to anything else.

"Are you okay?"

Jamison started to respond to Lee's concern when Sheriff Macke's squad car screeched into the parking lot. Sam stopped in the fire lane next to the emergency entrance. The engine shut off, but Sam already had the door open. Jamison didn't miss the expression of distaste before it quickly disappeared.

"I see good news travels fast."

"The wind was with me," Jamison quipped. "I figured you'd already be here. What took you so long?"

"I got a tip someone saw the girls out by Regis Mountain." Sam fell into step with Jamison and Lee, hitching her gun belt up to a more comfortable position. "Imagine my surprise when Gomez reported he found them in the middle of town."

"You gotta love eyewitnesses." Firsthand accounts were generally the least reliable source of information. Memory was a funny thing, with people often projecting personal biases onto descriptions of individuals and events.

Sam shocked her by saying, "Apparently, Casey North found them."

"Casey?" Lee asked. "Tim's little girl?"

"Yeah." Sam shrugged. "He called the dispatcher about forty-five minutes ago to say Casey was missing. I'd just authorized an Amber Alert when Deputy Gomez radioed that he'd found her."

They rounded a corner and Jamison spotted a small group up ahead at the nurse's station. A young child sat perched on the top of the counter. She looked tiny with a thin, white blanket draped around her shoulders. Unruly black curls stood out sharply against the paleness of her skin. A white bandage covered a wound on her cheek and Jamison spotted blood on the collar of the child's shirt. Casey North sported a huge grin that stood out in sharp counterpoint to the worried yet proud expressions on her parents' faces. Jamison noticed one of Casey's sneakers was soaking wet.

"Don't you ever take off like that again." Amy North sounded stern, but the gentle hand she ran through the curls gave away her tender emotions.

Sheriff Macke stopped to speak with the charge nurse and Jamison shamelessly eavesdropped. "How are they, Sharon?"

A small redhead smiled flirtatiously, but Macke appeared not to notice. "A tetanus shot and a couple of stitches for Casey. She's a lucky kid. Doctor Martin is checking the other girls out now. Their parents are with them."

"Good," Sam replied. "No one goes in other than medical personnel until I say otherwise."

Jamison had already turned away and was far more interested in hearing what Casey had to say. "I hear we have you to thank for finding Lindsay and Mira."

"Yeah," Casey said, ducking her head shyly before leaning against her mother's shoulder.

Lee stood closely beside her and Jamison could sense her

amusement. "Casey, how did you know to look over by the city yard?"

The child sat up and her face screwed up as she concentrated. "I heard Daddy say Mi...Mi...Lindsay's friend had a flat tire on the old hilly road. So I went to the hilliest road I knew of. It wasn't far from our house."

Lee snorted softly and Jamison couldn't look at her for fear of breaking into laughter. Instead, Jamison bit her lip to smother her smile. It wouldn't do to look so amused when Casey was so serious. For a long moment, she couldn't speak safely. Fortunately, Lee came to her aid.

"What made you look in the lumber yard?"

Casey kicked one heel against the counter and sat up straight. The blanket slipped off one shoulder. "'Cause I'm a genius, like Albert Frankenstein."

That was it. Jamison turned her head away and choked on her laugher. Casey's parents chuckled as did Deputy Gomez who stood sentry outside the examination room.

"It's not funny," Casey asserted, offended by their mirth.

"I'm sure it wasn't," Jamison agreed as soberly as she could. "What you did was very brave. It was also very dangerous. You could have been hurt going after the girls by yourself. You're very young."

"I'm seven and a half years old," Casey huffed. "'Sides I wasn't worried about that. I could see good but the chain was hard to untie. It was all gunky and stuff."

Jamison was relieved Casey didn't mention her abilities as a Panthera in helping her to see in the dark. Things could have become awkward with all the medical personnel standing around and passing through the area. Then Jamison realized what she had said. All humor vanished with the remark and suddenly everyone was interested in what the little girl had to say.

"What chain?" Jamison asked.

"The one Lindsay had around her. But I don't know how she got all twisted up in it or how her hands got trapped behind her." Casey raised one fist to rub tiredly at her eyes.

Jamison met Sheriff Macke's eyes over the top of Casey's head. She didn't miss the concern in the sable eyes. With an innocent comment, Casey had confirmed their worst fears. There wasn't any point in questioning the child further. She was too young to understand everything she'd witnessed and she looked exhausted.

"Can we take her home now, Sheriff?" Tim asked, hefting his little girl off the counter and into his arms. Casey buried her face in his shoulder.

"Sure, go ahead. I'm glad she's okay."

Jamison spotted a familiar figure approaching at a fast clip as the North family left. Detective Hex gave Casey a bright smile that quickly vanished as she passed them by. Her dark hair stood up in a tangle on one side and she sported a smudge on one cheek. Hex's usually immaculate garments looked rumpled and stained. Jamison thought it looked like she'd been crawling around in the dirt. Her eyes went straight to Macke and again Jamison had the sensation that she had missed the obvious.

"What'd I miss?"

"Not here," Sam responded.

The door to the exam room opened and Jamison's attention centered on Doctor Martin's demeanor. He didn't seem overly concerned. "How are they?" she asked before anyone else could.

"Lucky." Martin rubbed a hand over the back of his neck. "We're running tox screens on both of them, but I'm willing to bet we'll find out they were drugged. Both girls are showing signs of heavy sedation. Other than that, they have only minor bumps and bruises."

"We need to know as soon as you get the results," Sheriff Macke informed him.

Doctor Martin didn't look happy. "No offense, Sheriff, but there is such a thing as doctor/patient confidentiality."

Jamison felt anger wash over her at this minor impediment and spoke up quickly. "Doctor, this is an ongoing investigation. In order to find whoever did this we need as much information as possible."

"And I'm happy to give it to you," he responded. "But first you'll have to obtain a warrant or get the parents' permission."

"We'll give it," a deep voice stated. "I want this son of a bitch caught."

Jamison looked at Lindsay's father. He appeared to be as angry as Jamison. She understood that their response stemmed from a sense of outrage that someone would perpetrate such a crime against their community. It took only an instant for him to communicate his desire for Panthera justice. She also wanted vengeance, for everyone who'd become a victim in the last month. Still, she communicated the urge for caution.

"You'll sign something to that effect?" Martin asked.

"Don't worry, Doctor," Jamison said sarcastically. "We'll make sure you're absolved of any liability." Lee placed a restraining hand on her arm, but Jamison turned away from the physician to take in the rest of the group. "We need somewhere to talk."

Sam took a step forward. "Yes we do. Mr. Drake, do you mind staying with the girls for a while? We need to debrief Deputy Gomez."

"Wild horses couldn't drag me out of here."

"Why don't you use the hospital cafeteria?" Doctor Martin suggested. "It should be deserted at this time of night."

Jamison thought he would be disappointed if he thought the offer would earn him any points. She understood the need for protocol, but had little patience for anyone or anything that would obstruct their investigation. She turned on her heel and strode down the hallway toward the cafeteria, aware of the others following. Jamison shoved open one of the double doors and flipped on the overhead lights.

She flinched when someone touched her lightly between the shoulder blades. Spinning around, she encountered Lee's concerned blue eyes.

"Why are you so mad?" Lee whispered.

Jamison raked fingers through her hair. "I don't know. I'm just tired of being behind this guy and I've had the feeling all night that there's something we're missing."

"Like what?"

"I wish I knew."

Deputy Gomez followed up the rear of the group and stood near the exit until Jamison motioned him over. The others all gathered around him. Jamison wanted to demand answers from him, but allowed Sheriff Macke to take the lead. As his superior, she would command his respect and Gomez would more likely answer Sam without hesitation. If Jamison questioned him, Gomez might hold back out of a sense of loyalty to his boss.

"Tell us what happened, James."

Not exactly the tactic she would have taken, Jamison thought, but it proved effective.

"Well, I was patrolling around the square looking for suspicious vehicles when Casey North ran right out in front of my cruiser. It scared me to death; I almost hit the poor kid. She told me that the girls were over by the lumber yard. I radioed dispatch immediately to send out an ambulance and notify the sheriff."

Jamison's lips compressed. She could have obtained that much information from an impersonal police report. "What did you see when you arrived on scene?"

Gomez pulled a pack of cigarettes from his shirt pocket and shook one out. He placed the cigarette in his mouth but didn't light it. It bobbed slightly as he spoke. "The Drake girl sitting by the river bank. She was holding Mira in her arms. I almost didn't see them but then I saw the flashlight beam."

"Was Mira unconscious?" Jamison asked.

Gomez nodded. "Yes ma'am. She was sopping wet too, like she'd just been pulled out of the water."

Lee bit back a startled gasp and Jamison didn't know what to say. It belatedly occurred to her that Lee shouldn't even be in a debriefing meant only for law enforcement. She didn't care. As far as Jamison was concerned, all of this involved Lee to some extent and she deserved to know every detail.

"The killer discarded her," Jamison observed. "She wasn't the one he wanted."

"What about Lindsay?" Macke questioned. "Was she wet?"

"Just the front of her where Mira pressed up against her."

"Did you see anything that might point to the identity of a suspect?"

"No ma'am, but it was pretty dark and I was more concerned with getting the girls to safety."

Jamison couldn't fault his choices. She would have done the same. Still, they couldn't risk someone compromising a crime scene. Crap, she thought. She'd already called the forensics team out to Adirondack Park.

"Sheriff," she said, "you might want to send deputies out to secure the area until the crime scene technicians get there. Right now, they're in the park."

Macke's eyes narrowed. "Something you want to tell me, Kessler?"

"Unfortunately, with everything that's been going on, I haven't had time to update you."

"Well by all means, do so."

Fully aware that she had to be careful here, Jamison weighed her response. She couldn't admit to everything with Gomez and Hex in the room. "While we were searching the park for the girls, Lee and I found what I believe to be the spot where one of our victims died."

"And we're just now hearing about this?" Hex demanded sharply.

"Hold on," Sam said, holding up one hand. "We've all been pretty busy tonight. Go ahead."

"It's along one of the hiking trails about a mile from Pauline Reid's campsite."

"What exactly did you find?" Hex asked.

"A whole lot of blood," Lee provided, shuddering slightly.

"And a cigarette butt," Jamison added, glancing at the smoke in Gomez's mouth. "I collected the butt and called out the forensics team."

Macke nodded sharply and pulled out her radio. She notified dispatch to send personnel to secure the area around the city yard, not just the lumberyard but the entire lot. Macke ordered that forensics report on scene as soon as they finished with the park. Once she had everyone situated, Sam said, "It looks like it's going to be a long night for me."

"Why just for you?" Hex asked.

"Technically, Harmon is outside the Park Service's jurisdiction so that leaves you and Kessler out. Since I don't plan to let anyone check out the place where the girls were held without me, I guess I'll just have to wait for the techs with my deputies."

"Well, if you think I'm going to let you have all the fun you are seriously mistaken."

Jamison smiled at Hex's badgering tone. "I guess that makes three of us."

"Not a chance," Sam insisted. "I have to be there, but you don't. Besides, things are starting to heat up and I'd prefer some of us stay sharp. Since I plan on being awake all night that means you. Don't worry; I'll keep you informed if we find anything."

Jamison didn't like it, but Sam's logic made sense. Unfortunately, she had her own responsibilities this evening. "Looks like it's up to you, Detective Hex. Now that I know Lindsay and Mira are all right I need to get back out to the park."

"You don't trust the forensics team?"

"Trust has nothing to do with it. I'm just not comfortable leaving someone else to clean up my park."

"Fine, whatever. I could point out that the park is my jurisdiction too, but someone needs to be awake tomorrow when the toxicology reports come back."

The group disbanded. Jamison heard the sheriff order Gomez to find someone to relieve him. Hex waited for Sheriff Macke and the two walked away together. Lee kept Jamison behind with a touch on her sleeve.

"Do you really have to go back out to the park?"

Not this again. Couldn't Lee understand she had a job to do? "Honey, I'm sorry, but I don't have a choice."

Lee dropped her hand. "It's okay. I understand. I don't know why I feel so nervous about being at the manor alone. I guess I'm just being silly."

Jamison blinked. She'd assumed Lee was questioning her priorities. She felt like a heel when she realized Lee was afraid. Lee's feelings were only natural considering all she'd been through recently. Jamison wrapped her arms around Lee and pulled her in tight, closing her eyes to concentrate on the feel of their hearts beating together.

"I'm sorry."

"Don't be. Wake me up when you get home?"

"I'll be there as soon as I can."

Jamison kissed Lee on the forehead and then released her. Lee walked with her to the truck. They shared another embrace before Jamison slid into the Chevy. She drove back to the park feeling alert. At one in the morning, she should have been exhausted. Instead she felt wide-awake, hopeful they would fine something at the crime scene to help bring the killer to justice. Her concern for Lee kept nagging at her and Jamison was determined to finish up at the park as quickly as possible so she could return home. Regardless of the responsible party, someone had tried to kill Lee, and Jamison didn't want to be away from her for very long.

Thinking about the car crash that later proved to be no accident, Jamison felt even worse about her previous reaction at the hospital. Lee's fear was perfectly understandable.

Jamison drove into the park, struck by how dark it was tonight. Glancing overhead, she noticed the heavy cloud cover. The absence of ambient light caused the crime scene technicians' work lights to stand out brilliantly against the darkness. It was almost like someone had bottled a bit of sunshine and contained it to within a small area. Jamison squinted against the glare. She pulled over and parked a distance from where they worked to avoid contaminating the scene.

Ranger Roy Latimer met her before she crossed half the distance. He scratched absently at the perpetual dark stubble on his jaw. No matter how freshly shaved, he sported what appeared a full day's growth. He started talking as soon as he was within range.

"There wasn't much to find out here, Captain Kessler. Most of the scene was compromised by environmental factors and scavengers. The techs will be lucky to get anything out of this."

Jamison pulled a wadded sterile, blue glove from her shirt pocket. She unfolded it to show him the cigarette butt. "Maybe they'll have better luck with this. I need an evidence bag."

They walked to the edge of the crime scene where four technicians worked. Jamison took a small evidence bag, sealed it and filled in the information on the tag. She passed it off to Latimer and signed a chain of custody form to that effect. Once finished, Jamison kept watch over the proceedings, but there was little for her to do. Shortly after two-thirty, the crew started packing things up. The lead tech, Jamison had to admit she didn't know her name, spoke briefly with Ranger Latimer. She glanced cautiously toward Jamison and then walked away.

"That doesn't look good."

"It's not," he confirmed. "There wasn't much to find, but of course I'm sure that doesn't surprise you. The snow melt contaminated the scene. It's also been almost two weeks since the attack, assuming of course that this is related to the killings."

"It is. You better stop the techs before they get away, Roy. I know it's been a long night for them, but they need to head over to Harmon Lumber. There's another scene to process."

"The place where the Drake and Pye kids were found?" At Jamison's nod he said, "No disrespect, Captain, but these folks are tired. They might miss something."

Jamison was sympathetic, but her hands were tied. "It can't be helped. This isn't the big city and we don't have unlimited resources. I'd like to say it can wait a few hours but it just can't. We need them."

Roy nodded, but he clearly wasn't happy. "I'll let them know."

He walked away and Jamison pulled out her phone to call Sheriff Macke. She let Sam know the techs were headed her way and hung up after Macke's curt "it's about time". Jamison shook her head and climbed back into the pickup. She took another quick glance around and made a silent wish that the techs would find something leading to the arrest of a suspect. Then she started the truck and headed straight home.

For a long while after turning off the ignition, Jamison sat staring at the house. She could sense Lee's exhausted slumber and hesitated to wake her. Cleo exited the house from the kitchen dog door, the flap clicking sharply back into place. The beagle sat in the grass near the steps, watching her curiously. Jamison smiled and relented. Cleo's tail wagged a couple of times when Jamison scooped her up and carried her back inside.

Stay quiet, Jamison commanded. *She needs sleep.*

Jamison stifled a yawn as she placed Cleo on the floor. She took a quick shower in the guest bath so she wouldn't wake Lee. After toweling off, Jamison creeped into the bedroom and silently stood guard over her lover for a moment. The sound of Lee's gentle respirations quieted Jamison's restless beast, just as it always did. Finally relaxed after the days harrowing events, Jamison slid naked beneath the sheets.

Lee turned toward her as soon as Jamison stretched out. Jamison smiled and wrapped her arms around Lee's shoulders. Tenderness surged through her when Lee's cheek rested against her chest. Even in sleep, Lee snuggled against her. Jamison kissed her temple and inhaled her partner's scent. Arousal washed over her. Her heartbeat accelerated. It seemed like a lifetime since they'd last touched in a loving manner. She tried to still her passion, wanting Lee to rest but Lee must have felt her need.

Pulling away slightly, Lee's eyes opened. Gazes met and briefly locked. Words proved unnecessary. Jamison eliminated the small distance between them. What began as a simple press of lips quickly flared out of control. She rolled Lee beneath her. Strong arms held her near as legs encircled Jamison's hips.

Words alone hadn't been able to mend the small hurts between them. The physical reunion breached the remaining gulf. Jamison's cat calmed from their connection. Lee whimpered, a soft sound in the back of her throat and Jamison gentled her kiss. She tasted blood from a split lip.

"I'm sorry," she whispered. "I didn't mean to hurt you."

"You didn't. You never could."

Fingers in her hair pulled her back down. Jamison eagerly complied. Sounds of passion filled the manor. Jamison lost herself in the sensations of moist flesh, heated kisses and caresses that were sometimes rough but never harsh. She belonged here, in Lee's embrace. Jamison hadn't realized how adrift she'd felt lately until now. Their union gave her strength. Roaring out her satisfaction, Jamison gave voice to the joy Lee gave her.

Somewhere in the house, Cleo barked, startled by the roar. Jamison smiled. Lee chuckled and they settled down to sleep, wrapped in warm embrace.

Chapter Twelve

SAM PINCHED THE bridge of her nose in an attempt to stave off a headache. It was almost four in the morning and she couldn't remember the last time she'd had a full night of sleep. Unfortunately, there was still too much to do. Between processing the evidence at the river's edge where the kidnapper dumped Mira Pye and anything collected in the lumber mill itself, it didn't look like rest was in the forecast anytime soon. She resented the fact that Kessler was at home sleeping. She resented that Kessler had a partner. Hell, she resented Kessler's very existence.

Since finding out about the Panthera they'd been nothing but a thorn in her side. When Nicky still lived, Sam thought they had no secrets between them. Not for the first time, she wished the Panthera was one Nicky had kept. Realizing the truth of her nature left Sam with mixed emotions about their relationship. Most of the time, she cherished every moment of their lives together. On the rare occasion, like now, Sam considered Nicky's alter ego. She thought about how Nicky changed into a four-legged creature. No matter what she did Sam couldn't change the fact that she'd slept with an *animal*. What did that make her? Sam felt sick.

"Here, you look like you could use this."

Sam turned in surprise, automatically pressing her forearm to her pistol. She acknowledged the comfort she drew from its presence even as she realized it wasn't necessary. Shooting the cup from Detective Patricia Hex's hand wouldn't make her feel any better and might even be considered an overreaction. Scratch that, she thought. Definitely an overreaction.

"Sorry about that," Pat offered. "I didn't mean to startle you."

Sam grunted in response but took the hot paper cup. From the gleam in Pat's eyes, she thought that was precisely her intent. Still, she felt grateful for the coffee. "What the hell are you doing here?"

"You're welcome."

Sam's eyes narrowed. What secrets did Pat keep? Were they anything like Nicky's? Suddenly ashamed, she attempted to cover it by taking a quick sip of the scalding brew. Pat wasn't Nicky and Sam wasn't being fair. She shook off her suspicions. "Thanks for the coffee. I just meant why aren't you getting some sleep? It's still early."

"I guess I couldn't sleep, too keyed up wondering what you might have found."

"Nothing," Sam offered. "At least nothing that particularly stands out."

"What time did the techs get here?"

"Around three. At least Kessler didn't keep me waiting too long. I barely had time to collect Lindsay and Mira's clothing before she let me know they were finished out at the park."

Hex nodded. "You think the lab will find any trace on their clothing?

"I sure as hell hope so," Sam answered gruffly. "We have a better shot at it than finding some random fingerprint. Every schmuck with a television set these days knows to wear gloves. Hair and fibers are a whole lot harder to avoid leaving behind."

"Unless you're living in a plastic bubble."

Sam frowned, reminded of an old movie with a weak plot. "Uh huh."

"You know, you seem even crankier than usual. Why don't you go get some sleep? I can finish up here."

"Can't," Sam said. "Chain of custody."

Pat rolled her eyes. "So fill out a voucher. I am a federal agent, you know."

Why can't you just drop it? Sam wondered. This was her job and she wasn't leaving until the technicians completed their work. Fortunately, Grace Beaumont headed their way before Sam became rude. Handsome, middle-aged and extremely intelligent, the African American crime scene tech ran her team like a military command. Under her watch, Sam felt confident they wouldn't miss a thing.

Sam noticed Grace's bloodshot eyes and realized she wasn't the only one operating on little rest. Grace's team had investigated four separate scenes in less than twenty-four hours, beginning with Mira Pye's Buick. Sam chose not to insult the woman by pointing out how exhausted she looked.

"Grace Beaumont, this is Detective Patricia Hex from the U.S. Park Police."

Pat shook hands with Grace and offered a friendly smile. Sam wasn't surprised when she immediately cut to the chase. "Please tell me you found something."

"We did locate another tranquilizer dart down by the riverbank. It resembles the one Ranger Kessler found by the old train station. We'll run tests on the contents as soon as we get everything back to the lab."

"I imagine they'll contain some kind of sedative." Pat shrugged like it was a foregone conclusion.

"Maybe," Grace allowed, "but I don't like to speculate. Other drugs besides sedatives can induce the symptoms the girls described. At any rate, we collected the chain used to restrain Lindsay Drake and canvassed the mill and riverbank. Together with everything we've gathered tonight, we'll try to put some of the pieces together."

"You mean from the park and the train station, too?" Sam asked.

Grace nodded. "I wouldn't get your hopes up about anything from the park though, Sheriff. That area's been exposed long enough that any evidence is surely compromised."

"What about the rest?"

"If it's there, we'll find it," Grace assured her. "No one does these kinds of things without leaving something behind. The trick is being able to interpret the minutia. At any rate, we should be finished soon."

She was right, Sam thought. Had they been fortunate enough to discover the murder victims shortly after the event, Sam felt confident they'd already have a suspect in custody. The only reason law enforcement had nothing was a case of bad timing. Pauline Nielsen and Lauren Reid died days before hikers found the bodies. Nature obliterated any trace. Because of the community's heightened awareness and a plucky seven year old, that was no longer true. Rolling out forensics within hours of the kidnapping greatly increased the odds of finding key evidence.

"Thank you, Grace. Please keep me informed."

After she walked away, Pat changed the subject. "I contacted a reporter from Lake Placid after I left last night. She's coming up later today to meet with us."

"I'm surprised you found anyone awake. It was already pretty late when we wrapped up last night."

"You know reporters. They're always awake if there's a story involved."

"True," Sam allowed. "Now if things will just settle down enough for us to have a pow-wow with Kessler and get all our facts straight before we talk to the reporter."

Pat's expression turned pensive. It was one Sam didn't think she wore well since it didn't fit her usual cocky attitude. "Should I have waited to talk with you two before I set up the meeting? I thought we were all on the same page with that."

"We are. Kessler and I both agreed the media was a good idea. It's just we haven't had a lot of rest lately and I don't want one of us to slip and let out too much information."

"Right, we need to hold something back. That makes it all the more important for you to take off and get some sleep. I'll set the appointment up for around four."

"Speaking of Kessler, you just reminded me. How did things go with Seaver following Lee Grayson around?"

Pat snorted softly. "Not well, Seaver wasn't on the job more than five hours before Grayson flew away in a helicopter. The next thing we knew, those teenage girls were taken and that was the end of that."

"Maybe it's for the best," Sam offered, hoping Pat would let it go. Following Grayson or Kessler around could result in dangerous repercussions.

"I disagree. There's something funny going on around here, I can feel it, and I'm not talking about the kidnappings or the murders. Someone targeted Grayson, someone who hated her enough to cut her brakes. I'm not saying they know why, so don't start with me," Pat said quickly. "That being said, I'm sure that same person is our killer and that Lee Grayson is the key to this whole thing."

"What are you going to do about it?" Sam held her breath, fearing the worst.

"Honestly, I'm not sure there's much I can do. Grayson hasn't done anything wrong and all I have is a theory. Somehow I don't think she'll consent to being under federal protection."

"I doubt it. Besides, Lee Grayson can take care of herself."

Pat turned to her with a frown. "What do you mean by that?"

Sam thought quickly. "I just mean that she's fairly sharp, and now that she knows someone might be after her she'll be more aware."

The excuse sounded lame even to her own ears but Pat seemed to accept it. "Well, it doesn't matter anyway. Seaver and Chase will be combing through evidence and test results just as soon as the lab has anything. Considering that we're pouring all of our resources into this, I imagine that will start sometime later today."

Sam listened closely to Pat, but her eyes watched the forensic technicians. From their activities, she assumed they were shutting things down. Grace knelt down in front of a large silver case filled with evidence envelopes. While Sam watched, Grace signed a document, placed it inside the case and secured the lid. She looked up and met Sam's gaze, giving her a single nod.

"It looks like they're wrapping it up here. I'll contact the office and let them know I'm knocking off for the night." Sam rubbed her eyes briefly. "Four o'clock works fine for me. Do you mind letting Kessler know to meet at my office?"

"Not a problem," Pat assured her. "Would you like to grab some breakfast with me before you head home?"

Sam suddenly felt like she stood on shifting sand. Her entire body tensed. Since sharing a dinner with Hex that had unexpectedly become more, Sam had avoided spending time alone with her. Pat's invitation caught her unprepared. For a long infinitely uncomfortable moment, Sam searched for a way to decline. The fact that her mind went completely blank didn't help. Finally, she decided on the truth.

"I'm sorry, Detective. I'm just too tired to even think about food."

"Detective, huh?" Pat looked down, pushing at a loose board with her toe. "So we're back to that."

Crime scene techs began filing out of the lumber mill. Grace looked at Sam and smiled in a friendly manner before following her team. Left alone, Sam decided she could speak freely. The words tasted like ash in her mouth, but she needed to say them. "Look, I don't mean to seem abrupt."

"And yet..."

"Or self-centered, but I'm just not date material."

"Who said I was asking you on a date? Maybe I just wanted to get something to eat."

From the sudden high pitch of her voice, Sam didn't buy it. She thought Pat was trying to save face. That was fine. It was probably better if they pretended there was nothing more than a working relationship between them. It would be less awkward.

"Of course, my mistake. How about a rain check?"

"Sure, no problem. I'll get hold of Kessler and we'll meet you at the sheriff's office this afternoon."

Sam nodded, but Pat had already turned to go. She frowned and shook her head. This was exactly why she didn't get involved. Bruised feelings interfered with the job. Spinning on her heel, Sam left the lumber mill. She was more determined than ever to avoid involvement with Patricia Hex. Why couldn't people be more professional?

Driving across town, Sam noticed how quiet things were. She rarely traveled around Harmon before the sun rose, preferring to work the day shift. Calls for assistance usually came in during daylight hours and Sam liked staying involved with the community. From the way things were going, maybe she needed to switch to nights.

LEE STEPPED OFF the edge of the trail and emerged from the trees. She glanced down at Cleo panting by her side. A bit of grey at the muzzle and a slightly stiff gait were the only outward signs of her advancing age. At the same time the beagle's ears perked up, Lee heard an approaching vehicle. She didn't recognize the sound of the engine and Jamison was still at work.

Stay.

She didn't realize she'd given the mental command until halfway across the yard. Lee was impressed Cleo actually remained in place. She stopped about twenty feet from the front porch, her hands on her hips and curious gaze fixed on the property entrance. A beat-up brown station wagon came into view. Lee didn't recognize the vehicle but she did know the driver.

Ranger Brenda Thomas rolled to a stop less than ten feet away. Lee thought it inconsiderate that she drove off the lane and onto the grass. Though this was a rural area and her property not the manicured lawn of her father's mansion, it still bothered her. The engine sputtered and coughed before it finally died. Thomas had already exited the vehicle before it did. She waved and smiled at Lee over the top of the station wagon before walking around the front of the car.

"Good morning, Ms. Grayson."

"Ranger. I'm sorry, but Jamison is at work." Lee offered what she thought should be common knowledge, but allowed that maybe Thomas didn't know. Dressed in jeans and a pull-over t-shirt, she clearly had a day off.

Brenda shook her head. "Actually, I stopped by to talk with you."

"Really?" Lee hadn't expected that. "What about?"

"I just wanted to see how you were feeling after the accident. I heard it was pretty bad."

At that moment Cleo ran between the women, stopping a few feet from Ranger Thomas. She seemed curious but unafraid. Brenda smiled and squatted down to pet the dog. The wind gusted at that moment and Lee was certain she smelled cigarette smoke.

"Hey pretty boy. You're a sweetie, aren't you?"

"Actually she's a girl. Her name is Cleo."

Brenda looked up at Lee but kept one hand on the beagle's back. "I'm glad to see you weren't seriously injured."

Her sincere expression made Lee feel guilty. She'd teased Jamison mercilessly about what she called Brenda's "boss crush". Seeing how nice she was to Cleo and taking into consideration that she'd driven out to check on Lee put a new spin on things.

"Just a few bumps and bruises," Lee told her. "Would you like to come in for a glass of iced tea?"

Brenda gave Cleo a final pat and stood. "That's sweet of you, but I don't want to take up your time. I was just driving by and thought I'd stop for a minute."

"Are you sure? It's no trouble."

Brenda's face stilled. Her eyes seemed to go flat and the smile vanished. Her entire body tensed, giving Lee the sensation of a coiled spring. She had the distinct impression that Ranger Thomas was suddenly furious. The shadow in her dark brown eyes sent a shiver down Lee's spine. "No. Thank you."

Lee felt confused by the sudden shift in demeanor. "I didn't mean to offend you."

"You didn't."

Brenda's unexpected smile on the heels of her anger was equally bewildering. Lee struggled to keep up. "Um, okay. Well, thanks for stopping by?"

Apparently, that was the right thing to say. Brenda relaxed abruptly. Her shoulders slumped like a puppet master had cut the strings. Her grin stretched wider and Lee felt her own cheeks ache in sympathy. She pivoted on her heel and retreated to the far side of the station wagon. Her eyes darted down toward Cleo and then back up to Lee.

"Watch out for the pooch. I'd hate to run over her backing out."

There was nothing ominous in the statement. To the casual observer, Brenda merely expressed concern for Cleo's well-being. Lee wondered why the words sounded like a veiled threat. She squatted down and hefted Cleo into her arms, standing in place while Brenda drove over the grass in a wide circle before heading back down the driveway. Lee waited long after the sound of the engine vanished, somehow expecting Brenda to return. When she didn't, Lee let out a long sigh and looked down at Cleo.

"That was weird."

Lee glanced at her watch. It was almost five. Jamison should be home soon. She'd definitely have to speak with her about Brenda's unexpected visit. Lee turned Cleo loose and headed back into the manor.

Chapter Thirteen

JAMISON LOOKED AT her watch. Almost five, she thought. Lee would expect her soon. Unfortunately, that wasn't going to happen. The reporter was due to arrive in a few minutes and they still weren't ready. She sat in a hard wooden chair in Samantha Macke's office surrounded by Hex, Detectives Seaver and Chase, and Sheriff Macke herself. The room wasn't that big to begin with and having five adults inside made it feel positively claustrophobic.

"Got a date?" Hex asked curiously.

Jamison wanted to roll her eyes. She wasn't trying to hide the fact that she'd checked the time, but why did Hex see the need to point it out? "No, I was just thinking I should call Lee and let her know I'll be late."

"We'll be finished in a few minutes," Macke assured her.

Jamison nodded. "Right. Anyway, if we can have the reporter release her story in the morning that should give us time to set up phone banks. I hope you guys are ready because once that story hits the air, we're going to be slammed with useless tips from well meaning citizens."

"You're not wrong about that," Hex said. "The phones will be ringing off the hook. We'll need extra operators not to mention as much manpower as we can bring in to chase down leads."

"I can bring in all off-duty rangers from the park. That's about fifteen bodies and it's all I can spare. I need the rest to be working the forest."

"Isn't it the off-season?" Macke asked. "How many people do you need?"

"You're right. It is the off-season, but that doesn't mean there aren't still campers," Jamison pointed out. "Plus, there are always people willing to hunt when they think there's no one around."

"Poachers," Hex snorted. "I hate those guys. How many extra deputies can you pull in, Sheriff?"

Jamison noticed that Detective Hex wouldn't directly meet Sam's eyes. There was some tension going on there and she wondered what had happened between them. She tried to shift her focus back to the matter at hand. Their relationship had nothing to do with her and she did not want to get involved.

"Not as many as Ranger Kessler. This is a small station for a small town. Adirondack Park has more resources than the sheriff's department."

"It'll have to do," Jamison said. "Also, I have a suggestion in regard to the reporter. I think we should hold back some information from the public. This way we'll have something we can use to verify any tips."

"I take it you already have something in mind?" Sam asked.

"The lipstick. If any Good Samaritans say anything about the lipstick then we'll know they're actually involved. We all know that there are a percentage of these killers that like to inject themselves into the investigation."

"I can't argue with that." Hex folded her arms and leaned against the wall. She raised one heel and rested it on the paneled surface behind her.

Detective Hex hadn't sat once in the last hour, giving Jamison the impression that she would rather be anywhere other than here. Hopefully they'd catch this monster soon and she'd get her wish. Jamison turned her attention to the other two occupants. In a human investigation, lower level officers waited until directly included to volunteer information, but Jamison didn't work that way. She was accustomed to Panthera traditions and all members of the community were equally included.

"Have we heard anything from the labs yet?"

Seaver glanced at Hex in surprise as though asking permission to speak. Jamison noticed Hex merely awaited her response. That was a point in her favor, Jamison thought. She had nothing but respect for Hex. Macke could certainly do worse. Jamison realized where her internal musings had taken her and how dangerous things could become for the detective should such a thing happen. The Council already suspected Detective Hex could pose a threat to them. If she became involved with the local sheriff, who knew about the shape changers' existence, things could turn extremely ugly for Hex.

"Nothing from the local labs," Seaver answered. "Jack and I heard from the New York lab that they got a partial print off of Ms. Grayson's Mercedes. It's pretty smudged but they're running the print through all databases including the National Crime Index and Interpol."

"Interpol?" Sheriff Macke scoffed. "Surely you don't think we have an international serial killer on the loose in a National Forest?"

Hex frowned and Jamison easily sensed her irritation. Hex didn't like Macke taunting her people. Hex confirmed Jamison's suspicions a moment later.

"There's no need to get snarky, Sheriff. I'm sure Detective Seaver was merely pointing out that we might have a lead."

Jamison's eyebrows rose. This was getting interesting.

"It's okay, Sheriff," Seaver said quickly. "I think we're all a little tired. I know I can't wait for this to be over."

Chase nodded. "Agreed, I don't want to have to tell anyone else that they've lost a sister or daughter. I want this bastard caught and I'm thinking the sooner we get this story out the better."

"Jack, don't you have a birthday coming up soon?" Detective Hex asked.

"Not me, my son. He'll be seven in a couple of weeks."

"You're very lucky," Seaver said. "I don't have any kids, or a partner for that matter, this job takes too much out of me for that. Still, it would be nice to have some time off. I feel like I've been awake for a month."

Sam looked uncomfortable that the conversation had drifted onto personal topics. She cleared her throat and pushed back slightly from the desk. "When do you expect to hear back from the lab on the prints?"

An uncomfortable silence ensued. Jamison broke it by saying, "Detectives Seaver and Chase, why don't you two go ahead? Check in with the lab and see if they've found anything yet. The reporter will be here in a few minutes anyway."

The two looked surprised by the abrupt dismissal, but left when Detective Hex agreed. The reporter arrived less than a minute after the officers left. For the next hour Jamison forgot about calling home and immersed herself in the details of the case, what information they could safely release to the public, and concern that there would soon be another victim. Their suspect couldn't be happy about Lee surviving the car accident and then losing both Lindsay and Mira.

The sun had begun to set before they finished. Jamison stretched and left the reporter, Sherman Gibson, in the sheriff's capable hands. She still needed to go back to the office before heading home. On some days, Jamison regretted being in charge of the Paul Smith's Visitor's Center. She decided to call Lee after she left her office. Working late wasn't that unusual. Lee would understand.

Jamison drove the Range Rover into the park's main lot. The first thing she noticed was Brenda's car. Simultaneously, she saw that Jeanie Kraus had already left for the day. Strange, Brenda wasn't scheduled to work today. Jamison had given her the day off so she'd be ready to chase down leads after the story about the killer broke. She spotted Brenda sitting at the top of the steps leading into the ranger's station, but couldn't see her face. Brenda's elbows rested on her knees and her head was down. She appeared utterly dejected.

Concerned, Jamison pulled into her space and quickly shut off the engine. Absently, she locked the door and stepped around the back of the vehicle to look at Brenda. It took a moment to realize what was different. Then she saw the blood on Brenda's shirt.

"Brenda, are you all right?"

Jamison sprinted across the concrete lot and knelt down in front of her. She hesitated before resting a hand on Brenda's knee. "Look at me. What happened?"

Brenda looked up and Jamison saw tears flood her eyes. Her lower lip was split and swollen. A large bruise had formed on the lower left side of her jaw. "I didn't mean to upset her, honest." The words slurred a little, affected by her injury.

"Who did this to you? Who was upset?"

Blinking back the tears, Brenda glanced away and chuckled slightly. She grimaced from the pain and said. "I know it wasn't my place, but I went to see Ms. Grayson. I just wanted to say that I was glad she was okay."

Jamison recoiled in disbelief. "You're saying Lee did this? Why?"

Brenda shrugged. "I'm not really sure. I must have said something upsetting to her. To be honest, I can't really remember what it was. Maybe she thought I was looking for you or that we had something going on. It all happened so fast."

She realized Brenda had misunderstood. "I wasn't asking why Lee hit you. I was asking why you would say something like that."

"Excuse me?"

"Brenda, clearly someone attacked you but I highly doubt it was Lee. She would never do something like this. If someone made you say that, you need to tell me."

Jamison reeled backward when Brenda stood. Her position on the steps gave her an additional two feet over Jamison.

"You don't believe me? Even seeing the evidence with your own eyes, you still don't trust me?"

Brenda's voice echoed throughout the parking area and Jamison winced at the volume.

"I'm sorry, but I just can't. I know her too well."

"And you don't know me, is that it? I've worked with you for over a year. How can you say that? Why would I lie? Maybe she's jealous that we spend so much time together. Have you ever thought of that?"

In point of fact, she hadn't. Yet now that Brenda mentioned it, Lee had teased her relentlessly for the last few months. Jamison shook off the split-second of suspicion. It was possible that Lee harbored a bit of jealousy about Jamison spending time at work with Ranger Thomas, but she would never physically abuse someone. Jamison trusted her and that would never change. She felt sure that someone made Brenda blame Lee.

"Brenda, please tell me who did this to you. I can protect you."

"Forget it. I don't know why I ever thought you'd believe me." Brenda's face had turned red and the veins stood out in her forehead, obvious signs of her anger. She pushed past Jamison and started walking across the parking lot.

"Wait, where are you going? You need to get that cut looked at."

Brenda spun around and spread her arms wide, walking backward. "What do you care? Huh?"

She walked away then, but Jamison was sure she heard her mutter something that disturbed her greatly. She was sure Brenda said she was going to *fix* things. Fix what things?

Somehow the sun had set without her being aware of the event. The lights had come on around the parking lot and Jamison stood exposed directly beneath one. Her mind whirled in confusion and concern. She couldn't figure out why Brenda would make such an accusation, but she was adamant that Lee was the guilty party. Jamison thought Brenda might even believe it. Jamison didn't know what to think, but she was sure of one thing. Any paperwork could wait until later. Right now, she needed to get home.

Jamison pulled up in front of Mafdet Manor. Even in the unsure glow cast by the headlights she saw where tires had flattened the grass. The tracks made a wide half-circle before winding back around to the driveway. Neither Jamison nor Lee typically drove onto the grass. Pondering the implications, Jamison parked next to Lee's rental car in front of the garage. The insurance company had a while yet to settle the claim for the Mercedes. Jamison still found the car's absence unsettling. More disturbing yet were Brenda's claims of violence perpetrated by her partner. The tire tracks lent credence to the ranger's presence at Mafdet, but Jamison just couldn't believe Lee would strike the woman out of some misguided sense of jealousy.

She found Lee in the living room, curled up on the sofa with a novel. Cleo lay on the rug warming beside a crackling fire. Both of them embodied the picture of domestic bliss. Moreover, Jamison sensed only quiet contentment from her small family. As much as she trusted Lee, Jamison had to admit to a tiny kernel of doubt about Lee's innocence. Brenda had been so adamant and Jamison had seen the physical evidence of an assault with her own eyes. Yet seeing her now, any suspicions vanished like ether on the wind.

"Are you going to stand there or would you like to sit down?"

The teasing glint in Lee's baby blue eyes extinguished any lingering tension. Jamison smiled and settled next to her, placing an arm around her shoulders. She kissed Lee's temple and then her lips. For the first time since encountering Brenda on the steps of the ranger's station, the situation didn't seem so dire.

"Anything exciting happen today?" Jamison asked in a deliberately casual tone. She hoped Lee would bring up the topic on her own.

"Exciting? No, not that I can think of." Lee placed her novel on the sofa arm and snuggled closer. "Now that you mention it though, something strange did happen. I had a visit from Ranger Thomas."

"Oh?"

"Yeah, I thought she was looking for you but she said she came by to check on me. I don't really believe that's true. I think she wanted to see you and tried to save face when she found out you weren't here."

Her tone had assumed a teasing quality, as it usually did when the subject of Brenda Thomas came up. "Lee, surely you know you have nothing to worry about. I love you."

Lee pulled back to see her face. "Of course I know that. You don't think I'm jealous do you?" When Jamison didn't respond, Lee said, "You do!"

"It's all right if you are."

"Stop. Jami, I'm not jealous. I guess I make light of the situation because I feel bad for her. Joking about her boss crush is just my way of dealing with it."

"You feel bad for her?"

"Yes. It's not that confusing. Honey, you're an amazing woman and I can't blame her for how she feels about you. I feel bad for her because I know she'll never have what she wants."

Jamison cleared the lump in her throat. "Sometimes your capacity for compassion is staggering."

"Yeah, well I never said I was completely altruistic. I have no intention of stepping aside either. Why all the sudden curiosity about my attitude toward Ranger Thomas?"

This was about to become uncomfortable. Jamison turned toward Lee, raising one knee onto the cushion. She took Lee's hand.

"I went by my office after leaving Macke and Hex. Brenda was sitting on the steps when I arrived."

"So, did she say I was rude to her or something?" Lee asked, seeming amused.

"Actually, she had a busted lip and a bruised cheek. She said you punched her in the mouth."

"She said what?" Lee surged to her feet and Cleo growled, raising her head from the braided rug. "That's ridiculous, I would never hit her."

"I told her the same thing."

"You did?" Lee perched on the edge of the sofa. "What did she say?"

"She was pretty angry. I tried to get her to tell me who really hit her, but she insisted it was you."

Lee's expression turned pensive. She walked over to the hearth and stood staring down into the flames. Considering the recent unfounded doubt, Jamison thought she owed it to Lee to give her a minute. It didn't take long. She turned back to Jamison and slipped her fingers into the jean pockets.

"On the plus side, I don't feel so bad for her anymore."

"I'm sorry. I just can't figure out why she'd say such a thing."

"Do you think it's possible that Brenda hit herself?" Lee asked softly.

Jamison was shocked by the suggestion. "I hadn't considered it."

"Well think about it, honey." Lee ran a hand through her hair, leaving it slightly mussed. "Brenda shows up with a fat lip and I'm the prime suspect. Clearly she was trying to illicit sympathy from you. I guess admiring you from afar wasn't good enough anymore."

"It didn't work." Jamison walked over to Lee and hugged her close.

"What are you going to do now?"

"Nothing. I'm going to act like nothing ever happened. Regardless of her motives, now she knows that my loyalties are with you. I think it's better if we focus on keeping things at work strictly professional. As far as Thomas goes, the ball is in her court. We'll just have to wait and see what she does next."

"What if she files charges on me with Sheriff Macke?"

Jamison shook her head. "I doubt it will come to that. She doesn't have any proof because it never happened. Still, I think you should avoid being anywhere alone with her."

"Don't worry, I will."

SHE WORE HER rage like a heavy cloak. It covered both her mind and body, blinding her to her surroundings. Here, it didn't matter. Here, there wasn't anyone to see or tell. No one alive anyway. The smell of dried blood appealed to her on a primal level. Some might have recoiled at the scent of death, but to her it proved a balm that she needed in this crucial time, a reminder.

Eventually, her efforts would reap the rewards. On the day Jamison realized all she'd done to bring them together, that would be a glorious occasion. So why couldn't Lee Grayson just go away?

Every time Brenda and Jamison grew closer, the girlfriend interfered. Just a few weeks ago Jamison told Brenda what a good job she'd been doing. To another, Jamison's words would be only a meaningless compliment, but not to Brenda. She understood what her intended couldn't come out and say. She knew Jamison wanted to be with her too. They'd already be together if not for Lee Grayson.

Brenda threw her head back and screamed, giving voice to her anger and thwarted passion. She realized the door still stood ajar but didn't feel threatened. Deep in the Adirondack forest, the trees and brush absorbed sound. More than that, the forest had the strength to quickly and quietly reabsorb manmade structures. Nature had almost reclaimed this old hunting cabin, though it wasn't really that ancient in the scheme of things. Trees hugged closely around the frame, limbs growing out over the roof and looping down. Branches and leaves twined around cracked windows. High, thin grass and scrub helped conceal the building. A crumpled and rat-eaten bit of paper, a single page from a man's hunting magazine during the 1970s testified to its age.

No, not that old really. Yet in this forest, damp from constant rain and the mountain elevations, it was a miracle of workmanship that a single board still stood, much less the bulk of the outer shell. Brenda saw the discovery of the abandoned cabin as another sign that she had found her soul mate. Twin mountain peaks towered over the structure. Legend had it that the mountaintops had once been a single structure and that an earthquake split the terrain in two. Whatever the truth of the situation, the peaks separated at sheer cliff faces and dropped into the valley below. The cliffs created a natural, narrow walkway between them referred to by locals as the Devil's Snare. Fortunately for Brenda, officials had closed this section of the park years ago.

Thoughts of Jamison helped Brenda feel more centered. For long moments she closed her eyes and indulged in her favorite fantasies. She smiled as she created a home for the two of them. Not the place she had now, only a mile outside the park. The old rental house would never do for Jamison. Maybe Lee would be gracious enough to let them have the manor once she realized how wrong she'd been to keep them apart.

Brenda's smile faded and her lips twisted cruelly as she contemplated her rival. Clearly, Lee didn't understand the messages she'd received. Either that or she didn't care. Yeah, it was probably that. That was why Lee often kissed Jamison in front of her. She was telling Brenda that she didn't care what she did, that she would keep Jamison from her at all costs. So why couldn't Jamison see that Lee was playing her? Why did she keep defending the woman? More importantly, why didn't Jamison believe her when Brenda showed her the bruises? She should have believed Brenda's story about Lee striking her without question. That Jamison still chose Lee over her when Brenda had provided the way out infuriated her beyond reason.

Suddenly she calmed, the rage in her breast quieted. She felt stupid for forgetting how loyal Jamison was and that she wouldn't leave a partner, no matter how justified. Brenda's eyes narrowed as the answer occurred to her. Jamison might not leave someone, but what if that person died? She would have a way out that wouldn't reflect on her reputation. A predatory smile graced her lips. She was wrong to leave warnings. Lee was too selfish to understand and bow out gracefully.

"I made a mistake before. Just because they looked like you didn't mean anything. But it'll mean something next time, won't it? Oh yes it will. Now when...?"

She needed a lure, something sure to draw Lee into a trap. The dog. Brenda had already made friends with the mutt so it would probably come right to her. She'd have to be careful though. Grayson and everyone around her had an uncanny way of escaping tragedy. The teenage girls were proof of that. It still irritated her that a squalling brat had discovered them before Brenda had time for some fun. She was smart to drug them; at least they couldn't describe her.

She'd have to work fast though, and going to work tomorrow was out of the question. With the press release intended for the next morning, the park was going to become crowded. Even though it was technically the off-season, thrill seekers would be everywhere. The Adirondacks would be as busy as the height of tourist season. The time for cat and mouse was over.

Feeling better than she had all day, Brenda set about readying the cabin for a guest. Getting Lee here was the hard part, but once that happened she would never leave. Somehow, it seemed fitting that Grayson would join the heap of dead animals under the cabin's floor.

She would be a permanent trophy. Brenda liked that idea.

While she worked, Brenda entertained herself with fantasies of getting even with little Casey North. Maybe a bicycle accident right in front of her parents would be the way to go. She could just imagine how contrite she would appear.

"I'm so sorry. She raced right out in front of me and I just couldn't stop in time."

Brenda snickered in delight, sure her reputation as a hard working, trustworthy park ranger would prevent anyone from suspecting the truth.

Chapter Fourteen

LEE AWAKENED AND sat up quickly on the sofa. She felt like something was wrong, but she couldn't imagine what. She could hear the birds singing outside and watery sunshine streamed into the living room through the large bay window. She had worked hard all day in her basement darkroom and decided to take a nap in the early afternoon. When Lee lay down everything was fine. Jamison was at work and Cleo sleeping on her rug by the hearth. Something had changed since then.

She held her breath, listening. There weren't any unexpected noises in the house, no footsteps or bangs to indicate an intruder. A light clicking sound came to her ears and she turned her head to watch Cleo pad into the doorway. The beagle cocked her head inquiringly.

"I think I'm getting paranoid, Cleo." Lee pushed away the gnawing sensation and threw back the light throw. "Are you hungry?"

She sensed satisfaction coming from her canine companion and took that as a negative answer. Cleo wasn't interested in food right now. Apparently she was just curious about Lee's activities. Leaving Cleo to her own explorations, Lee headed for the bathroom. She needed a shower to clear away the sleep fog. Maybe it would help with this uneasy feeling as well. Lee thought it possible her feeling stemmed from an unremembered nightmare. Cranking the heat on high, Lee stripped as she waited for the water to warm. Then she stepped under the spray, already mentally planning what to do with the rest of the day. The media release had originally aired that morning, but would probably be on a repeating loop. Lee considered watching the news, but quickly changed her mind. Rehashing the gory details wasn't her style.

Steam filled the room by the time Lee emerged from the shower. Feeling more relaxed, she rolled her shoulders relieving the last of the kinks. She toweled off and then wiped the steam from the mirror with the damp cloth. A noise caught her attention and Lee listened intently for a moment. Was that a car engine?

"Huh." Her hearing was getting better all the time. Now she could hear the occasional sound of vehicles traveling down Black Mountain Road.

Feeling far too impressed with herself, Lee whistled as she dressed and then headed for the kitchen. She found Jamison's empty cup sitting in the sink. Though it had been rinsed out, Lee caught the lingering scent of chamomile tea. She wrinkled her nose a bit and grabbed a soda from the fridge. Glancing around the kitchen, she noted Cleo's absence and smiled indulgently.

Even after a year of living in the country, Cleo loved exploring outside though she rarely spent more than a few minutes at a time doing so. Her favorite area was over near the edge of the woods where Lee had discovered an old game trail. Last year Cleo often accompanied Lee on a run through the forest, but she didn't seem as interested lately. That didn't prevent her from nosing out all the interesting scents there, however.

With a cold Pepsi can in hand, Lee took the steps off the kitchen to the basement. The temperature dropped several degrees from the sun-filled first floor as she descended to the subterranean level. Lee felt chills break out over her arm and run down her spine. Though she kept her darkroom down here, it often reminded her of last year's exploits. Having an insane rogue lion-shifter using her basement for a lair would do that, she supposed, but had expected the feelings of dread to fade over time.

Lee spent quite a while looking through her recent shots. An offer from an outdoor enthusiast magazine for a cover photo had her considering the possibilities. Unfortunately, the search proved fruitless. She just didn't have anything that spoke to her. Pondering where she could capture just the right image, Lee sipped from the can only to discover it empty. On her way back to the kitchen, she realized Cleo hadn't come to find her once finished outside. That wasn't like her. The dog always wanted to be with Lee when not engaged elsewhere.

Curious but unconcerned, Lee dropped the can into the recycle bin and then strolled to the back door. Taking a light jacket from the peg on the wall, Lee slung it over her shoulder and stepped outside. She stood on the porch searching for Cleo near the tree line. She wasn't anywhere in sight.

"Now where did that dog go?" Lee muttered.

Cleo had a tendency to blend into her surroundings. Lee often had to really look and then she would find the beagle standing practically in front of her. That didn't happen this time. She stepped off the porch and down into the yard but still didn't see Cleo. Thinking Cleo had wandered down the trail, Lee pulled on the jacket and headed into the woods. There weren't any recent canine tracks in the damp earth. All she found were impressions from a small deer. Lee explored a quarter of a mile into the trees before she decided Cleo had not gone this way.

Smirking, she thought the dog was probably inside the house by now. She turned around and started home. Halfway across the yard, Lee caught movement from the corner of her eye. She expected to see Cleo sniffing at the car tires but instead she noticed a scrap of paper under the windshield wiper. The encroaching shadows caused by night coming on caused the white to stand out sharply.

Had someone left her a note? Why wouldn't they just knock on the door? Forgetting about Cleo for the moment, Lee went to the car and picked up the slip of paper. What she read caused the breath to catch in her throat.

> I have the dog. Come to where it all began. Destroy the note and come alone. Tell anyone or fail to follow these instructions and I will gut her like a fish. You have until sundown.

Heart pounding, Lee looked around the yard again. Somehow she expected to find Cleo wandering nearby. This had to be some kind of sick joke. Only she didn't find her dog. More disturbing still, she couldn't be sure how long Cleo had been missing. Was it while she was in the shower or later while she was in the darkroom? Suddenly, Lee remembered the sound of the car engine. She had assumed it was a vehicle out on the highway, but now she couldn't be sure. Glancing at her watch, Lee realized that had occurred more than two hours ago. She'd lost track of time while looking through photos in the darkroom.

Lee wadded the hated note into a ball and raced back into the house. She grabbed the phone off the kitchen wall and then froze in her tracks. Her first instinct was to call Jamison and enlist her help in the search for Cleo, but she couldn't. The note said not to tell anyone and Lee wasn't taking the chance that her movements were being monitored.

Come to where it all began. What could it mean? The instructions were far from clear. Where what all began?

Thinking furiously, Lee could only come up with one incident that would stand out from a recent perspective. The murders of the women in the park flashed through her mind. The killer had Cleo and had baited a trap for Lee. The only thing she couldn't figure out was why. Why not just come for Lee directly? Surely whoever took Cleo had to know Lee was alone out here.

"Coward," Lee grated aloud. "You should have faced me yourself instead of taking my dog."

Pissed, Lee didn't intend to wait around for inspiration. She was going to get Cleo back now. Still, reason cautioned her to follow the printed directions. She wouldn't take a chance with Cleo's life. Lee strode over to the fireplace and knelt down. Reaching for the box of eleven-inch fireplace matches, she lit the corner of the paper and watched the flame take hold. Once she was sure the paper would burn completely, Lee dropped it into the hearth.

Lee ran into her bedroom and grabbed an extra pair of jeans and a long-sleeved shirt. She had the feeling she would shift to her more natural form before this night ended and intended to be prepared. This asshole didn't know who he was dealing with. That thought gave Lee comfort. Though required to act alone, the kidnapper had seriously underestimated her and expected Lee to act like a human woman. That single miscalculation would be all she needed to get Cleo back safely.

With clothes in hand, Lee jogged back through the manor and

scooped the rental car keys off the foyer table. She was already in the car and speeding onto the blacktop before she realized she'd left the cell phone behind. For a half second she was tempted to turn around, but almost as quickly discarded the notion. She still wasn't sure exactly where to go and didn't plan to waste time by turning around. Thomas might want Lee to meet her at either victim's campsite or at the killing field she and Jamison had discovered a few nights ago. On the heels of that thought, Lee realized she'd identified Ranger Thomas as the murderer.

She had no proof of that, but her supposition felt right. In this case, she had to trust her instincts. It would certainly explain the woman's odd behavior. A low, guttural growl rose from deep in her chest. Her fingers itched and Lee felt the urge to change into her jaguar form. Her fingertips ached as though claws would erupt at any second. Lee shook off the sensation and concentrated on driving. If she shifted now she would crash. That didn't prevent her fangs from elongating or the pelt from erupting on the backs of her hands.

Changing effortlessly wasn't usual for her, but Cleo was her baby and Lee's outrage over the kidnapping threatened her control. Not even taking Lindsay and Mira had caused such a visceral reaction. Lee wondered at that but then realized the difference: Cleo was practically defenseless, a middle-aged dog who was helpless against a human aggressor.

In less than ten minutes she entered the Adirondack Park. Lee pulled to the side on the park road and thought about what Jamison had told her of the killings. For a moment she couldn't remember the campsite where park visitors found the first body. Panic beat at her and her fingers trembled. Where was it?

Deerlick Falls!

Lee gunned the engine and took off, raising a cloud of dust in her wake. She wasn't sure of the exact campsite and the campgrounds were extensive. She would have to explore both campsites as well as the place along the hiking trail where she and Jamison had found the blood. At the same time, Lee would have to be on the lookout for Brenda. She didn't intend to become a victim. The canopy of tree branches overhead further diffused the waning sunlight. Lee switched on the headlights and bounced over the uneven terrain in the rental sedan.

Though trying to remain confident, a part of Lee worried that she was way off base and wouldn't find Brenda. If that happened, she would lose Cleo. Lee felt her heart harden. Losing Cleo wasn't an option. She would kill Brenda first. A primal part of Lee rejoiced as the sun began to set. She would be in her element, but Ranger Thomas would not.

An hour later, she wasn't any closer to finding the ranger or the beagle. Lee hadn't even seen a park service vehicle. Sitting in the front seat of the rental, Lee waited on the side of the park road. A few vehicles passed, headlights blinding her briefly in the rearview mirror. Each time she tensed in anticipation, but each time they passed without slowing. Lee's palms slipped a little against the steering wheel, slick from nervous perspiration.

"Come on, where the hell are you?"

Lee huffed in impatience and checked her wristwatch again. In the darkness, she could just barely make out the illuminated details. Almost seven, Jamison should be home by now. Lee had been sitting outside the entrance to the Deerlick Falls campground for the last forty minutes and was beginning to worry that she was in the wrong place. She realized that maybe she'd made a faulty assumption. Whoever left the note never said they'd be arriving by car. Lee had only assumed they would be. More than that, the note did not state a time for their meeting, although they had mentioned it would be after sundown. That wasn't a very specific time reference. She could be out here half the night with no one the wiser.

Squinting her eyes, Lee concentrated on trying to adjust her vision. After a few moments, she figured it wasn't working. The heat of the moment had passed long ago and with it her spontaneous ability to transform. Lee didn't understand why shifting seemed so effortless when the situation proved life threatening, but had difficulty changing otherwise.

She opened the car door and hurriedly closed it, worried about the glare from the dome lights. Lee reached up and switched off the lights before opening the door again. She stepped out into the night. Closing the door softly, Lee hip checked it to ensure it closed completely. She didn't want the dome light to switch on and inadvertently inform an onlooker of her actions. She took a few steps into the brush. Lee thought that if she moved away from anything manmade it would help her connect with her more instinctual abilities.

Lee smelled the acrid scent of vegetation crushed under her hiking shoes. She opened herself up to hearing the nocturnal sounds and the feel of cold air against her exposed hands and face. When she'd gone far enough that the car disappeared in the gloom, Lee stopped and squatted down. Placing one hand against the cool ground, she closed her eyes and tried to let everything else go. She took two long breaths and then raised her head. Finding Cleo was the ultimate goal and centering her emotions the key.

Blood rushed through her veins. Lee felt gooseflesh erupt on the backs of her arms. The center of her spine tingled and she expected pelt to erupt. She opened her eyes a few moments later when nothing happened. Frustrated, she struck her thighs with her fists. What good was a shape changer who couldn't change shape?

"Dammit!"

Tears flooded her eyes when Lee thought about Cleo being held by a psychopath. Her imagination happily supplied her with gruesome scenarios Cleo was experiencing at that very moment. Lee buried her face in her hands, feeling like a total loser for not finding her friend. After a few minutes, she dropped her hands and sat back on her heels.

"All right, Grayson. Get it together. You can't help her if you fall apart."

Lee had always found talking to herself helped her concentrate. She needed all the assistance she could get now and didn't worry about sounding crazy. No one was out here anyway.

"Okay, if I were a psychotic killer where would I go? I've checked out the campground so where next?"

Lee climbed to her feet and returned to the rental. She sat thinking for a moment and then switched on the engine. She considered the possibility that Brenda hadn't been talking about the park at all. Lee had met Ranger Thomas for the first time at the visitor's center, but she didn't think that was the answer. She decided to check the area near the hiking trails between here and Cherry Falls Reservoir. It was a fair hike on foot, but wouldn't take long to drive over. If she didn't find anything there, Lee would try Paul Smith's Visitor's Center.

Within minutes Lee arrived and turned off the Chevy. She left the headlights on for a brief time, but then realized that was ridiculous. No one was stupid enough to pass right in front of the beam. She clicked off the lights and climbed out, walking over to the spot where they'd found the dried blood. Lee could smell the coppery scent long before she arrived and grimaced at the irony. Any abilities that didn't require conscious thought came easily. Unfortunately, those same faculties were useless for finding Cleo.

Lee strolled passed the scene, her eyes taking in everything around her. The moon floated overhead, illuminating the trail between the trees. She felt like she stood under a spotlight. The trail disappeared around a bend and Lee started walking. The turf under her feet absorbed any sound. The wind seemed louder than usual as it sang through the branches and leaves. Pleasant scents of cool earth, dry grass and impending snow teased her nostrils.

Lost in the sensations of nature, Lee didn't realize her sight had expanded. She stopped dead on the hiking trail, suddenly able to see as clearly as she usually could in the daylight. In relaxing she had accomplished what sheer will alone could not. She'd simply been trying too hard. Jamison had been telling her that all along, but Lee hadn't really believed her.

Now, she paused to savor her newly formed visual acuity. Colors faded, taking on a washed out appearance while things at a distance seemed to rapidly rush closer. It was her enhanced night vision that created the effect and Lee appreciated being able to see better than her human alter ego. The jaguar in her sensed that she could easily cross the final barrier and transform completely, but she currently held the element of surprise. The ability to shift to cat form was her ace in the hole. Lee intended to keep it that way for as long as possible.

She heard a slight noise off to her left, merely a rustling in the brush. She inhaled deeply, seeking an indication that Cleo was near. Only an animal could have heard the sound. The muscles below her ears twitched, but in her human condition Lee couldn't utilize directional hearing. Instead, she turned her head. At the same time, Lee spotted a small object zooming toward her. She could hear the swish of displaced air as it whizzed toward her.

Lee threw her body to the side, attempting to avoid the projectile. She wasn't quite fast enough. Reflexively, she reached up and yanked the dart from her shoulder. The needle didn't really sting. In fact, her whole arm felt numb. Lee's vision swam and her eyes returned to their usual appearance. When they did, the world seemed to shrink around her. She stumbled a little and then dropped to one knee.

Footsteps approached and Lee watched Ranger Thomas strolling casually toward her. She held a rifle by the pistol grip, the barrel pointed toward the sky as the weapon rested against her shoulder. A smile gently curved her lips. As she approached, Brenda started to whistle. Lee wanted to rush at her, to grab her by her jacket and shake her until she revealed Cleo's location. Her body didn't obey her commands to move and Lee fell over onto her side.

"Took you long enough to get here," Brenda said. "I was starting to think you didn't care about the damned dog."

"Wh...," Lee swallowed and tried again. "Where is she?"

"Impressive. I gave you enough to drop a buffalo. Most people would be unconscious by now."

Lee had trouble understanding Brenda's words. Her brain felt disengaged. "Jami will find me."

Brenda's smile vanished, much as it had the day she told Jamison Lee had struck her. Anger washed over her like a tide so strongly that even in her insensate condition Lee sensed it. The full moon highlighted Brenda's face as it hardened.

"Shut up. You don't deserve to say her name."

Lee shook her head, not understanding. She wanted to ask why Brenda was doing this, but didn't get the chance. As Ranger Thomas grasped the rifle in both hands and raised it high into the air, Lee realized what was about to happen. She didn't have the motor control to avoid it when Brenda brought the weapon down hard and struck her between the eyes with the rifle butt.

Chapter Fifteen

"JEANIE, I'M HEADING out now. I've got to run over to the sheriff's office before I head home."

"It's kind of late for that isn't it? I'm pretty sure the office closes at five."

"They'll be there," Jamison assured her tiredly. Although it was going on six-thirty, the media release had people coming out of the woodwork with helpful tips. Jamison was exhausted from chasing down leads that went nowhere and expected the local deputies were doing the same. Macke wouldn't go home until things died down.

Since the tip hotline was running inside the sheriff's office, Jamison didn't see that happening anytime soon. At least Macke had Hex and her crew in addition to twenty full and part-time deputies as well as ten park rangers to help out. Jamison had considered calling in extra help from the other park headquarters but decided against it. Unless they came up with anything useful, all of the extra bodies would have people tripping over each other.

"Did you ever hear from Ranger Thomas?" Jeanie asked curiously. "It isn't like her to just not show up for her shift without calling."

Jamison hesitated before answering. She could tell her secretary about the incident with Brenda yesterday, but didn't feel comfortable doing so. Jamison felt like she had bungled handling that whole situation and blamed herself for the outcome. She hoped that by giving Brenda some time to deal with her emotions things would blow over. All things considered, she shouldn't have expected her to show up for work today.

"No, but I'm sure she's fine. She's just...going through some things."

"What things?" Jeanie sounded curious, but didn't look up from her typing.

Rather than answer directly, Jamison changed the subject. "Why are you still here? Don't you get off at five?"

Jeanie stopped what she was doing and looked up with a grin. "You busted me. All right, I admit it. With everything on the news this morning I wanted to hang out and see if you learned anything."

"Hoping to be around when we catch the bad guy?"

"Is that so wrong of me?" Jeanie sighed in a deliberately melodramatic fashion.

Jamison chuckled. "No, it's not wrong. Unfortunately these things rarely work out quickly and usually not at all."

"Then why do it if it doesn't work?"

"We use every tool at our disposal." Jamison shrugged. "Just because it doesn't usually work like we want it to, doesn't mean that we don't try. Why don't you head home? I won't be back tonight and there's no reason for you to just hang out."

"Let me log off and get my coat."

Jamison waited patiently and then walked Jeanie to her car. The headlights blinded her a little but she waved in Jeanie's generally direction as her secretary drove away. She took her own vehicle to the sheriff's office since she didn't plan to return to the park. This late in the evening Jamison almost expected the sheriff's lot to be deserted. Instead, she finally had to park on the grass. People crossed at random across the lot and it looked like midday at a busy supermarket. The melee inside the building was even worse. Jamison absently caught snatches of conversation from operators brought in specifically to handle calls on the tip lines.

"Harmon County Sheriff's Office, how may I help you?"

"No sir, we're not asking volunteers to scour the forest at this time."

She smirked at little at the last one, but also appreciated the caller's enthusiasm. It might just come to that. Down the hall, she caught sight of Sheriff Macke inside her office. The sheriff was also on the phone but looked up and caught Jamison's eye through the window. The building boasted an open floor plan and where the walls weren't load bearing they were constructed of glass. Macke waved for her to enter the office while she continued with her call. She hung up a few seconds later.

"How's it going?" Jamison asked. "Is there anything we can use yet?"

"Not unless a report of a Yeti roaming the backwoods is helpful. I actually had someone tell me that Bigfoot is responsible for the murders. Another guy said it's a government conspiracy designed to distract the public so they can take over everyone's computers without anyone noticing."

Jamison shook her head. "How gullible, don't they know that it's not the government doing that? The Panthera are planning to perform that little stunt at New Year's Eve. The ball dropping in New York is really the perfect time."

Sam stared at her for a moment without blinking. Clearly she didn't appreciate Jamison's humor. "Why are you here?"

"I came to see if you need any help chasing down these hot tips. Bigfoot roaming the Adirondacks is pretty impressive and should be looked into."

This time Sam sighed aloud. "You're in a particularly good mood."

"I take it you don't approve."

"I'll let you know when I've decided. In the meantime, Detective Hex went into town to pick up some pizzas for the crew out there. Care to join us?"

"No thanks. What's the deal with you two anyway."

After a moment, Macke replied, "I'm not sure I take your meaning and if I did, I'm not sure that's an appropriate conversation."

"Are you telling me to butt out?"

It wasn't lost on Jamison that Macke was entirely right. They barely knew each other and usually interacted with ambivalence at best. It did seem odd for them to be discussing the sheriff's love life.

"Yes I am. However, since I'm sure you intend to pursue the subject anyway just let me tell you for the record that there is nothing going on between us."

"And even if there was you wouldn't say? Fair enough." Jamison nodded. "It's none of my business. I don't know why I even brought it up. It must be Lee's domesticating influence. Anyway, I just came by to see if you needed any help."

"No, not really, I've practically got an army on standby and so far there isn't a damn thing we can use. Go on home. I'll call you if we hear anything worthwhile." Macke hesitated. "Come to think of it, there might be one thing you can do. Would you mind making a little patrol out by the campgrounds utilizing your...special skills?"

"Come again?"

"Hear me out." Sam raised a hand. "All of this publicity might shake things up for our psycho. This might be the perfect opportunity."

"Or all this media attention might drive our killer into hiding. Besides, how would I even know where to start? Do you know how big the Adirondacks are?"

"That's actually not so hard to figure out," Sam assured her. "Each of our two victims was taken from the Deerlick Falls Campgrounds. It makes sense that he would be looking for his next target there."

Jamison snorted. "Sure, it makes perfect sense. That's why he cut my partner's brakes and kidnapped Lindsay Drake and Mira Pye, neither of which happened in the park. The truth is that we don't have any idea what this guy is going to do next. Still, if it'll make you feel any better, I'll take a *stroll* through there on my way home."

It wasn't lost on Jamison that they were utilizing euphemisms in discussing her shifting abilities. She appreciated Macke's tact considering the crowd in the next room.

With nothing further to say, she returned to the pickup. She hadn't expected another trip into the park and realized it would be a while before she returned home. Jamison pulled out her cell phone and tried to call the manor to inform Lee of the delay. The call went to the answering machine. Thinking she had gone outside for some reason, Jamison tried Lee's cellular. Again there was no answer. Jamison left a short message and then started the pickup.

Surprisingly, Jamison didn't see many people out as she drove to the falls. With the press release, she'd expected the area to become crowded fast. Then again it was the middle of the week and any New Yorkers out for a thrill would have to wait until after work to make the drive up. Of course that didn't count the locals who would probably be just as curious. She had agreed to this little excursion, but would have to be very careful not to be spotted.

Jamison shut off the engine and headlights and then sat for a moment. Just the thought of transforming had the adrenaline rushing through her veins. Her eyes constricted and the pupils elongated. From the safety of the vehicle's cab she scanned the darkness into the woods for as far as she could see. No one lurked in the shadows. Jamison pressed a switch on the mirror to turn off the interior lights. Only then did she open the door and step out. Shivering a little, partly in anticipation of the change and partly in response to the cold, Jamison began stripping down.

She folded her clothes and set everything on the seat. Once ready, Jamison stepped off the park road. Dirt and twigs slid against the bare soles of her feet. She squatted down and placed her palms against the ground. Jamison relaxed, allowing her human mind to go quiet as her beast sprang forward. The great cat was eager to pounce and for once, she allowed it. Normally, Jamison savored the process, relishing each alteration beginning with the thickening and shortening of her spine to the eruption of claws. In this instance, she didn't have that luxury. Some camper might come along at any moment and while trapped between forms, she'd be vulnerable. A rush of endorphins and dopamine joined the adrenaline pumping through Jamison's system. The flood of hormones made the change painless, bordering on the sensual.

A fully formed, midnight black jaguar stood where a woman had only moments before. In this animal shape, Jamison retained her higher reasoning. Her mighty head swung from side to side, ensuring no one had encroached while she changed. Razor sharp claws ripped into the turf as she loped away, the scent of leaf mildew and damp earth in her nostrils. The full moon peeked at her through the branches, darting out periodically through the clouds. Jamison smelled snow on the wind and something else.

She entered a clearing near a deserted campsite. Near the edge of the weeds someone had dumped their garbage. A rustling sound emerged from the pile of refuse and after a moment a white form backed into the moonlight. The possum turned its head and hissed at her. Although she'd heard that the little creatures had migrated all the way up into Canada, it was rare to find one in the interior of the Adirondacks though they did occasionally make an appearance. Sometimes Jamison would receive calls from frightened campers thinking the little beasts were giant rats.

Rather than fall over into a stupor, the possum scuttled off into the weeds. Jamison sneezed in distaste. As a jungle cat, killing and ripping into prey was part of her makeup but she had no desire to eat this little scavenger. With the scent of rot in her nose, she shook her head and explored the balance of the large campgrounds. Staying to the brush and avoiding the few scattered campfires, Jamison spent hours scouting the area. The campers she did see stayed close to the fire, whether because of the nip in the air or the threat of a killer in the woods she didn't know.

She crossed back and forth over the hiking trails multiple times but discovered nothing to raise her suspicions. Lost in the sensations of powerful muscles sliding over bone and tissue, Jamison roamed the woods. She stopped near the lake for a drink of water and for a moment felt tempted to enjoy a swim. Unlike most cats, jaguars appreciated the water. A sudden, sharp gust of cold wind prevented her excursion. Casting sharp eyes overhead, Jamison realized how far the moon had traveled. The vision of Lee formed in her mind and Jamison turned back toward the truck. With all her speed and agility, it required another half hour to reach the vehicle.

Back in human form, dressed and sitting in the truck with the heater blowing, Jamison considered trying to call Lee again. She rejected the notion after glancing at the dashboard clock. Few cars were out on the road. She pulled in front of the manor house a short time later. Lee's rental car was nowhere in sight and no lights burned in the house. Jamison wondered if Lee was upset with her for working late and decided to go for a midnight shoot.

The house was cold and quiet when she entered and Jamison wondered how long ago Lee had left. She tried to call her partner again and jumped in startled reaction when she heard a phone ring somewhere in the house. Jamison tracked down the cell phone sitting on the dining room table. Frowning, she walked through the house looking for signs of something out of place. The only thing that really stood out was that Lee had left her cell phone at home, something she never did, and Cleo was also missing. With her advancing years, Lee had started leaving the dog at home. On the surface, these two factors weren't exactly a smoking gun but Jamison's instincts told her something was off.

Jamison wandered back through the living room and turned on a table lamp. A scrap of white paper lying in the fireplace caught her eye. Curious, she knelt down and reached into the hearth. Just enough of the paper remained unburned for her to see that it contained no stationary header, meaning it didn't come from the notepad beside the phone. The edges of the page were burnt and crumbled to the touch while the middle was blackened with soot. Jamison rubbed a thumb over the smoke residue. Most of the words were completely obliterated. Holes had burned through in places, but just enough words remained to make Jamison's blood run cold.

Her heart felt like it skidded off a rib and began to hammer in her chest. Fear dried the saliva in her mouth. She jumped to her feet and raced to the house phone, dialing a number from memory. Jamison listened to the ringing on the other end and began to despair that it would never be picked up.

"Hello?" Sheriff Macke's groggy voice answered.

"The killer has Lee."

Jamison heard Macke clearing her throat. "Who is this?"

"Sheriff, wake up. This is Jamison Kessler. The killer has Lee."

Macke suddenly sounded wide awake. "How do you know that, what happened?"

"I just got home. Lee and her dog are both gone and I found a burnt note in the fireplace. Most of it's burned beyond recognition but there's enough there for me to see that someone told her to come alone."

"That's not much to go on. Do you have any idea where to start?"

Jamison swallowed hard, trying to keep the panic out of her voice. At least Macke wasn't trying to convince Jamison she was over reacting. "She took the rental car. It's equipped with a GPS tracker in case of theft. We need to get hold of the company to track the signal."

"Kessler, I don't mean to be insensitive but it's the middle of the night. The rental companies are closed."

"Then wake them up!" Jamison's voiced ended on a high trembling note. "Call Hex, she's a federal agent. She has the authority to force the issue."

Jamison's imagination was in overdrive. She could visualize the second hand on the clock sweeping around its face. Time was a luxury Lee did not have. Every moment wasted arguing with Macke ratcheted her fear up another notch.

"All right, I'm convinced. The car company might demand a warrant, but I'm sure we can argue exigent circumstances. I'll call Detective Hex as soon as we hang up."

"What am I supposed to do in the meantime? Sit on my hands?"

"Unless you have an idea where to start looking. If you do, I'm all ears."

Unbelievably, Jamison's mind went completely blank. She felt numb and couldn't think of a response. Shock, she thought. She had to pull it together. Lee and Cleo were counting on her and now wasn't the time to fall apart.

"Kessler?"

"I'm here. Call me back as soon as you get off the phone with Hex."

"Yeah, okay. Bye."

Jamison held the receiver to her ear until the shrill tones of a disconnect signal began to blare. She winced and hung up. She didn't think the sheriff sounded sincere about calling her back. Almost dazed by the recent turn of events, Jamison stumbled over and fell onto the sofa. Sheriff Macke's comment resonated in her mind. Did she have any idea where to start looking?

Did she?

A gnawing sensation pricked the edges of her consciousness. Jamison thought carefully about any small detail that might indicate who could have done this. She looked at the singed note crumpled in her fist. Smoothing out the paper, Jamison frowned over the few legible words. Mutt... come alone... gut like...fish.

It didn't take much to perceive the threat in those few words, or the anger. They reminded her of Brenda Thomas's hostility when Jamison didn't believe her about the altercation with Lee.

The breath caught in her lungs. A flood of disjointed images assaulted her. Taken separately, none of them amounted to much. But as a whole, the events took on a menacing cast. Jamison envisioned Brenda entering her office unannounced a few weeks ago. She'd passed the infraction off as the product of exhaustion, but there was no good reason for Brenda to be there. Added to that, Jamison wasn't even supposed to be at work that day. What was she looking for?

Jamison also recalled Brenda's haggard appearance the night Lindsay and Mira disappeared. Jamison had attributed it to calling the woman in unexpectedly on her day off. Why then had she smelled of old diesel oil, the same type used in the machinery at the defunct lumber mill? In combination with these small things was the look of absolute fury when Jamison defended Lee against the assault charge.

She realized she skated on thin ice by even contemplating this possibility. A few inconsistencies and a misguided bid for attention were hardly grounds to accuse Ranger Thomas of murder and kidnapping. Still, there was one last piece of evidence that Jamison found compelling. She and Lee discovered a cigarette butt engulfed by a puddle of blood in the park. They suspected the site marked the killing ground of one of their two victims. Jamison knew Brenda was a closet smoker, she'd smelled it on her uniform on occasion. It wasn't often and the lab results on the cigarette hadn't come back yet, but Jamison had a sinking sensation in the pit of her stomach.

Placing her hands on the sofa, Jamison pushed herself up and headed for the phone. If she was wrong, she would apologize later. Jamison quickly redialed Macke's home number. She growled in frustration at the busy signal beeping in her ear and slammed the receiver back in place. Checking her watch, she realized only a few minutes had passed. It certainly felt longer than that. Sheriff Macke was probably still filling Hex in and deciding on their next move.

Think, Jamison. She hesitated to rush over to Brenda's home and confront the woman with nothing more than suspicion to go on. Finally, she decided that Lee's life was more important than offending Thomas. She hadn't removed her jacket when arriving home, which saved time now as she headed for the front door. Jamison's hand was on the knob when the phone rang. Thinking it was Lee, she sprinted back across the room.

"Hello?"

"Detective Hex has access to federal GPS tracking software. She'll have to call the office in New York, but she needs the license plate number and VIN of the car."

"Hold on, I'll grab it." Jamison dropped the phone onto the table and ran into Lee's office for the rental paperwork. She dug around in the desk's top drawer before realizing the contract lay right on the surface. She sprinted back to the living room and gave Macke the information.

"Right, I'll tell Hex and I'll call you back as soon as I know anything."

"Wait," Jamison said quickly, afraid that Macke would hang up. "I thought of a place to start looking."

She filled the sheriff in on everything she'd thought of, tripping over words in an effort not to leave out any pertinent details. Jamison expected Sheriff Macke to argue with her and she wasn't disappointed.

"As much as I appreciate your instincts, that's not enough for a warrant. We need probable cause."

"That's for a search. There's nothing that says I can't go over there and knock on the door," Jamison argued. "If she comes to the door wearing pajamas and carrying a stuffed bear, I'll assume she's innocent."

"A stuffed bear? Where do you come up with this stuff?"

"Don't humans sleep with stuffed animals?" Jamison asked hesitantly. The Panthera weren't strictly human and many of their customs differed. Sleeping with inanimate objects was one.

"Only little kids do that. You have some pretty weird ideas."

Jamison shook her head. "It doesn't matter, we're getting off track."

"Yes we are, but you still shouldn't go over there. Thomas is the suspect, at least she is in the kidnappings. I'm not sure about the murders but the point is that she might see you coming. She could kill Ms. Grayson before you even got close."

Jamison knew she was right and resisted arguing the point. "We can't just do nothing."

A small silence ensued and Jamison allowed the sheriff a few moments to gather her thoughts. "How about this, you go to the park and search her locker. You guys do have one of those, right?"

"Of course all park rangers have a locker so they can change into their uniforms."

"Good. You go do that and see if you find anything incriminating."

"That's brilliant," Jamison complimented. "As a federal employee, there's no assumption of a right to privacy for a locker at work. It can be searched for contraband at anytime without a warrant. What are you going to do?"

"I'm going to wake up Judge Mills and get a warrant. She owes me a few favors and believe me, I'll be calling in every one of them to get her to sign off on this. We don't exactly have a smoking gun. I'll get Detective Hex and her people to help serve the warrant. I doubt she's stupid enough to keep Grayson at her home, but we might get lucky."

"Since when? Forget I asked," Jamison contradicted quickly. "I'm on my way back to the park now. I suppose I don't have to ask you to stay close to a phone?"

"You do the same."

Jamison thought it likely that Macke was just trying to keep her busy, but in reality she had a better chance of finding something in Brenda's locker than the others did at her home. No one would be that careless and the killer had been very careful up to this point. There was no concrete evidence to go on, only supposition. Conjecture would not hold up in court, but Jamison wasn't worried about legal procedures at the moment.

She jumped in the truck and gunned the engine racing back toward the Paul Smith's Visitor's Center. With the streets deserted, it didn't take long to turn back into the park entrance. Jamison bounded out of the vehicle before it stopped completely and jogged up the steps. She fumbled for a second to get the key into the lock. The lights were out in the building, but it didn't occur to her to flip them on. Instead, she hurried toward the women's locker room.

As the station's commanding officer, she had more freedom to come and go so didn't require keeping a locker. For that reason, she rarely visited this part of the facility. Upon entering, Jamison smelled old soap, humidity and mildew. Water dripped from the shower area, striking ceramic tiles and echoing throughout the empty space. Out of habit ingrained by years of safety awareness, Jamison glanced toward the noise. She didn't see anyone over the top of the short, half walls. That didn't mean someone couldn't be squatted down, hiding, but her instincts told her that wasn't the case. She was alone.

Jamison walked quickly along the row of lockers, checking the tags on the front for Ranger Thomas's name. She reached the end of the single row before realizing it wasn't there. Frowning, Jamison started back along the distance. Like most members of law enforcement, men significantly outnumbered women. There were less than twenty lockers to inspect. After going through a second time, Jamison concluded the name wasn't there. Regardless, she considered that Thomas wasn't as smart as she thought. Only one locker was unlabeled so it was process of elimination.

Reaching for the latch, her hand froze in mid-air. Brenda had placed a padlock on the locker. Jamison cursed herself for not anticipating this. She grabbed the lock and yanked hard. She didn't hold back, pulling with all her Panthera enhanced strength. The lock held. Brenda had shelled out for a quality, top of the line padlock.

Irritated but far from defeated, Jamison headed for the building's rear exit. A gardener's shed stood out back. Utilizing the small key on her ring, she easily opened the door. The irony wasn't lost on her that Brenda had purchased a better lock than the state did for the tool shed.

Jamison could have snapped this one.

The small room was extremely crowded, requiring her to switch on the lights this time. After digging through bags of fertilizer, dead plants and rusty tools, she found what she needed on a back corner shelf. The bolt cutters were almost rusted into place, but she didn't hesitate to snatch them up. Jamison left the door to the shed open and the light burning as she raced back to the locker room. The bolt cutters made short work of the lock despite their rusty condition. As soon as the lock snapped, Jamison dropped the tool. She ignored it bouncing onto the floor and reached for the latch.

She expected to have to dig through sweaty clothes and piles of old papers. Instead, the locker was almost obsessively tidy. What Jamison discovered as soon as she opened the door made her blood freeze. Despite the tidiness of the contents, photographs covered every square inch of surface space along the locker's walls and the inside of the door. She'd known since the car accident that someone had their eye on Lee. Since the supposed altercation Brenda had told her about, she'd even suspected on some level that Ranger Thomas was that person. Given the circumstances, the photographs weren't all that unexpected. However, what was unexpected was that Jamison was the subject in the pictures...not Lee.

At first glance, there appeared to be close to a hundred photographs. They were in all shapes and sizes, some cut from newspaper articles relating to the park. Others were candid shots, taken when Jamison wasn't aware. She'd have remembered these. One large photo took up the rear wall of the locker. This one she remembered. It was taken the day Jamison graduated from the FLETC academy in Brunswick, Georgia. She sat proudly facing toward the camera wearing her full dress Forest Service uniform. Brenda must have taken the photo from Jamison's official file and had it magnified hundreds of times.

There was one picture of Lee. This single shot was easily as large as the one from Jamison's file and rested on the backside of the locker door. Brenda had drawn concentric rings with what appeared to be a red marker around Lee's image. A bull's-eye rested over the center of Lee's chest and the implications were obvious.

Brenda was fixated on Lee, but not for the reasons Jamison had supposed. She was a target.

Chapter Sixteen

BLOOD ROARED THROUGH her veins like a freight train. Each throb of her heart reverberated through her head. Lee's eyes cracked open to mere slits. The small amount of light allowed in sent daggers of pain into her skull. Lee groaned and closed them again. Absence of light only slightly diminished the headache. She attempted to raise a hand to her forehead, but couldn't move.

Why couldn't she move?

Lee worked her tongue around in her mouth, trying to relieve the uncomfortable feeling of dryness. She blinked and opened her eyes, combating the pain. Her vision swam and then began to clear. She could see directly in front of her, but objects at the edges of her vision remained blurry.

Lee didn't recognize the room. It was dark except for the soft glow cast by an oil lamp. Lee couldn't see the lamp, only the flickering of shadows on the wooden walls. A large hearth dominated the room, framed by irregular, natural looking chunks of stone. Soot liberally coated the inside of the fireplace making it appear to be a doorway into space. Cobwebs and dust obscured every surface. Judging by the log walls, wooden floors and twelve-point buck trophy over the fireplace, she was in a hunting cabin. A heavy rope wound around her body several times, holding her to a chair with her hands tied behind her back.

Raising her head, Lee inhaled deeply and then gagged. The air reeked of death. For several long moments, Lee resisted the urge to vomit. She had to breathe through her mouth to void the worst of the stench. Where was that smell coming from?

Something whined from nearby. Lee's head swiveled toward the noise and a tendril of pain traveled from her left eye upward into her forehead. Cleo stood beside the chair, almost right at her heel. Lee frowned, realizing she hadn't been aware of the beagle's presence until she heard the sound. From what Lee could tell, Cleo wasn't confined in any way. A tendril of breeze lifted the hair on Lee's forehead and she noticed the door to the cabin stood partially open. Her loyalty kept Cleo from leaving the cabin.

A shadow moved from the opposite side of the room and Brenda Thomas stepped into the weak circle of light. "I'm impressed. I shot you with enough ketamine to drop a bull moose. You shouldn't even be awake, much less able to move."

Brenda walked up directly in front of her and stood staring down at Lee. She rested her hands on her hips. Her eyes looked black in the semidarkness. Lee tried to sense Thomas's emotional state, but couldn't get a read on her. It was true that Lee had problems shifting on occasion, but she'd always been able to intuit the emotional atmosphere. Now she couldn't.

"Why'd you hurt those women?" Lee barely recognized the sound of her own voice. The effort to speak left her weak. "They were innocent."

"No one is innocent!"

Brenda's anger made her shout and Lee's headache intensified. Lee's vision swam for a moment and it occurred to her that she might be able to use Brenda's agitation against her. If Lee could rile her up enough, Thomas might make an error that would allow her to escape. She stretched her shoulders a little, testing the ropes that held her confined and nearly rejected the idea. The bonds were too strong.

Lee had the feeling that it wouldn't matter. Brenda wasn't concerned about her escaping or anyone else finding them or she wouldn't have left the door open. She hung her head, feeling defeated, and met Cleo's eyes. If she couldn't get free, maybe Cleo could. Lee felt confident that all she required was a momentary lapse in judgment from Brenda. Once Cleo made her getaway, Lee would be able to focus on her own dilemma. She felt her strength returning by the moment.

"Are you just some sicko that gets off hurting people," Lee paused to take a breath, "seeing the fear in their eyes?"

Brenda's fists clenched. Her jaw tightened and her body stiffened, but she didn't react any further.

"Did you enjoy it when they saw your uniform and thought they could trust you?"

"It was an accident," Thomas shouted.

She lunged forward and grabbed Lee by the collar. Brenda shook her until Lee saw darkness hovering. She was shouting something, but the words ran together until Lee couldn't understand. Lee's head reeled to the side and she realized Brenda had slugged her. She didn't feel any pain and wondered if that was a side effect of the ketamine. If so, she was grateful for small favors.

Cleo lunged for Ranger Thomas, growling low in her chest. Her sharp teeth latched onto a jean-clad calf. Brenda shouted and released Lee. She tried to kick the dog, but couldn't maneuver well in the confined space.

"Cleo, run!" Lee shouted.

Brown eyes swiveled toward her, but Lee couldn't get a read on her reaction. She thought she saw stunned disbelief in the chocolate brown eyes. Cleo's jaw flexed and she bit down harder. Brenda grunted and bent over. At first Lee thought the woman was in serious pain, but quickly determined that wasn't the issue. Ranger Thomas grasped at the side of her boot and withdrew a wicked looking hunting knife.

Cleo, run! Now!

Lee projected as much urgency as she could into the mental

command. Cleo lunged away from the ranger like she'd been scalded, reacting to the order. Brenda swiped the blade toward the dog and Lee expected to see blood arc across the room. Instead, Cleo barely managed to avoid being filleted to the bone. The glint of light off the edge showed Lee the instrument was razor sharp. She breathed a sigh of relief when Cleo shot between Brenda's feet and tore out of the cabin into the night.

Brenda shouted and started after Cleo. Lee thought she'd pursue the canine until she lost her in the darkness. Unexpectedly, Brenda stopped at the threshold and turned back to Lee. The fury on her face vanished, replaced by a cruel smile.

"It doesn't matter. I was going to get rid of the hound anyway. I just needed her to bring you here. How does it feel to know you've signed her death warrant?"

Lee thought Brenda was taunting her, trying to get a rise out of her. It wasn't going to work. "You don't know what you're talking about. She's out of your reach now."

"Sure, out of my reach but what about the animals she's bound to run into?"

A niggling bit of doubt wormed its way into Lee's heart. She didn't respond, unsure what to say.

"We're miles from anywhere, in a valley surrounded by mountain peaks and heavy forest. There's only one road in and it ends over a mile from here. How long do you think that mutt of yours is going to last?"

Brenda stalked a few feet away. She giggled and Lee felt a chill skate down her back. The woman sounded unhinged. When she turned around Lee saw her gleeful smile. In that instant, clearly Lee saw the insanity lurking below the surface.

"She's smarter than you think," Lee responded defiantly. She had to stay positive or she would begin to doubt that she'd done the right thing in telling Cleo to leave. If she allowed any pessimism to invade her spirit, Lee was afraid she would give up. "She'll find that road, someone will find her."

"We'll see."

Brenda sounded eerily contained. She squatted down in front of Lee but her eyes were on the hunting knife. She turned the blade this way and that, allowing the lamplight to reflect of the surface. Lee grew concerned that Thomas would think of another use for the knife and sought something to keep the woman talking. Surreptitiously, she began to work the knots tying her wrists together.

"You said the road ended over a mile away. Did you carry me here?"

Brenda threw her head back and laughed. "No, I didn't carry you. Are you stupid?"

"But you said..."

"I used a brush hog to cut a path." Brenda's eyes lit up as she described her activities. "This place was a real find and I knew no one would discover me here. Even the main road is rarely used. Hikers aren't even allowed in this part of the park anymore, it's too dangerous. I cut the path myself and I'm the only one who knows about it."

Lee attempted to play along. "That was very clever of you. I can see why Jamison values you so much as an employee."

She quickly saw that was exactly the wrong thing to say. The humor vanished from Brenda's brown eyes. She jumped to her feet and lurched toward Lee, grasping her again by the collar and holding the knife edge against her throat.

"Don't patronize me and don't you *dare* say her name. You want to know why I killed those women? Because they were just like you, so smug and sure of yourself. The first one was an accident. She pissed me off, ordering me around like I was her flunky. I got so mad I didn't even think about it." Brenda's eyes glazed over as she spoke. Her voice softened and Lee thought she'd actually forgotten where she was. "The next thing I knew she was just laying there, bleeding out."

"You enjoyed it, didn't you?" Lee risked retaliation by asking the question, but her outrage for the victim demanded a response.

"She got what she deserved." Brenda pushed Lee back into the chair and stood up. She walked over to a round table and picked up a small, gray object. When she began drawing the knife along the length, Lee figured out it was a whetstone. "After she was dead, I realized she could serve a purpose."

Lee swallowed thickly. "What sick purpose?"

"A warning to you, of course." Brenda looked up from her task, her gaze completely devoid of emotion for the first time since Lee had awakened. "Only you were too stupid to pick up on it and another woman had to die."

Lee's eyes widened as Brenda replaced the stone and started in her direction. Ranger Thomas held the knife tightly and the look of intent in her eye was hard to miss.

"Wait, tell me why. You at least owe me that. Don't you want to tell me what warning you were trying to send?"

Confusion swam in Brenda's gaze, but she stopped walking. Lee let out a soft gasp of relief. The ploy seemed to work. Brenda rocked back and forth on her feet, just a second of indecision. Then she started talking.

"You were supposed to go away so Jamison and I could be together."

Lee blinked. She hadn't expected that. She knew Brenda had a small crush, and had teased Jamison about it often enough. She thought that infatuation the root cause of Brenda making up the story about Lee assaulting her, as a way to get attention. Lee had even figured out Brenda was the murderer, but she never expected the two events were related.

"Brenda, that doesn't make sense. How could killing those women warn me to leave?"

"Because they look like you! You should have known that I would come for you if you didn't allow us to be together."

Lee stretched her hands apart. She had some slack in the ropes now. Flexing her muscles, Lee was disappointed that she still couldn't break free. Her body still felt sluggish, heavy. She had tried everything she could think of to work the bonds loose and distract her captor, but sensed time running out. Lee had no doubt that Jamison was coming for her but worried that she wouldn't be in time. She had to keep Brenda talking until Jamison found her.

"Why didn't you just tell me? You didn't have to hurt anyone."

"That wouldn't have worked," Brenda argued. "You're too selfish and Jamison is too loyal. That's the only reason she's still with you, you know? If it looked like you walked away on your own, she would have let you go."

"What if I agreed to leave now...now that I know?"

Lee held her breath, hoping Brenda would consider it. For some reason she couldn't break the ropes but if Ranger Thomas untied her, Lee would have a fighting chance. Lee offered what she hoped was a friendly smile.

"You think I'm an idiot, don't you? You'll just run and tell Jamison." Brenda shook her head and raised the knife high into the air. "Can't have that, now can we?"

"Fine, whatever. I'm tired of trying to reason with a psycho. If you're going to kill me then just do it and get it over with. At least I won't have to listen to this lunacy anymore."

Fury tightened Brenda's face. Lee shivered slightly, chilled by the expression and the evil it revealed to her. She'd thought that goading Brenda might cause her to slip up, give Lee a chance to make a break for it. Instead, she thought perhaps she'd gone too far.

"You've got guts," Thomas said harshly, lowering the blade. "Before this is over, I'll be playing with them."

Lee tasted fear. Desperation caused her to take another track. "If you kill me, Jamison will hate you."

The words tumbled out before Lee realized what she was saying. Her heart pounded, but Brenda stopped again. Lee had finally gotten through to her. Jamison was the one thing Brenda cared about. Maybe she could get out of this after all. She just had to be smart and play off this psychopath's emotions.

"She won't know." Thomas didn't sound very sure. "She'll think you left all on your own when no one finds the body."

Lee shook her head. "My clothes are all there and I didn't leave a note. Jamison will be worried and she'll look for me. Don't you want her all to yourself without any distractions?"

"Yes," Thomas hissed, clearly reluctant to give Lee even that much.

Brenda turned away from Lee and placed the knife on the table. For a moment, Lee thought she'd actually convinced Brenda to let her go. Her hopes vanished when the woman walked over to the corner of the cabin and hefted a rifle from out of the shadows. Lee watched her work the weapon's bolt and then retrieve a dart from her shirt pocket. Brenda slipped the dart into the chamber and then returned to stand directly in front of the chair.

"What are you doing?"

"You talk too much. I need to think."

Brenda raised the tranquilizer rifle to hip level and squeezed the trigger. She didn't bother to aim, seeming unconcerned where the dart hit. Lee grunted when the needle drilled into the right side of her chest, just above the breast. The drug flooded her body and Lee sagged against the rope. She tried to speak, but managed only a gurgling noise. Lee fought to keep her eyes open. When that failed, she made a last ditch effort to shift. The rush of hormones released from changing into a jaguar should allow her body to expel the toxin and rid herself of her bindings.

Lee hadn't tried earlier because her beast would have no compunctions about killing Brenda. She would simply see it as survival of the fittest and eliminating a threat. Lee's higher reasoning abhorred the thought of killing another, even to save her own skin. However, talking hadn't worked and she wondered why she ever thought it would. Her altruistic compunction to save Brenda from death at the hands of her jaguar counterpart changed with the tranquilizer shot. Now it was kill or be killed. Lee had no illusions what Brenda's ultimate plans for her were.

Lee strained, trying to force the change. It was very likely she wouldn't get another chance. Unfortunately, her effort at changing now produced the same outcome it had earlier in the evening while waiting for Cleo's kidnapper to show up. Lee sagged against the restraints, unable to hold her body upright. From somewhere far away, she heard Brenda laughing.

WITH GRAYSON FINALLY quiet, Brenda heaved a sigh of relief. She stood directly in front of the woman, the rifle dangling forgotten in her hands. Just before losing consciousness, Grayson had struggled against the rope. By itself, her resistance wasn't all that unusual. Anybody would fight, given the same circumstances. What surprised Brenda was that Lee actually expected to break free. Brenda could see it in her face. The sheer audacity was enough to anger her further.

Brenda raised the rifle, reversing it with the butt end forward. She tensed in preparation of striking. One sharp blow to the bridge of her nose would drive bone shards into Grayson's brain. It would be over in an instant. That thought alone prevented her from following through. She didn't want things to end so quickly. Grayson deserved to die slowly for keeping her and Jamison apart.

Spinning on her heel, Brenda walked over to the single hardback chair near the hearth. She dropped into the seat, grunting slightly. Her hard, flat gaze traveled over Grayson's unconscious form. Brenda wanted to pull her flesh from her body in strips, slowly, so she could listen to Grayson scream. She'd have to wait for the woman to wake up first and that would take hours.

Brenda sighed in disappointment and then frowned. Lee had said Jamison would be looking for her. She wouldn't believe Lee left town on her own. That was true. Brenda knew how stubbornly loyal Jamison could be. It was one of her most adorable qualities. It was also one of her most annoying. If Jamison had just accepted that they belonged together and walked away from Grayson, none of this would be necessary. In a way, the death of three people was on Jamison's hands. Brenda acknowledged that fact and forgave her anyway. That's what you did when you loved someone.

Once Lee was out of the picture, Jamison would be free to be with her. Brenda stared unseeing at the front door considering what she'd have to do if Jamison chose not to embrace their opportunity. She didn't want to hurt Jamison; the woman was her soul mate. Brenda shook her head. It wouldn't come to that. She was worrying about nothing.

Something slapped against a cracked windowpane. Brenda started, convinced her cabin had been discovered. She realized it was only a tree limb. The wind was starting to pick up. Looking through the dusty glass, Brenda noticed the moon beginning to set. She'd need to take the dog out or the damn thing would be pissing all over the cabin. Brenda looked around, but didn't see the mutt anywhere. She searched the entire cabin before remembering that the animal had skittered out through the open door earlier. She had taunted Lee about the dog, saying that forest animals would kill it. Now Brenda wasn't so sure. Jamison would be out looking for the Grayson woman. If she managed to find the beagle, it would lead her to the cabin. The structure was the only one around for miles and showed on the old park maps. That was how Brenda had found the place to begin with.

"Damn."

She had to find that damned dog. Brenda glanced toward Grayson. The woman hadn't moved since she'd shot her with the tranquilizer dart and it would be hours before Lee woke up. Cleo couldn't have gone far. Remembering the rifle, Brenda retrieved it and slipped another dart into the pipe. The dosage was fine for Grayson, but this much would kill the dog. Brenda didn't care. She'd just dump the carcass with the rest of the dead animals in the root cellar. Without another look at Grayson, Brenda headed out of the open cabin door.

Brenda headed toward the road at a steady jog. She glanced all around while she called to the dog in what she considered a sickly, sweet tone.

"Here boy, that's a good dog." Wait, Grayson said it was a girl. What was her name? "Here, girl. Come here, I won't hurt you...much. At least not for long," she added under her breath.

Brenda passed the remains of the white van she'd used to transport the two teenagers, wrinkling her nose from the stench of burnt wiring and upholstery. The vehicle stood out in the darkness, but Brenda couldn't see the dog. She whistled and called for the beagle but didn't see any signs of her. The tall grass on either side of the rough path didn't help. Cleo could literally be lying right beside her and Brenda would never know it.

When Brenda reached the edge of the hard packed park road she stopped to think. Cleo took off at least an hour ago, maybe two. Brenda had lost track of time while talking with Grayson. She cursed herself for not shooting the dog right then. Or stabbing her, Brenda silently amended. She'd been holding her knife at the time.

"I tried," she whispered. "She jumped out of the way. It's not my fault that she jumped out of the way."

Brenda stood looking out into the forest, wondering where the dog had gone. She heard birds beginning to stir in the treetops. Crickets still chirped but not as loudly as before. The wind rustled in the high grass but still she didn't move. Brenda felt numb, an all too familiar sensation that usually occurred just before a sense of panic would wash over her. The trepidation was a familiar sensation, usually experienced briefly after killing someone. She didn't care about the person whose life she'd snuffed out. Brenda cared only that someone would catch her. If she didn't find the dog, it would lead someone to her and it would all be over.

The shadows lightened and Brenda blinked. She realized she'd been standing in one spot long enough for the sun to begin to rise. Brenda stirred and ran for the park jeep. She'd left it near the edge of the cabin and would need it if she was going to hunt down the beagle. First she'd shoot it with a tranquilizer and then she'd slit its throat for causing her so much trouble.

Chapter Seventeen

JAMISON FORCED HERSELF to breathe deeply. As disturbing as the photographs were they wouldn't help her get Lee back. She needed to find something useful. Jamison reached into the locker and started sifting through the contents. Much of what she found wasn't that unusual for a workplace locker; a hairbrush, a packet of hair ties and even a can of black shoe polish for Brenda's work boots. A paperback novel rested upon a stack of loose papers. The cover was battered and torn on one corner. Jamison tossed the book into the floor with barely a glance. As far as she was concerned, the photos alone were justification for probable cause and it didn't bother her to ransack the contents as she went. She didn't know if a judge would agree considering that she found the incriminating photos after breaking into the locker, but the exigent circumstances of a life hanging in the balance should do the trick. That was assuming it ever came to a courtroom.

Finding the bull's-eye drawn around Lee's chest was enough to enrage Jamison. If she got to Thomas before Macke and Hex did, she didn't know if she'd be able to refrain from tearing the woman apart with her bare hands.

A few loose articles lay under a pile of papers and Jamison picked up a shiny, gold button. She puzzled over its meaning, but her fist clenched when she realized the object's significance. Jamison had lost the button off her dress jacket during last year's Christmas party. She shuddered to think Ranger Thomas had become preoccupied with her so long ago and Jamison had missed the signs. Jamison felt her anger ratchet up another notch, but forced her ire into submission. Lee was the focus, and anything that would lead to her whereabouts. She slid the button into her trouser pocket and reached back into the locker.

Most of the loose papers were useless, various blank report forms used by the park, a ticket book and an empty and wrinkled old manila folder. Jamison noticed the folder sat canted and bent at an odd angle. Whatever rested beneath had a hard, rectangular shape. Cautiously, Jamison raised the folder to find a small box of tranquilizer darts. Although it wasn't uncommon for park personnel to use ketamine on unruly, rampaging or displaced animals, she didn't expect to find them inside a personal locker. Their presence was a blatant breech of protocol, made further disturbing by recent events.

Jamison had discovered a dart just like these on Old Mill Road next to Mira Pye's Buick. Later, police found another in the high grass next to the defunct lumber mill. Outrage pumping through her body, Jamison snatched the box from the bottom of the locker and flipped it open. The container was empty. Rolling her eyes, she pitched it onto the floor. The box bounced off the discarded book and slid across the narrow aisle. Only a few scraps remained inside the locker. Jamison decided the silver chewing gum wrapper was probably worthless so chose the final, folded square of paper.

Her cell phone vibrated and Jamison jerked in surprise. She flipped open her phone as the paper fluttered to the floor. "What is it?"

"We've got a warrant," Sheriff Macke said by way of hello. "Hex and I are headed over now."

"I'll meet you there. Other than several dozen pictures of me and an empty box of tranq darts, there's nothing here."

Jamison bent over to pick up the dropped page. She almost tossed it back inside, but changed her mind. Slamming the locker closed, Jamison exited the room with the paper clutched in her hand. She shoved it into her hip pocket so she could lock the office door.

"Did you say tranquilizer darts?"

"Yep and I'm willing to bet they're the same kind used on Lindsay and Mira. I don't suppose we have any lab results back on their tox screens?"

Jamison could hear Macke speaking to someone in the background before she said, "Detective Hex is calling the hospital to see if the results are back yet. I'll fill you in when you get here."

"Copy that, I'm on my way."

Jamison jumped into her Chevy and pulled out, leaving the Range Rover sitting in the lot. Halfway to the park exit she remembered to switch on the headlights. The moon was full and her primitive side so close to breaking free that she could see as clearly as she could at high noon. Unfortunately, that didn't mean an oncoming driver would see her truck in the dark.

Tires squealed a little when Jamison hit the blacktop. Only then did Jamison notice she could see her breath. The temperature had dropped considerably in the last few hours and it was beginning to mist. The light rain froze almost instantly upon contact with the windshield. Jamison glanced down for just a moment to turn on the wipers and the defroster. When she looked back up she flinched from the glare of lights from a vehicle rapidly approaching from behind. Black Mountain Road was a narrow two lane that led straight into Harmon. Accidents occurred frequently on the road even during the best of conditions. In this weather, driving so recklessly was almost suicide.

Headlights disappeared from her sight in the rear view mirror. If she touched her brakes or slowed in the slightest the other driver would ram into Jamison's bumper. There wasn't a shoulder for her to move over to and get out of the way. Suddenly, the following car drifted into the other lane. It wasn't a quick move, like it would have been if the driver decided to pass. Instead, the move seemed lazy and uncoordinated. As though in response to her observation, the car wandered toward the guard rail. The driver quickly corrected the vehicle and leapt forward.

Jamison heard the engine whine in protest as the driver poured on the speed. As the vehicle passed, she glanced over but the driver sat below Jamison's sight line. She could just make out the bulky sleeve of a coat worn by a passenger sitting in the front. The other car's engine coughed a little and she smelled the smoke that belched out of the tail pipe. At first irritated, Jamison's emotions quickly changed to surprise and confusion when she recognized Brenda Thomas's beat up brown station wagon.

With the worsening of the weather, clouds now obscured the light cast by the full moon. Jamison could see shadows moving inside the car, but little detail. What she could see told her that Brenda was not alone. Jamison had the impression of a heavy coat covering a figure sitting in the front passenger seat. Lee was in there with her.

Adrenaline surged through Jamison's veins and dark pelt erupted over her arms. The seams of her shirt strained at the shoulders and she heard a ripping sound, easily ignored over the sensation of claws erupting from her fingertips. Jamison's teeth elongated into wicked, threatening points. Her vision sharpened even more as she pressed her foot down on the accelerator. She didn't intend to lose them on this windy mountain road.

The station wagon returned to the proper side of the highway, but the driver appeared to have little concern for staying there. The vehicle drifted over the white line several times. She could almost believe the driver was impaired if she didn't know to whom the car belonged. Suddenly Brenda poured on the speed and the gap between the vehicles began to widen.

"Oh no you don't," Jamison muttered. "You're not getting away from me that easily."

Jamison pressed down on the pedal, trying to be careful on the slippery road but not willing to allow Brenda to escape. That Jamison could see an unresisting passenger told her that Lee was either unconscious or injured. If Thomas managed to give her the slip, she would kill Lee. Jamison didn't know why she hadn't already, but didn't want to dwell on the answer. She was just happy that Lee was still alive.

Going around a sharp curve adjacent to the high embankment, Jamison's tires slipped a bit. She gritted her teeth and held on tightly to the wheel, allowing the pickup to drift slightly over the line to compensate for the speed. A car coming from the other direction made her over-correct. She had to fight for control as the rear end fishtailed. The driver of the oncoming car blew the horn and Jamison caught the vague impression of a hand offering an obscene gesture.

Because she had to let off the gas to get the pickup back under control, Thomas had put considerable distance between them. Jamison roared her anger, the sound reverberating off the inside cab of the pickup. She tromped down on the accelerator even as the shoulder seams of her shirt and coat split. Pelt the color of midnight burst from her forearms and lethal claws erupted from the tips of her fingers. The change was so abrupt that it was almost painful, further fueling her rage.

Cat-like vision allowed her to measure the narrowing distance between the vehicles. Jamison's bumper edged nearer to the rear of the station wagon and for a brief instant she considered ramming the jalopy. In its current condition, another dent would hardly stand out. Jamison eyed the rusty bumper in front of her but changed her mind at the last instant. Even a light tap in these hazardous conditions could send the car flying out of control on these treacherous mountain roads.

The freezing mist tapered off until the wipers thumped back and forth across cold, dry glass. She hardly noticed the sound until the rubber blades began to stutter without moisture to help them glide. Jamison switched the wipers off without taking her eyes from the station wagon. Concentrating hard, she tried to peer into the vehicle's interior and identify Lee. Jamison could clearly make out three figures: the two in front and another in the back. She wondered if the third occupant was an accomplice.

Black Mountain Road abruptly crested as Jamison negotiated yet another sharp curve. For the next mile and a half, the terrain was steadily downhill. The driver of the other vehicle wasn't quite as skilled in navigating the turn and Jamison held her breath as the station wagon drifted across the center stripe. Only a galvanized steel guardrail would prevent someone from leaving this road and in this particular spot, that unfortunate individual would encounter a one hundred and fifty foot drop to the canyon floor. At the last second, the driver whipped the vehicle back across the roadway to the proper lane.

Jamison frowned, struck by the lack of control evidenced by the driver. As the station wagon crossed back into the right lane, she watched the very scene that she had feared unfold. The bald rear tires of the vehicle slipped in the light build up of ice accumulated on the blacktop. Thomas's station wagon fishtailed briefly and then went into a sideways slide down the two-lane road.

"Lee," Jamison whispered in sudden dread.

Unable to do anything but watch helplessly, Jamison let off the accelerator and allowed her pickup to slow naturally. She put distance between herself and the out of control station wagon but stayed close enough once the deadly tableau had played out. Thomas's car spun around as it slid until the headlights faced back toward her. As it continued around, the station wagon began slowing and sliding toward the edge of the abutment. Bouncing off the rocky mountain wall would send it ricocheting back toward the cliff and Jamison highly doubted the driver would be able to regain control if that happened.

Up ahead, Jamison spotted a highway breakaway ramp. Intended for semi-trucks that lost control, any vehicle that hit the ramp would stop quickly as it became buried in a foot of plowed soil. In normal conditions that was true, but Jamison didn't know when the highway department had last maintained the ramp or the hardness of the ground considering the weather.

Thomas apparently saw the breakaway ramp at the same time. For a moment, the station wagon righted itself and headed directly toward the emergency exit. Jamison estimated that the vehicle was doing at least forty when it hit the plowed soil. Almost immediately, the station wagon lurched to a stop. Encased at an angle by reddish sand, only the front doors of the vehicle were capable of opening.

Jamison pulled to the edge of the breakaway ramp and rammed the truck into park. She jumped out and ran to the station wagon as fast as she could on the icy terrain. Adrenaline pumped and blood poured into her muscles. Claws punctured metal when she reached out to grab the door lever and Jamison yanked backward with all of her enhanced strength. The top hinge strained and gave way with a shriek. Jamison let go of the sagging door and reached inside to grapple with the driver, afraid that if she didn't act quickly Brenda would harm Lee.

Claws tangled in the thick down covering an arm. She held the driver still while she reached in with the other hand to grab the neck of the jacket. Since the driver hadn't bothered to secure the seat belt, Jamison found it easy to haul them from the vehicle. At the same instant that she dragged the driver from the station wagon, Jamison released a roar of triumph. Higher order reason had given way to primal animal instinct. She held her prize dangling a foot off the ground with one hand and prepared to slash her claws across the prey's face with the other.

Some last whisper of rationality prevented her from killing and Jamison staggered slightly as three things hit her all at once. The smell of booze was overwhelming, the driver was a teenage boy barely old enough to grow facial hair, and he was laughing so hard tears were rolling down his cheeks. Jamison blinked and glanced inside the wrecked station wagon. Another boy sat in the front seat and a girl in the rear. All three were hammered and laughing in delight.

"Man, that was great," the teenager dangling from her inhuman grip asserted. Still grinning, his eyes narrowed as he peered at Jamison. He seemed to have trouble focusing on her features through the alcohol induced haze. "Did you see that?"

Jamison dropped him into the sand. She stomped through soil toward the back of the station wagon, sinking up to mid-shin with every step. Finally at the rear of the vehicle, she peered through the tinted glass into the cargo area. The teenagers were the vehicle's only occupants. Jamison turned back toward the boy attempting to regain his footing. He wasn't having much luck, staggering around in the dirt. She grabbed him by the lapels of his coat and hauled him close to her face.

Allowing him a close-up of her fangs, Jamison grated, "Where did you steal the car?" By finding out where they'd boosted Ranger Thomas's station wagon, she hoped she could narrow down a search area.

"You're purdy." The youth belched unexpectedly and Jamison winced from the stench of stale alcohol.

This was pointless. Until they sobered up a little, these kids wouldn't be able to tell her anything. Jamison dropped him back into the red clay sand and headed for the car. She pulled the keys from the ignition and slipped them into her pocket. The car wouldn't move short of a wrecker pulling it free, but she wasn't taking any chances. After briefly attempting to question the other two, Jamison returned to her initial conclusion. She kept an eye on the three while she called for a patrol car on her cell phone. Fortunately, they didn't seem interested in going anywhere.

The sun was just beginning to peak over the horizon and Jamison felt the seconds tick by. Every moment she wasted here was more time Brenda had to torture and kill her partner. With worry eating at her insides, Jamison called Macke.

"Are you there yet?"

"Yeah, we're waiting for you. There aren't any lights on and I don't see her car."

"And you won't."

Jamison quickly filled the sheriff in on her latest adventure and finished up just as a black and white came into view. "I'll be there in just a few minutes. The deputy is here now and as soon as I turn these guys over I'll be on my way."

"Hurry it up, Kessler. I've waited out of professional courtesy, but we don't have all day."

"Thanks, Sheriff. My day wouldn't have been complete without a little of your sarcasm. I'll be there as fast as I can."

Jamison closed her phone and slid it into her jacket pocket. Deputy Robinson, a brunette somewhere in her mid-thirties coasted to a stop beside her. Light sable eyes tracked over her form, the expression more curious than concerned.

"You okay, Ranger?"

"Of course, why do you ask?"

Robinson nodded toward Jamison as she put the patrol car in park. "Your jacket's torn."

Jamison had forgotten she'd partially shifted while following the station wagon at breakneck speed down the mountain road. "It's just an old coat. Come on and I'll show you what we've got."

Robinson didn't attempt to keep Jamison on the scene for any longer than necessary as a lot of arresting officers would have done in her place. She helped Jamison practically pour the joyriders into the back of her patrol car, took a brief statement and the car keys and then hopped back into the department vehicle.

"Sorry, I don't mean to rush off," Robinson apologized, "but shift-change is in two hours and it would be nice to actually get off on time for once. I figure the paperwork on these three is going to take that long."

"No problem, I have somewhere I need to be. Can you do me a favor, though? Hold these three at the station until they sober up. I need to ask them some questions."

Abruptly suspicious, Robinson's eyes narrowed. "I thought this was about a couple of joyriders. Is there something you're not telling me, Kessler?"

"Not necessarily. This car belongs to Ranger Thomas. She's a person of interest in another ongoing case. I need to find out where they stole the car from and if they saw anything that might help in that other investigation."

"I don't suppose you're at liberty to tell me what that other case is, are you?"

From the way she worded the question, Jamison knew Robinson didn't expect her to be especially forthcoming. She shook her head. "Sorry."

"Uh huh, I thought so. Fine, I'll keep them at the station. It makes no difference to me."

"Thanks, I owe you one."

Robinson carefully checked the road for oncoming traffic and then turned back toward Harmon. Jamison wasn't far behind, but veered off as soon as they hit the city limits. She knew Brenda Thomas lived in the trailer park near the south-west edge of town. Minutes later, she pulled up behind the sheriff's department issue patrol car and turned off the lights and engine. Macke greeted her as soon as she stepped out of the truck.

"About time you got here. We're freezing our butts off."

Jamison ignored her, but didn't miss the amusement in Detective Hex's eyes. Looking around the area, Jamison didn't see how a search of Ranger Thomas's trailer was going to help. "Lee won't be here."

"I agree," Sheriff Macke responded. "The neighbors are too close for her to get away with dragging a kidnap victim inside. Someone would have seen something."

"That doesn't mean they'd report it," Hex pointed out. "Most people avoid getting involved."

Jamison shook her head. "Not here. This isn't New York and these people know each other. If a strange car parks on the street for more than an hour, someone calls it in."

"Regardless, we're not getting anything accomplished standing here and I didn't wait for you all this time to just walk away. Besides, even if they haven't been here we might find something inside that will point us in the right direction."

Jamison didn't agree with Sheriff Macke, but they had little else to go on. Her expression grim, she followed the other two up onto the small porch and waited for the sheriff to knock.

"Harmon County Sheriff's Department, Ranger Thomas. We have a warrant. Open the door."

No one responded. The curtains didn't flutter from an unseen observer and the setting seemed preternaturally silent in the early dawn chill.

"Think she's playing possum?" Detective Hex asked in a stage whisper.

Jamison strained to hear the slightest sound. All she could hear was the wind in the trees. "No, the place is empty."

Macke tried the door but found it locked. Before the frustration finished forming on her face, Jamison raised one booted foot and kicked the door open. She didn't have time to play with humans as they fumbled for another way inside. To her credit, Sam didn't say a word as Jamison led the way into the trailer. She saw the barrel of Macke's drawn pistol out of the corner of her eye as the sheriff broke away to her left. Hex headed the other direction toward the back of the trailer, where Jamison assumed the bedrooms to be.

Jamison's eyes adjusted quickly. What she saw in a scant few moments was enough. "This is nothing more than a crash pad. Thomas doesn't live here."

"I agree," Hex shouted from the master bedroom. She spoke again as she headed back up the hallway. "There's not a stick of furniture in the place and not one photo on the wall."

"More fun, still. There's not so much as a cube of ice in the freezer." Sam re-holstered her Glock. Now what, Kessler? If this is a wild goose chase..."

"It's not. I didn't imagine that note or Lee and Cleo's disappearance."

"But how do you know it's Thomas?" Hex clearly didn't want to question Jamison, but it was important.

"A lot of little things that don't add up," Jamison admitted. "Besides, I know Thomas's handwriting and she was the one who wrote that note."

Sam rolled her eyes. "That's really thin. I hope you've got more than that because it isn't exactly incriminating evidence."

Jamison started and reached into her hip pocket. She'd forgotten about the slip of paper.

"What's that?" Hex asked, leaning over Jamison's shoulder to see.

"I'm not sure. I took it from Thomas's locker at work."

Sam walked over beside her and glanced at the page. "Huh, looks like some kind of property deed."

"What makes you think that?" Jamison asked sarcastically. "The words 'Title Deed' printed at the top?"

"Now just a damn minute, it's not my fault your partner is missing."

Sam's hands were fisted at her sides, a sign of rising temper with which Jamison was unfamiliar considering the source. Sheriff Macke prided herself on maintaining self-control and her obvious tension was enough to make Jamison think twice. It wasn't that she worried that Sam could best her in an altercation. The outside signs of forced restraint just reminded Jamison that the entire community was on edge. People they all knew and cared for had been injured recently. They were going to have to put aside their differences and work together to find Lee.

Jamison deflated like a balloon pricked by a needle. "You're right, I'm just worried. Anyway, it looks like this deed is for a small plot inside the Adirondack Park."

"Let me see that." Hex snatched the deed from Jamison's hands, studying it intently. "Look at this, Kessler. Now, technically the whole area is Adirondack Park but this property looks like it's inside the national park boundaries."

"How can that be?" Sam asked. "I thought there weren't any private residences inside a park."

Jamison briefly considered the conundrum. "There used to be. A long time ago, before the state set aside the land, cabins and homesteads filled these woods. When the park was established most of the cabins were purchased by the state."

"Most?"

"Yeah." This time Detective Hex answered the sheriff. "There are always a few hold-outs though. If this deed is valid, one of the owners must have held onto their property and passed it down through the family. Since Thomas's name is on it, she either inherited the land or purchased it outright."

"That doesn't make sense. Wouldn't the government have seized the land if they wanted to establish a park, whether someone wanted to sell or not?"

Hex looked at Sam like she'd lost her mind. "You do remember the Bill of Rights? No state shall deprive any person of life, liberty or property without due process?"

Sheriff Macke snorted. "Right, and that was from the same government that herded Native Americans onto reservations and seized their land."

"Are you always this suspicious or is it a social disorder?"

"No, I'm always this suspicious. It's part of my natural charm."

"If this is charm, I'd hate to see—"

"Hey!" Jamison interrupted. "As cute as this banter is between you two, save it for the honeymoon. Bigger fish, people."

With her cohorts duly chastised, Jamison took advantage of the silence to study the deed. At the bottom corner of the old title was a tiny map intended to outline the boundaries of the property. Under the map, she could just barely make out some small print.

"Edward Anson addition. It could be a few square acres or a few hundred miles."

"I'll give Seaver a call and have her run it through the computer," Hex offered. "Let me see it so I can get a lot number off it for her to reference."

With Hex on the phone, Jamison had nothing pressing to occupy her mind. Each time she was left without something to concentrate on in the moment, she felt like she might lose it. Fortunately, Hex didn't take long.

"She's on it. I told Chase to be ready to join us just as soon as we know where to start looking."

"Good idea," Macke approved. "I should call the station and have some deputies standing by for a grid by grid search."

Jamison remembered Deputy Robinson's parting words when she'd picked up the inebriated teenagers. "Great, Robinson is going to love me."

"What's Robinson got to do with anything?"

"She picked up the joyriders for me and booked them into lockup. Robinson made a comment about looking forward to getting off shift on time."

"If Deputy Robinson has ten sixteens," Macke said, using the police code for detainees, "then she's going to be too busy to help us out. Besides, I'm not sure an exhausted deputy is going to be much good to us anyway."

"Especially if this area is where I think it is," Jamison added, studying the deed.

"What do you mean?"

Rather than answer, Jamison handed the page to Hex. "Does that look like the Devil's Rim area to you?"

Hex looked over the page, a baffled expression on her face. She shrugged. "From the legend, I'd say so but I don't really know the area. What's the problem?"

"Oh nothing much, except that the Devil's Rim section of the park was closed to tourists years ago. It's full of unexpected drop offs, sheer cliffs and heavy undergrowth. It's far too dangerous for weekend campers or novice hikers."

"Sounds like the perfect place to hide out with a captive," Sam pointed out.

Jamison shook her head. "How would she get in there? The area isn't maintained."

"Are there any roads going into Devil's Rim," Hex asked.

"I'm not sure."

"Well, you'd better find out. Even if the area isn't maintained, Ranger Thomas has access to park vehicles, doesn't she?"

"Yes," Jamison said slowly. "She does, and they're all equipped with four-wheel drive. Maybe that's why she didn't need her car—she traded up."

"You did say they passed you as you were leaving the park," Sam said. "I know it's not the height of camping season, but a couple of high school kids wouldn't care about that. Chances are they were out looking to have a bonfire or something in the park and found the car with the keys still in it. Either way, we need to narrow down the search."

"At least we have a place to start. The Devil's Rim and Devil's Peak areas are on the northeastern edge of the park. The region is hard to get to, but I think I know just the person to give us a bird's eye view."

"Who?" Detective Hex asked.

"Do you think she'll do it?" Macke questioned.

"Of course, Lee is practically her sister in law. I'll call to fill Dinah in on what's happening."

Jamison reached for her cell phone as the sheriff filled Hex in on the family situation. She had dropped her phone into the coat pocket earlier while speaking with Deputy Robinson, forgetting that she'd grabbed Lee's cell off the phone table earlier. Both phones resided in the same pocket and one of them began to ring just as she touched it.

"Hello?" Jamison listened as a nervous woman began to speak. From her voice she sounded young, perhaps in her late teens or early twenties.

"Hi, you don't know me but I found a beagle in the woods and this number was on the tag."

"You found Cleo?" Excitement caused her to speak loudly as the blood sang in her veins. Macke and Hex stopped talking and watched her expectantly. "Is she okay?"

"Yeah, I guess so. I was just out on a day hike and the poor little thing ran right up to me. She's soaked to the bone and cold, but I don't see any injuries."

Jamison felt so relieved that tears pricked her eyes. She had to clear her throat before asking, "Where are you now?"

"At the base of Colbert Mountain. I just finished the M22 loop trail and was heading back for my car when I saw the dog."

Loop M22 wasn't far from the old Myers logging road, out of use since the area was named a national sanctuary. It also wasn't far from the remains of a town, abandoned in the late 1800s. Jamison didn't think any of the original structures still existed, but that didn't mean that a few of them hadn't been rebuilt in the centuries since. That area was well within the borders indicated on Thomas's deed. If Jamison could get Dinah to investigate from the air, they might be able to hone the search grid to something more manageable.

"Can you meet me at the Paul Smith's Visitor's Center? I'm in Harmon right now but I can meet you there in..." Jamison checked her watch. "Fifteen minutes?"

"That's fine. It'll give me time to warm up a little. Can you believe this weather?"

Jamison rushed the young woman off the phone, belatedly realizing she hadn't even asked for a name. "I've got to get Cleo, but I can tell you that we're on to something. She must have either escaped or Brenda let her go. I'm betting she didn't expect anyone to find her. In any case, Cleo couldn't have walked far in the woods. It helps us narrow down the area."

"Right, Detective Hex and I will start searching where the dog was found. You take care of the dog and then meet up with us."

"I have a better idea. I think it's time to split up. Do you have a hiking map of the park, Sheriff Macke?"

"Of course, what kind of police officer would I be if I didn't have a map of something near my jurisdiction?"

"Good question," Jamison allowed. "You and Hex start at the western trailhead of the M22 loop, that's where the girl said she found Cleo. Have Chase meet you there. As soon as we hear from Seaver we can narrow the search parameters."

"What are you going to do in the meantime," Hex asked.

"I'm leaving Cleo at the visitor's center and I'm going to start from the north. There's an old logging town in the area and I'm guessing that Thomas has Lee down there somewhere."

Hex pulled a notebook from her hip pocket. "Draw me a map. You've worked here for years and probably know the area better than anyone. Instead of wasting time starting miles from anywhere, we'll start searching as close to that site as we can get."

"Sounds good to me," Sam said. "If we don't find anything there, we can always fan out."

"Just be careful. You won't be able to go far on foot and if you get split up, someone is liable to end up lost. We don't need more people to search for."

Chapter Eighteen

JAMISON SCRIBBLED FURIOUSLY on the pad before she pressed it into Detective Hex's hands and rushed out of the door. Fate had returned Cleo and along with her, a hint as to where Brenda had taken Lee. Foregoing all caution, Jamison dialed her sister with one hand as she pulled away from the trailer park. Her hands felt numb from a combination of the cold and the dread that had settled in her heart.

Before Dinah finished answering the call, Jamison began to speak. She filled her sister in on everything that had occurred in the last few hours. Barely pausing for a breath, Jamison outlined what she needed in order to get her partner back safely. Dinah's reaction was not what she anticipated.

"Are you crazy? I mean seriously, that's the only possible reason you didn't call me before contacting the local police."

"Dinah, I hardly think this is the time."

"It's exactly the time. You should have put the Panthera patrols on this as soon as it happened."

Dinah was right. As a medicine woman for the community, Panthera protocol dictated that their own people would jump in if anything happened to Lee. They had some of the best investigators on the planet and their enhanced senses of sight, smell, and incredible strength were attributes not to be ignored. Jamison only wished things were so cut and dried, but living with humans set the stage for unpredictability.

"I didn't have time. Honestly, since I found out about this I haven't slowed down. Besides, this is a human killer and not an out of control shifter like last year." Jamison realized she was babbling and took a steadying breath. "That's not important right now. Will you help me?"

"Of course, she's my family too you know. Give me five minutes to throw some clothes on. I'll call Mom and have her get the hunters into the park."

With Dinah covering details that she couldn't even wrap her mind around at the moment, Jamison felt the first bit of hope that she had all night. "That's a great idea. I'd call the patrols myself, but I think they'll mobilize faster if their *Caber* issues the order."

Dinah actually chuckled. "Would you go up against Mom when she gets her dander up?"

"Not a chance."

"Exactly, and when she hears what this is about she's going to go postal. I think she loves Lee more than she does both of us."

The comment elicited a laugh, but it ended on a sob. "I can't lose her, Dinah. I love her so much."

"You won't. Lee just became a part of our family and we aren't about to let that happen. Right now, she needs us to be strong so pull it together, Elder."

Jamison nodded unseen by her sister. "Okay." She took another breath. "Okay, I'm all right now. I guess I'm just freaking out a little."

"Anyone would in your place. We just have to focus on getting her back. Where are you headed now?"

"A woman called. She found Cleo wandering in the park. I'm going to meet her and find out exactly where she was when that happened. It'll give us a starting point for a ground search. In the mean time, I need you to start from the air and help us narrow the area down. We think Thomas found somewhere to hide out near that old logging town."

"Shipper's Village? Is there anything left standing there?"

"There must be. Her trailer hasn't been lived in and I don't see her as the type to hole up in a cave. Fly around the area and look for any signs of life, smoke from a fire...anything. That area is off limits so if you see something like that, that's where she'll be."

"Got it. Keep your radio on you and I'll contact you as soon as I know anything."

"Same here, and Dinah? Thank you."

Jamison closed her cell phone and started to toss it beside her onto the bench seat. At the last second she changed her mind and slid the phone back into her jacket pocket. She didn't want to be without the phone, just in case Lee called or there was some important break in the situation that would lead to her whereabouts. Pulling into the parking lot of the Paul Smith's Visitor's Center, Jamison experienced a strong sense of déjà vu. She rolled her eyes a second later when she recognized the sensation arose from her fourth arrival at the station in as many hours.

A canary yellow Volkswagen Beetle sat idling near the steps. A steady stream of exhaust plumed from the tail pipe, a visual reminder of the dropping temperatures. Jamison refrained from shaking her head at the impracticality of such a vehicle in poor weather on mountainous terrain. She resolved to make the exchange for Cleo and find out as much as she could from the female Samaritan before conditions worsened.

Jamison pulled up sideways beside the Beetle, with her door adjacent to the other driver. She spotted an open, smiling face and a pink scarf before a woman climbed out of the car holding Cleo. Jamison was so relieved to see the beagle that tears unexpectedly flooded her eyes. Soulful brown eyes met her gaze as Jamison hopped out of the pickup and she had to dash away the moisture that caused Cleo to appear blurry.

"Thank you so much for taking care of her," Jamison said, opening her arms up to accept the happy dog. She could sense Cleo's excitement at seeing a familiar face and hugged her close. Jamison noticed how badly Cleo was shivering and unzipped her coat with her free hand. Then she shoved the beagle under the flap and against her own warm body.

"No problem, I felt so sorry for her out there all alone. How'd you lose track of her, anyway?"

"Actually, Cleo is my partner's dog. Lee went missing several hours ago and I was wondering if you wouldn't mind showing me exactly where you found Cleo. It would really help narrow down our search radius." Jamison held her breath, hoping this woman wasn't in too much of a hurry to be somewhere.

The stranger cast a glance overhead at the gray sky before responding. "Sure, okay. I suppose I have time. Do you want to follow me?"

Jamison looked briefly at the Volkswagen. "Uh, why don't we just take mine. I promise to come straight back."

The woman shrugged and then walked around to the passenger side of the truck. Once safely on their way, Jamison said, "I didn't get your name."

"Oh right, Sarah Parker. I guess introducing myself would have been the polite thing to do. Since you're wearing a Park uniform, I'm assuming you know the way to the M22?"

Jamison nodded. "Just point me in the right direction once we get to the trail."

It didn't take long to reach the trailhead and then they had to go in the rest of the way on foot. Jamison held onto Cleo the entire time, unwilling to let her out of her arms. Cleo rested her head on Jamison's shoulder and appeared to be sleeping though Jamison doubted that was the case. She could still feel a great deal of tension in the small body. The M22 loop wasn't wide enough to accommodate Jamison's pickup and she didn't relish getting stuck in the mud up to her hubcaps. Sarah led her about a quarter of a mile farther down the path before stopping near a felled Sycamore.

"This is it. I stopped to tie my shoe and she came out of the trees over there." Sarah pointed toward the highest nearby mountain. Devil's Peak.

Jamison nodded. She had expected as much. The trouble was that she didn't know how long Cleo had been wandering in the woods and this was still a big area. Still, the information would help narrow things down some. Cleo lifted her head and sniffed the air before returning to her previous position. She showed no sign of wanting down.

"Thanks you've been a big help. Come on and I'll give you a ride back. Then I've got to start calling out some people to help start a search."

"Uh, I could stay and help if you want. I just stopped by the park for an early morning hike before I have to go to work. I figured it would be the last of the season what with the storm coming in, but I really wouldn't mind helping you look."

Jamison smiled, truly touched by the offer. "Thank you, I appreciate that. Unfortunately, the front is moving in pretty fast and I'd hate for you to get stuck up here. No offense, but your car doesn't look like it's designed for driving in the snow."

"You're right about that," Sarah laughed. "Oh well, it would have been a good excuse to get out of work."

Jamison focused on the road, pondering Sarah's comment. She doubted getting out of work was the real reason Sarah wanted to stay. The remark was more self-deprecating than truthful, an attempt at deflection. Thinking about it, Jamison realized Sarah had done much more than was strictly necessary. Many people would have ignored a dog wandering alone in the woods, even one wearing a collar and tags. Now she offered to stay and look for someone she'd never met in the worst weather of the year that threatened to become more so. Yet she couldn't see any angle in it for Sarah.

There were those in the Council of Elders convinced that humans had no redeeming qualities. Marie Tristan was one of those and if she had her way, none would be allowed to live in the Harmon city limits. Then people like Sarah Parker came along and proved her wrong, wanting to help just because it was the right thing to do. Jamison had to remind herself that Sarah didn't know about the Panthera either. She was offering to help search for a fellow human being, not a shape changer that could rip her lungs out without any effort.

Jamison decided to let the remark go without comment. As much as she appreciated the offer, she wanted only Panthera hunters or trained law enforcement involved in the search. The last thing they needed was to bring in civilians that would get lost in an impending snow storm and add to their problems. She dropped Sarah off at her Beetle and offered her a wave before the young woman drove away.

As soon as they were alone, Jamison hefted Cleo up and looked into the curious brown eyes. "I don't suppose you want to tell me where your mom is?"

Cleo leaned forward and touched her wet nose to Jamison's. Jamison could tell that the dog was worried, no doubt picking up on her own dread. Unfortunately, without the ability to speak Cleo couldn't give Jamison the information she so desperately desired. Jamison could get impressions from the beagle, but dogs and cats communicated in fundamentally different ways. About the only thing she could determine for sure was that Cleo was cold. Considering how badly she shivered, that didn't take much of an interpretation.

"Well, come on. Let's get you inside and warmed up."

Jamison unlocked the station and settled Cleo in her office. An old pad taken from the gardener's shed served as a makeshift dog bed. By the time she had Cleo settled, the sun was up and Jamison was more than ready to get started looking for Lee. The sky was still heavily overcast and she didn't expect to actually see the sun anytime soon. Jamison's phone rang as soon as she placed her hand on the front door in preparation of leaving the visitor's center. Taking advantage of the warmth inside the building, Jamison stayed where she was to answer Detective Hex's call.

"Do you have something?"

"Yes," Hex answered promptly. "It looks like you were right to suspect Ranger Thomas. Detective Seaver just called to let me know that the lab got a hit on a partial pinkie print left on your partner's Mercedes."

"And?"

"Her real name is Bethany Brenda Waters. She changed her name after her release from juvenile custody. Thomas is her mother's maiden name."

"Do I want to know why she has a juvenile record?"

Hex didn't respond to the question. Instead, she chose to give Jamison the full rundown. "How about stalking and petty theft followed by a restraining order filed by an ex-girlfriend? After her ex filed the restraining order, your girl killed her. Thomas was convicted of second degree manslaughter, mitigated for psychiatric reasons. She did four years in juvie with mandatory psychiatric counseling and was released at twenty. By all accounts she was a model prisoner."

"Why wasn't this discovered before?" Jamison asked in anger. "She's a federal law enforcement agent. How could something like this slip through the cracks?"

"You know how it is," Hex offered rationally. "A juvenile record is sealed and because she changed her last name, nothing flagged on a background search."

"That's a piss-poor excuse and you know it."

"Maybe, but it's all we've got. It's also enough to show a pattern. Now we just have to see where that pattern leads us."

Jamison considered Hex's information for a moment. "It explains why we couldn't find any evidence at the crime scenes. Thomas knows forensic countermeasures."

"True, and the victims would have seen her ranger uniform and would have trusted her. Thomas could have been right on top of them and those women wouldn't have suspected a thing."

"I think that fact makes me even more furious," Jamison responded honestly. "Those women trusted her and Brenda took full advantage of her authority. Sometimes I wonder if Marie wasn't right about humans."

"Who's Marie, and what about humans? I'm not following."

"It's not important," Jamison said quickly, worried that she had said too much. "I'm getting ready to leave the station. Sarah, the woman who found Cleo, showed me exactly where she found her. Tell Sheriff

Macke to meet me at the trailhead for the M22 loop, she knows where it is. My sister is a helicopter pilot and she's already started flying over the area looking for signs of life. In this cold weather, the heat bloom from a fire should stand out like a flare."

"Will do. Look, Ranger Kessler...I know we don't know each other very well, but we will get Ms. Grayson back in time."

"How do you know?" Jamison realized she sounded desperate, but she felt like clinging to anything that might offer a bit of hope. She and Lee had fought so much lately and if she lost her now, Jamison would carry the guilt for the rest of her life. Meeting Lee had been like coming full circle, the completion of herself that she'd been looking for since she could remember. She loved Lee with every fiber of her being and intended to spend the rest of eternity proving it. If only they could get Lee back before it was too late.

"I have an instinct about these things. Trust me."

Jamison snorted and sniffed against the tears. "Classic overachiever, right?"

"First in my class."

"I'll try to keep it in mind."

"You should. Listen, Macke says we're about five minutes from the park. We'll meet you at the trailhead and finalize the details from there."

Jamison hung up and put her hand on the push bar. Again, she was interrupted by an external source but this time it wasn't the phone. Cleo had sunk her fangs into the hem of her right trouser leg and hauled backward with her stumpy body to prevent Jamison from leaving. Cleo tugged hard and threw her head from side to side like a bulldog with a ragdoll, a low growl emanating from her throat.

"Cleo, stop. What's your problem?"

It didn't take much to figure out that Cleo didn't want Jamison to leave her alone. What took a little more work was putting the piece of the puzzle together. Click, click, click...they fell into place. Cleo was just as concerned for Lee as Jamison. She wanted to help find her master to make her pack complete.

"You want to help find her, don't you girl? I wanted to leave you here to warm up, but that isn't gonna work, is it?"

Jamison rubbed Cleo's head, but the beagle didn't flinch. Brown eyes met her own, full of purpose. Jamison realized that her idea of leaving Cleo behind in a warm, soothing sanctuary wasn't going to fly. The dog was determined to accompany her. On reflection, maybe that was a good thing. Cleo knew where she'd come from. Perhaps she could retrace her steps. Humans often didn't give dogs enough credit and Jamison thought Cleo had a better chance of leading them to Lee than if they went on a blind search without more information.

"Okay, girl, you win. Let's go find Lee."

Chapter Nineteen

"TELL ME AGAIN why we're going in on foot," Sam groused. "I thought Park vehicles were equipped with four-wheel drive."

"That doesn't mean they can fly. The terrain here is too rough for a vehicle and besides," Detective Hex paused to take a panting breath, "it's too slippery."

The brief flurry of freezing rain during the night had left a light coating of ice over the ground. Sam could hear it crunching underfoot as they walked and her toes already felt numb. She couldn't believe they'd only been out of the car for about ten minutes. Sam sniffed against the cold and adjusted the scarf covering her face.

"Are you sure we're in the right place?"

Pat shrugged. "You tell me, you're more familiar with this area than I am. All I know is that Kessler said to head east overland from the trailhead."

"We're in the right place then." Sam glanced down and checked the compass. "Dinah reported seeing something near that old mining town Kessler mentioned, but the trees were too thick for her to get very close."

"Dinah...she's Ranger Kessler's sister?"

"Yeah, she runs a helicopter service to fly tourists around the area and she's been known to help law enforcement out in a pinch." Sam stumbled slightly and had to clear the moisture from her eyes with a thumb.

"In that case we probably don't want her to get too close to Thomas anyway. There's no telling what would happen. It's too dangerous for a civilian."

Sam's lips twisted with distaste beneath her scarf. "Yeah, dangerous," she mumbled.

"What does that mean?"

"Nothing, can we just not talk about it?"

"Talk about what?" Hex sounded curious but a little distracted as she navigated around a steep drop.

Sam remained silent, following the other woman into the tree line.

"Fine, whatever," Pat finally said. "If you don't want to talk about that, can you tell me why you won't go out with me?"

Sam froze and stared at Pat's back. The detective had stooped over slightly in preparation of stepping over a felled tree trunk. She sounded slightly distracted and Sam determined Pat wasn't really paying attention to her. When she reached the other side of the tree, Pat turned and met her eyes.

"Why can't you just take no for an answer?"

"It's not in my nature."

Sam smiled a little despite the uncomfortable nature of the conversation. She knew it wasn't fair to keep blowing Pat off without any kind of explanation and so far she'd gotten away with it because of the case. That excuse was wearing thin. Sam had a feeling they'd find Thomas soon and she would turn out to be their killer. Though everyone was already convinced of that fact, Sam didn't like leaping to conclusions. Still, she had to admit things looked pretty incriminating for the park ranger. Once that happened, Pat would leave.

"All right, you win. I won't go out with you because there isn't any point. This case will end, probably today, and you'll leave. Why start something that doesn't have a chance of going anywhere?"

"I'm not asking you to marry me," Pat pointed out. "What's wrong with having dinner together and having a little fun?"

Oh, Sam thought. She certainly hadn't expected such a cavalier attitude from Pat. Sam wasn't the type to have casual sex, which sounded like what Pat had in mind. Sam wanted what she'd had with Nicky, a committed monogamous relationship. Apparently, she was the only one. This was just further proof that getting involved with Pat was a bad idea.

"It's not in my nature."

Sam walked past Pat and headed toward the canyon at Devil's Snare. Disappointment prevented her from being able to look at Pat anymore. She refused to respond to any other comments and eventually Pat stopped trying. They continued on in silence and Sam forced herself to concentrate on finding Lee Grayson and Brenda Thomas.

JAMISON KEPT HER eyes on Cleo as the beagle trotted through the woods with her nose to the ground. From the moment she had taken the dog in her arms, she'd been able to smell Brenda. That the woman's scent was all over Cleo was further proof of Brenda's culpability in all of this.

Find her. Jamison gently touched Cleo's canine mind with her stronger presence, careful not to overwhelm the dog while continuing to encourage. Cleo's desire to locate Lee resonated within Jamison and she watched as Cleo suddenly threw her head back and bayed loudly. Jamison smiled as the dog took off at a run, clearly on the scent. Jamison's nostrils flared as she attempted to pick up the spoor. Cleo had picked up on her own trail from earlier in the morning hours and now used it to backtrack her starting point.

"Smart girl."

Jamison picked up the pace, jogging through the high grass in pursuit of the beagle. Like most National Parks there were vast open areas as well as heavily treed regions. At the moment, Jamison felt exposed without the protection of the forest canopy. Her boots felt heavy, pulling her feet down and preventing her from keeping up with the dog. If Cleo kept up the pace, Jamison would lose her in the grass. Jamison shivered at the thought of having to shed her clothing and assume her cat form. Panthera were no different than the average housecat when it came to the cold. She decided to wait until they came in sight of whereever Brenda held Lee, otherwise she'd be running naked through the wilderness from an undetermined distance if she had to shift back to human form.

Within ten minutes, Cleo stopped and looked back over her shoulder for Jamison. She trembled from the cold, but still seemed determined to continue looking for Lee. She stood beneath the shadows cast by a grouping of four giant pines. Here the grass ceased to grow, but ice had accumulated at the base.

"What is it, girl?"

Jamison squatted down and lifted Cleo to her knees to get her feet off the frozen tundra. She peered through the trees and shrubbery and could just barely see the outline of an ancient man-made structure. Rough-hewn boards outlined a cabin that had been all but reclaimed by the forest. Jamison could smell a fire from inside the structure and something else that made her feel sick. She hadn't seen smoke from a fireplace because the trees were too thick. The cabin sat at the base of where the heavy forest resumed.

She fumbled for the radio in her pocket and depressed the call button. "Dinah, are you there?" A second later she heard her sister's voice over the noise of helicopter rotors.

"I'm here, did you find it?"

"Yes, there's a cabin here. I can smell Lee. Relay the coordinates on the radio's GPS to Macke and the hunters. I'm going to check things out."

"Jamison, you wait for backup!"

Jamison heard, but had no intention of waiting. Even now, Brenda could be killing Lee. She refused to contemplate the thought that she already had. Jamison switched off the radio so that an unexpected communiqué wouldn't alert Brenda to her presence. She placed Cleo on the ground and headed for the cabin. Cleo led the way, her tail wagging. The little dog was in such a hurry to return to her master that she started to run.

"Cleo, wait." The order did no good.

Jamison didn't waste time calling after her again. Cleo was a loyal friend who had lost patience and gone to help Lee on her own. Jamison couldn't fault that loyalty but she approached the structure more cautiously, straining to listen for any signs that another was nearby. There was no sign of a vehicle and she couldn't hear anything coming from inside. Cleo stood on her hind legs, scratching at the closed door before casting a look over her shoulder to Jamison. Jamison got the clear projection from Cleo demanding that she clear the way.

Putting her ear against the door, Jamison listened intently. There was no sound. She could tell Lee was inside because her scent was stronger here, but Brenda's mark wasn't as intense. Jamison put her hand on the knob and hesitated when it turned easily. This could be a trap.

She pushed the door open enough to peer around the frame. When she didn't see Brenda and didn't trigger a booby trap, she edged inside. Lee was alone and sat tied to a chair. She lifted her head when she heard the door, a look of wariness in her eyes that faded when she identified the newcomer. Jamison rushed across the room and dropped onto her knees beside Lee. She checked quickly for signs of injury but found nothing.

"I'm all right," she mumbled.

Lee's words slurred a little and Jamison noticed her dilated pupils. A rope held Lee tightly to a chair and Jamison realized Lee would never be able to break her bonds. Jamison gagged a little from the heavy stench of rot coming from under the floor. She shook her head and tried not to think what Brenda had been doing in the cabin. Jamison made a mental note to have a forensics team sweep the cabin and surrounding area for bodies. Trying to ignore the offensive odor, she tugged at the bindings around Lee's wrists. Judging by the thickness of the braiding, it would take a while to untie them. Brenda could return before she finished.

"You have to get me loose." Lee sounded desperate, just at the verge of starting to panic.

"I can't get it. My hands are too cold," Jamison admitted, her teeth beginning to chatter. The cabin wasn't exactly airtight and the dwindling fire in the hearth did little more than take off the worst of the chill.

"My front pocket, I still have Dinah's knife. She loaned it to me to open something and I never gave it back."

Jamison reached for the top of her pocket while Lee leaned back as far as she could. It wasn't much room to work with. Jamison slid her finger tips into the narrow opening and pinched the end of the knife between her thumb and index finger, pushing at the object from the outside with her other hand.

"Where's Brenda?" she asked as she worked.

"She went looking for Cleo. We got into an argument and the cabin door was open. Cleo escaped and then Brenda got worried someone might find her and lead her back here."

"She was right." Jamison finally freed the knife and began sawing through the heavy rope. "Cleo led me straight to you."

"Good girl," Lee whispered. Her eyes closed and she swallowed heavily.

"Are you okay?"

Lee shook her head. "I kept trying to change into my jaguar, but I couldn't. Why can't I change like you can? I should have been able to free myself."

She sounded so miserable that Jamison felt bad for her. "It's not your fault, it's the ketamine."

"Keta what?"

"You've been drugged. I noticed your eyes are dilated and there's a dart still sticking out of your chest."

Lee's eyes fixed on the orange feathers at the tip of the now empty tranquilizer dart. "Brenda shot me with a sedative, I know, but if I could just change I could get the drugs out of my system. Isn't that right?"

"It's not that easy." One of the loops finally let go. "Ketamine is a paralytic. I'm not so sure anyone could change after being shot with that stuff."

Cleo suddenly started barking. Jamison knew there weren't any roads nearby and she hadn't heard a vehicle. If anyone was approaching, they had to be coming in on foot. Jamison didn't know if it was Macke, the Panthera hunters or Brenda returning. She did know that odds weren't in her favor.

"Is it her?" Lee asked fearfully.

Jamison unwound the rope as far as she could, freeing Lee's body from the chair, but her hands remained tied. Jamison gripped Lee by the upper arm and encouraged her to stand. She was worried that Brenda would shoot them both with another tranquilizer before they could react. Jamison was pretty confident her quick reflexes could evade the dart, but Lee wasn't quite herself. From what Jamison could piece together, Lee had already been hit twice. She didn't know if even a jaguar could shake off a third dose of ketamine in less than twenty-four hours.

"I don't know, it might be nothing, but unless our luck undergoes a serious change I'd guess it is her. I can't pick up a scent from inside the cabin. Let's get out of here."

Cleo whimpered and Jamison scooped her off the floor. Lee leaned forward and briefly buried her face in the fur at Cleo's neck.

"I'm not letting you out of my sight ever again."

Jamison wanted to give Lee time, but she didn't know how much they had. She placed a hand at the small of Lee's back, encouraging her to move. "Come on, baby. I'll untie your hands once we get under some cover."

The crunch of ice under her boots helped Jamison feel more centered. Although not fond of the cold, it was far more preferable to the stench of death permeating the inside of the cabin. At the moment, Jamison had experienced enough death over the last several weeks and wanted to concentrate on life. Specifically, she wanted to ensure that Lee stayed alive.

She kept a grip on Lee's upper arm to prevent her from slipping on the ice. Halfway to the woods, Cleo began to squirm and Jamison had no choice but to set the dog on the ground. Tongue lolling out of the left side of her mouth, Cleo happily trotted toward the trees. She vanished into the shadows. At almost the same instant, Jamison heard a hissing sound. The sound abruptly stopped as something slammed into the ground at their feet. Jamison stared at a small, smoking hole in the ice.

Lee hunched over and started for the place where Cleo had disappeared. "Jamison, hurry, she's shooting at us."

Jamison followed Lee into the brush, grabbing her around the waist when she tripped and almost fell. Strength flowed into Jamison from the adrenaline pumping through her veins and she felt her cat throwing itself at the cage door in her mind. Jamison grabbed the ropes around Lee's wrists and ripped them asunder, the muscles in her forearms bunching. Bullets continued to tear into the trees where they crouched and it was only a matter of time until their luck ran out.

"We can't stay here," Lee pointed out.

"No, but if we leave the woods she'll have a clean shot."

Jamison looked around frantically. The place where they hid was an oasis of trees and high brush surrounded by tall grass. Once they left this spot, they would not stand a chance. If they would survive this, they had to act quickly. "Stay here."

Lee placed a restraining hand on her arm. "What are you going to do?"

"The only thing I can."

Jamison reached for the top button of her coat, but Lee quickly stopped her. "She'll shoot you before you get within two feet of her. You may be strong Jamison, but a bullet is just as deadly for us as it is for any human."

"Then what do you suggest?" Jamison asked in frustration. "I don't want to die, but I won't sit here and let her kill you."

Brenda let off another round of shots and they dove toward the frozen ground. Jamison could hear the crunch of ice as she approached their location. She approached from their left and the hiking trail. The cabin lay off to their right. That only left straight ahead or toward the rear. Brenda would easily spot whoever moved forward. Time was running out and Jamison couldn't think of an alternative plan.

"Fine, but I go first. Head back through the shrubs and make your way around to the main road. Dinah has already called for reinforcements and you should run into either Sheriff Macke or the Panthera."

"They're together?"

Jamison didn't really think that was important at the moment, but answered anyway. "No, of course not. Macke doesn't know they're out here and they're smart enough to avoid her. Especially considering that Hex is probably with her."

Jamison watched Brenda raise the rifle to her shoulder and aim in their direction.

"Go now." She didn't give Lee time to talk her out of her next move. She planted her feet and quickly eyed the best route to distract Brenda.

She jumped to her feet and ran at an angle between Brenda and the M22 loop. The loop was far from here, but she thought Brenda must have taken it until she got close to the cabin. At any rate, Jamison counted on forcing the woman to turn her back to the old logging structure so that Lee could get away unseen.

Jamison watched Brenda as she ran. From the corner of her eye she caught a flash of color as Lee darted from beneath the branches. She assumed Cleo followed her master, but shifted her attention back to the threat. Drawn by her movement, Brenda's head swiveled in Jamison's direction and she automatically raised the rifle. When she caught sight of Jamison, Brenda's eyes widened and she froze, the weapon dangling uselessly in her hands. Jamison took advantage of her shock by sprinting away toward the dense forest undergrowth.

Heart thumping in her ears, Jamison cast a look back over her shoulder. She expected to see Brenda either hot on her trail or aiming at her with the rifle. To her surprise, Brenda had turned away from Jamison and headed toward the cabin. Clearly, she had no intention of shooting the object of her affection. Instead, she was looking for Lee.

What the hell was she thinking? Jamison wondered. Did Brenda honestly think that if she killed Lee she would have a chance with Jamison? Was she truly that delusional? If so, how could Jamison have missed the signs? She was supposed to be a trained observer. Jamison watched Brenda spin around and bring the rifle to her shoulder. At first she couldn't understand why Ranger Thomas had turned toward the mountain range when Lee had headed in the opposite direction. Then she caught sight of Lee's blonde head bobbing as she climbed the lower escarpment. She followed a small trail that wound around the base of Devil's Peak, leading toward the summit.

Jamison couldn't help wonder why Lee had headed toward the mountain. She flinched when the echo from the gunshot rang throughout the valley. Brenda stood much closer to Lee, but Jamison had been running toward the forest. Now she was too far away to be of much help to her partner. She expected Lee to stiffen and fall from the modest height, but she didn't. Lee raised her arms to cover her head and ducked, slipping back a little in the small accumulation of ice.

Brenda started up the trail about a hundred and fifty yards behind Lee and Jamison quickly changed direction. She briefly hoped the weapon would be out of rounds soon and then noticed the magazine extending from the bottom of the rifle. Even if the magazine ran dry, Brenda probably had another tucked into her coat.

Too far away to prevent Brenda from shooting at her partner, Jamison released her beast all at once, throwing off the shackles of humanity. Blood sang in her veins, heating her core temperature as muscles bulged and rippled. Midnight pelt erupted from her pores all at once, leaping into existence. Endorphins flooded her system as bones reformed and a lashing tail extended from the base of her spine. Her sense of smell expanded, as did her vision, and she no longer felt the cold.

Jamison roared in challenge to anyone who would threaten them. As the sound echoed throughout the canyon, bouncing off the three sides of mountain walls, Jamison leapt from the tree line and raced toward Brenda, intent on ripping out the human's throat.

Chapter Twenty

PAT SHIVERED AND huddled into her thick down parka. It felt like they'd been walking forever and she was chilled to the bone. The silence stretching between Sam and her served only to compound her misery. As fascinating as she found the rural sheriff, Pat couldn't argue with Sam's reasons for not wanting to get involved. Pat was stationed in Lake Placid and while that wasn't exactly the far side of the moon, it was still a respectable distance. In Pat's experience, long-distance relationships never worked. She didn't know if she liked Sam enough to become entangled in an actual relationship, but that was the point of dating. Not that it mattered. Sam had apparently already made up her mind and Pat had no idea how to counter her logic.

"I think we're getting close. Here, hold this."

Pat realized Sam had stopped walking and held out the compass. She took the device while Sam unfolded her map. Sheriff Macke gave the map a half turn to reorient the terrain and then studied the lines. She looked up and stared toward the mountain range for a moment.

"Yeah, I think it's just up ahead."

The bark of a shot being fired punctuated Sheriff Macke's comment. Both women jerked at the noise before sprinting toward the bang. From the proximity of the shot, Pat knew they weren't far away. Pat pulled her Glock from her hip holster as she ran, careful to keep her finger off the trigger since the weapon wasn't equipped with a safety. Her breath plumed around her in sharp counterpoint to the frigid mountain air. Pat's heart thundered in excitement at what they might find and she forgot about the temperature and sidelined romantic thoughts concerning Samantha Macke.

Pat rounded a small copse of maples and skidded to a halt, quickly taking in every detail. She spotted Ranger Brenda Thomas high up on a trail. Pat's expertise in weapons assisted her in identifying the AR15 equipped with a high-powered scope. For all that the weapon seemed rigged for deadly accuracy, Thomas didn't bother to utilize the scope. She merely threw the weapon to her shoulder and fired off another round from an extended clip. Pat brought her Glock to bear when she saw Thomas aim at Lee Grayson's fleeing back.

"You'll never hit her from this distance," Sam said quickly.

"I have to try."

Pat took aim as the shot from Brenda's rifle ricocheted harmlessly from a large boulder. Pat trained the front sight of her handgun on Ranger Thomas's torso and began slowly squeezing the trigger. Before she could fire, Ranger Kessler raced into her line of sight and Pat quickly released the trigger. She started to shout for Jamison to get out of the way when the most confusing, bewildering and frightening thing happened.

The expression on Jamison's face froze the blood in Pat's veins. To call it feral would not have done the anger and sheer ferocity justice. Pat was sure she didn't blink, but everything happened so fast she must have. Jamison's clothing seemed to fall from her body, accompanied by an intense ripping sound. Since Kessler ran as it happened, clothing trailed behind her on the frozen ground. Her black boots also split up the sides and went flying, but Kessler wasn't naked. In fact, Kessler wasn't Kessler. Suddenly, a jet-black jungle cat raced up the base of the mountain toward Ranger Thomas.

The animal was *huge*. Muscles rippled and weak sunlight shimmered off the ink-black pelt. Massive paws boasted claws that dug furrows into the hard ground as she moved, throwing up bits of frozen dirt. Wicked fangs as white as new-fallen snow curved from the beast's upper and lower jaws as she issued a growl of challenge. The sound bounced off the mountain walls and echoed throughout the canyon, sending a shiver down Pat's spine that had nothing to do with the cold. A part of her mind seemed to curl up in a dark corner, gibbering in insane panic. This could not be real, she argued internally.

Something grabbed at her arm and Pat pulled desperately away, convinced another creature was about to have her for lunch. For a moment she didn't recognize Sam and she tried to raise her pistol. Sam batted the Glock aside with the back of her hand before she shook Pat by the lapels of her jacket.

"It's just me, stop it."

"You knew?" Pat found it difficult to recognize the harsh sound of her own voice.

"Now isn't the time. Thomas is about to kill someone."

Sam pushed Pat back on her heels before she turned and ran toward the confrontation. Pat thought it far more likely that Brenda Thomas would meet a grisly end, but she pushed the thought aside and chased after Sam. Thomas had murdered two women and was actively attempting to kill another. Pat focused on that fact. Less than a hundred yards from the base of the elevated, windy trail, Pat saw Brenda raise the rifle for another shot. Automatically, she raised her Glock into position.

"Stop, U. S. Park Police. Put the rifle down," Pat shouted.

Brenda looked around in surprise and briefly glanced at Macke and Hex. A determined expression settled on her face. Thomas turned back to Lee who had apparently run out of room on the mountain trek. A small rock fall sometime in the past had left the path impassable. Far from sporting defeat, Grayson faced the ranger proudly, with her chin held high. If she was afraid, Lee did a fantastic job hiding it.

When Thomas turned her back to raise the weapon, Pat had no choice. She fired the .40 caliber handgun. The round passed inches from

Brenda's head, driving into the granite wall of Devil's Peak. Rock and dirt flew from the bullet hole and Brenda recoiled from the spray. Before anyone had a chance to react further, the huge jungle cat rounded the trail and raced toward Brenda at breakneck speed. A roar of triumph issued from her throat at the same time that her body coiled for a massive leap.

Brenda turned and saw the cat. Terror gripped her visage and she raised the rifle once again. Pat heard the echo of a hammer falling on an empty chamber. Ranger Thomas had run out of ammunition. The cat's paws took Brenda high in the shoulders, pushing the woman backward. As Thomas fell to the ground, Lee Grayson raced forward. She paused long enough to kick the rifle from Brenda's hand. The weapon sailed over the edge of the cliff and shattered as if made of china when it hit the canyon floor.

Grayson grabbed the midnight colored feline around her thick neck and Pat expected the animal to turn on her. Rather than rip Lee to shreds, the animal paused with razor-sharp fangs so close to Thomas's neck that from where Pat stood it looked ready to rip the helpless woman's throat out. She didn't know what Grayson said and doubted that she ever would, but the black jaguar slowly backed up until Thomas could stand. Brenda regained her feet and cowered back away from Lee and the jungle cat.

"Keep it away from me," Brenda shouted in fear. Her hands were up in a defensive position as she backed up even farther.

"Thomas, freeze," Sheriff Macke shouted up at her. "You're close to the edge."

Although not far up the side of the mountain, Pat knew a thirty-foot drop would still do some damage. Whether Brenda heard the Sheriff or not it didn't matter. Her foot slipped in the ice near the edge of the trail. She fought for balance, casting a terrified look over her shoulder. Brenda fell forward and tried to grab at anything to stop her slide over the edge, but came away with a handful of dead grass. Pat closed her eyes when Brenda fell but she couldn't shut out the sound of her scream.

Macke was already running toward the injured woman. Brenda lay moaning when Pat arrived. Her eyes were open, but Pat could tell by her expression that nobody was home. Shock, she thought.

"Stay still," Sheriff Macke said. Pat heard the authority in her voice but detected little compassion. Considering Ranger Thomas was responsible for the death of two women and had kidnapped a couple of teenagers, Pat didn't blame her. In fact, she had to give Sam points for being so professional.

A noise from behind made Pat spin around. She found herself face to face with Lee Grayson and a feline Jamison Kessler. The only thing familiar in the cat's face were the intense green eyes that studied her with unsettling intelligence.

"I think...," Brenda Thomas rasped thickly. "I think my back is broken."

Lee Grayson fixed eyes as hard as flint on Thomas. She lacked the compassion that Sheriff Macke had displayed. "That's impossible. First you'd have to have a spine."

Still a little freaked by Jamison Kessler's alternate nature, Hex chuckled at the comment. Then the jaguar took a step forward and Pat raised her Glock. If anyone asked, Pat would swear she did so instinctively. Sam quickly stopped her from shooting by placing a hand across the top of the pistol.

"Easy, Annie Oakley. Kessler, maybe you should change while we call for an ambulance."

The green gaze fixed on Sam's face and Kessler made a sound somewhere between a cough and a growl. She tossed her massive black head at the same time. Sam looked at Lee to translate.

"She says to radio Dinah for the chopper. It can't take all of us, but it can get Brenda to the hospital. Oh, and you should ask her to bring a change of clothing for Jami. Hers are ruined."

Pat shook her head to get the bangs out of her field of vision and to shake the cobwebs loose enough for her to speak. "You got all of that out of one growl?"

Lee shrugged and her cheeks flushed a little. "Most of it is mental projection."

"Are you...?" Sam stopped her before Pat's head exploded.

"We'll play twenty questions later. We still have a case to wrap up."

"Right," Pat muttered. Somehow, she just didn't know how to say anything. If Kessler was a shape shifter, werewolf, or whatever, did that mean the rest of her family was too? What about Lee Grayson and the other town residents? Suddenly, Pat wasn't so sure she wanted to know. "Right."

"THIS WOMAN IS a threat!"

Marie Tristan's shouted words reverberated around the Council of Elder's closed chambers. The elder was on her feet, her hands fisted so hard on the tabletop that her knuckles were white. She leaned her weight on her fists, every line of her body tense. Jamison understood what wasn't said, that Marie wanted Detective Patricia Hex eliminated. From Jamison's perspective the woman might as well be saying "off with their heads!".

"She saw you shift. Once she reports this Harmon will be filled with humans that want to exterminate the Panthera!"

"Elder, calm yourself."

Darlene Kessler sounded almost bored and Jamison hid her smile by looking down at the table. As the *Caber*, or Elder in Charge, Darlene was the only one who could put Marie in her place. But that didn't mean that Marie had to like it. Her eyes shot daggers in Jamison's direction.

"This is your fault, Elder Kessler," Marie spoke to Jamison. "I realize you are a junior elder, but you were a *pieta* for years. Your carelessness is criminal."

Jamison felt her hackles rise. "My partner was in danger, by a human. I would think that you of all people could understand my reaction given that you hate humans so much."

Marie ignored Jamison's argument. "Since this is your mess, how do you propose that we clean it up? Clearly you don't want the threat eliminated."

"You mean killed. Stop sugarcoating it, Elder."

So far, no other elders weighed in. Dominick Crane, Cole Verity, Gail Henson, Lydia Booker and Darlene kept silent as Marie and Jamison made their cases. Everyone knew that Marie had no use for humans and found them an abomination, a plague on the face of the earth. Conversely, Jamison saw their good points and had no problem with humans. She clearly saw the threat they could pose if the population at large discovered the Panthera's existence, but didn't think that possibility justified cold-blooded murder. Jamison believed the Council felt as she did and gave silent thanks that her mother was *Caber* rather than Marie, yet she knew she had enemies.

Lydia Booker still hadn't forgiven Jamison for the fiasco last year that ended with Aaron Dalton's death. Jamison thought it a distinct possibility the woman would side with Marie simply out of spite.

"Is there any other option?" Lydia asked, proving Jamison's worst fears.

"If we have her killed, Sheriff Macke will expose us. Besides, who's going to believe Detective Hex if she does tell someone?"

"All it takes is one person to believe her and our entire community will be at risk." Elder Tristan drove home her point by slamming her fist into the table top.

Jamison immediately saw the flaw in her argument. "That would have to be one seriously well-placed person and if we do kill her we'll have feds crawling all over Harmon investigating her death. Then we *will* be exposed. Hex has already given her word that she will keep our secret and I trust her."

"How can you trust the word of a human?" Marie spat the word.

"Because she's more concerned with looking insane in front of her colleagues. It's the same with alien abduction stories and UFO sightings. Claiming she sees shape shifters would cast doubt on her sanity and hurt her career."

"And what of this Ranger Thomas?" Lydia asked. "Should we just ignore her as a threat as well? After all, she saw you in your jaguar form up on the mountain."

So now they wanted to murder two humans? Jamison felt a growl rumbling in her chest. If this was how the Council of Elders operated, she wanted no part of it. "Thomas didn't see me change, she just saw the aftermath. Then there's the fact that she's delusional to begin with. I'm sure Elder Kessler, as the hospital's Chief Resident, can sign off on the fact that hitting your head after falling from a great height can cause people to see things."

The meeting went on for another hour with Marie vehemently arguing against allowing Hex and Thomas to live. Jamison countered with every logical argument she could think of. In the end, the Council decided against eliminating the two women but there were concessions. All but one agreed that Thomas was not a serious menace given her mental state, but someone would be assigned to surreptitiously keep tabs on Hex. The surveillance would continue until such time as the Council no longer considered her a risk.

Elder Tristan wasn't happy with the decision but the Council operated on a democratic, majority rule basis. The final tally against the more bloodthirsty solution was 5-2. Only the final compromise appeased her. It was one Jamison happily made though she doubted it would be enough to satisfy the elder for long. Marie couldn't suppress her dislike for humans anymore than a jaguar could become a vegetarian.

Finally it was over and she heaved a sigh of relief. Jamison left the Council chambers, closing the door behind her. She felt sure that the others still had issues to discuss, but whatever they were, they no longer concerned Jamison. Turning to walk away, Jamison froze in surprise. Lee's presence wasn't unexpected, but Jamison wasn't prepared to face Sheriff Macke.

"What are you doing here?"

"Nice to see you too, Kessler."

"I mean, *how* are you here?"

"You mean how did I know that an abandoned concrete bunker barely on the edge of downtown Harmon is where your Council hangs out? I am an investigator. I found this place three weeks after moving here."

Jamison nodded sagely. "I guess the giant sign saying 'Bomb Shelter' was hardly misleading."

"Hardly. Now that the pleasantries are out of the way, what have they decided?"

Jamison experienced another troublesome jolt. She knew exactly what Sheriff Macke was asking but felt inclined to do what she always did, protect the Panthera community. "What are you talking about?"

"Don't give me that," Macke growled. "I'm not stupid. What are they planning for Hex because if they plan to knock her off, I'll call everyone I can think of and tell them about your kind. Hell, I'll call the damned White House."

Jamison rolled her eyes at the melodrama. "They aren't going to do anything. You have my word."

"They aren't? No unexplained auto accident on the way to Lake Placid?"

"No car accident."

"No gargling with broken glass or staged suicide?"

Jamison heaved a tired sigh and wrapped one arm around Lee's shoulders. "I told you, Sheriff, they won't do anything."

Sam nodded, clearly baffled but willing to accept Jamison's word. "Okay for now, but if anything happens down the road, I'll make your life hell."

"If anything happens down the road, I'll make the responsible party's life hell," Jamison promised. "Now if you don't mind, it's been a long day."

"Actually, by my calculations it's been two full days since anyone has had any sleep," Lee pointed out, leaning her head against Jamison's shoulder.

Sheriff Macke hesitated before she looked down at the floor. "Fine, I'll let you go get some rest." She looked back up and held her hand out. As Jamison shook hands with her, Sam said, "Thank you. I know this was your doing and I'm sure it wasn't easy."

Jamison merely nodded, too tired for anymore verbal sparring. "What about Thomas?"

"She's been charged with double homicide and three counts of kidnapping, including Ms. Grayson here." Sam looked at Lee. "I'm sure with your testimony, plus mine and Detective Hex's there won't be any reason to put Casey North on the stand."

"Thank goodness for small miracles," Lee responded.

"Agreed, the kid's been through enough. Of course, if she pleads guilty to the charges it'll save the state the cost of a trial."

Jamison snorted. "What are the chances of that?"

"Slim. Any good lawyer would use the insanity defense, but it won't matter. She's off the street and she's going away for a long time. How's your pooch, by the way?"

Lee smiled. "Cleo's at home and the dog door is locked. I'm not taking a chance on her disappearing again."

"I'm sure you'll be keeping a close eye on her for a while. It's only natural, all things considered. Well, I'll let you two get some rest. Thanks again, Kessler."

Macke walked away without a backward glance and Jamison felt nothing but relief. The last thing she needed was for the other elders to see Sheriff Macke in the meeting hall. She turned to Lee and wrapped her protectively in the circle of her arms, resting her head on the top of Lee's head. Jamison closed her eyes and allowed the tension to drain from her body.

Lee held her quietly for a long moment and then asked, "What did you have to give up for them to agree?"

"Can't get anything by you, can I." Jamison tried for sarcastic but succeeded in sounding amused, perhaps because what she gave up wasn't much of a sacrifice.

"You're stalling."

Jamison took a deep breath. "You are looking at the Panthera's newest, oldest *pieta*."

"They demoted you?" Lee pulled away to look at her.

Jamison shook her head. "I willingly gave up being an elder. I'd rather be an investigator any day. The decision is one I would have chosen anyway and it made Marie Tristan happy. She felt like she scored a point against the Kesslers. Or something. I can never figure that woman out."

Lee nipped Jamison's chin. "Are you sure this is what you want?"

"It's where I belong."

"No, where you belong is with me."

Jamison squeezed Lee and then released her. "You're right about that. Now let's go home. I feel like I could sleep for a week."

"Aren't you supposed to be at work?"

For the first time in a long time, Lee's questions didn't seem like opposition. Jamison recognized the words as concern. Lee would never just accept things at face value. She would always question, not because she lacked faith in Jamison but because her active mind naturally sought answers. Lee was Jamison's equal in all ways and Jamison welcomed that astuteness. She'd almost lost sight of that over the last few months and swore that she never would again.

"I'll call in sick. Jeanie can run the office."

"Good answer," Lee responded. "I have plans for you for the rest of the day."

"Do those plans include sleep?"

"A little, but I can promise that you won't be getting out of bed."

More S.Y. Thompson titles

Under the Midnight Cloak

Lee Grayson is a nature photographer whose father is a senator in New York. She's never felt close to him and her faith in people as a whole is lacking. She moves to the town of Harmon deep in the Adirondack Mountains after inheriting her great aunt's estate, but the local townspeople seem a little...off. Then she meets Ranger Jamison Kessler and learns there's a killer running rampant around the area. Jamison seems to be hiding things from her and Lee is starting to become suspicious.

Lee discovers that her aunt was a central part of this community and that she possesses the woman's unique abilities. She and Jamison are falling for each other, but things take a turn for the worse when the murderer sets his sights on Lee and a cure for his condition which he believes her to be harboring. Their situation is further complicated by the fact that the killer isn't even human. Neither is Jamison.

ISBN: 978-1-61929-094-5
eBooks 978-1-61929-095-2

Fractured Futures

Detective Ronan Lee has just solved the crime of the century, or has she? The case of the copycat killer plunges her into an ancient mystery, but solving the murders raises questions about the world government's true objectives. An unexpected invention gives her the chance to travel to the past. Her target is the 21st century and her mission is to save the woman at the heart of issue. This same woman, Sidney Weaver, is a warm, personable and accomplished actress that Ronan would give her life to protect.

Unaware of what fate has in store, Sidney's life is boringly predictable until a mysterious stranger comes out of the darkness of night to protect her. She knows there's something unusual about Ronan, but despite her misgivings, she can't deny the mutual attraction. All of this takes a backseat when she's plunged into a harrowing game of cat and mouse that could destroy everything she holds dear.

ISBN: 978-1-61929-122-5
eBooks 978-1-61929-123-2

Now You See Me

Corporate attorney Erin Donovan has nothing on her mind except representing her clients to the best of her abilities. One fateful day, she shows an irritating new client, Carson Tierney, around the tenth floor space of her own building and her life takes an unforeseen direction.

Carson is an awe-inspiring woman by anyone's standards. Possessing genius-level intelligence that has allowed her to become a self-made millionaire of a computer software company, Carson still has a dark secret that could be her undoing.

When the two are thrust together to escape a deadly killer in a high-rise office building while a blizzard rages outside, they have no one to count on but each other. So begins an unexpected yet tender romance. However, unchecked love and desire isn't in their future. The murderer is still out there and he's coming for them. Will Carson's street-wise skills protect them both as Erin attempts to discover the killer's identity just as relentlessly as he is seeking their demise?

ISBN: 978-1-61929-112-6
eBooks 978-1-61929-113-3

Destination Alara

In the 24th Century technology has evolved but greed and war are constant. A rookie starship captain but a veteran of the recent Gothoan War, Vanessa Swann searches the outer rim of the galaxy for any sign of rebel activity. Her favorite pastimes are kicking enemy butt and making time with the ladies. The last thing Van wants is to team up with the Andromeda System's heir apparent and leader of the Coalition flagship, Princess/Admiral Cade Meryan.

Coal black hair, piercing grey eyes and skin the color of fresh cream threaten Vanessa's professional boundaries, but focus she must when faced with repeated attempts on Cade's life. The fate of millions and the threat of galactic war rest on Van's shoulders. Whatever the outcome, their lives will never be the same.

ISBN: 978-1-61929-166-9
eBooks 978-1-61929-167-6

Coming Soon from
S. Y. Thompson and Regal Crest

Woeful Pines

While undercover agent Emily Baptiste is investigating a rash of disappearances in rural Kentucky, she discovers something that strains the limits of credulity. The kidnapped are being hunted for sport. When she is also captured, Emily discovers an insane truth. The missing are taken through an inter-dimensional portal to a place where fantastic creatures reside, predominant among them are a race of vampires. The vampires use other species to hunt as well as for sex and slave labor.

Now Emily is among the hunted. Her only hope is Sheriff Jenna Yang from Woeful Pines, Kentucky. Unfortunately, Emily and Jenna hardly know each other. Will Jenna even realize Emily is missing? If she does, will Jenna be willing to risk everything to cross into an unknown land and face enduring hardship to rescue a virtual stranger?

Scheduled for February 2015 release

Illusive Witness

Who can you turn to when everyone betrays your trust? This is an especially important question for Ruth Gallagher. Severely injured at the same time that her best friend is killed in a mountain climbing incident, she later learns it was no accident. Repeated attempts on her life are made when a mobster believes she knows more about his criminal enterprises than she does.

Riding to the rescue is U.S. Marshal Emma Blake, but after all the perfidy can Ruth trust Emma? Barely healed from her previous encounters, she may not have a choice.

Scheduled for July 2015 release

Other Mystic Books You Might Enjoy

Return of An Impetuous Pilot
by Kate McLachlan

When Jill's latest time-travel experiment goes awry, no one but Jill is surprised. But when Amelia Earhart suddenly pops out of RIP, everyone is stunned-and delighted! Everyone except Jill, that is, especially when Amelia decides she likes the future too much to return to her own time. History without Amelia Earhart? Unthinkable! But how do you return an impetuous pilot who doesn't want to go home?

It's Bennie and Van to the rescue! Together with Kendra and Jill, they try to return Amelia to the right side of history. Their motives might be mixed, but their hearts are in the right place...or are they?

Reunite with the RIP gang in Return of an Impetuous Pilot, the third book in the RIP Van Dyke Time Travel series, and find out where their hearts are leading them now.

ISBN: 978-1-61929-152-2
eBooks 978-1-61929-153-9

Ban Talah
by A. L. Duncan

From the crumbling pages of ancient Celtic scrolls comes a vivid world of mysticism and unflinching valor. Ban Talah is the daughter of Tlachtga, Goddess of the Thunderbolt. Unbound by mortal laws Ban Talah must find strength in her own moral constitutions in all their depths and complexities and not distance herself from the deep undercurrent of her immortality in order to fulfill her Geasa, her duty, as a strength and legend to her people. It is the time of King Henry II, ruler of England, where Celtic-Christianity struggled with Rome's papacy and the legitimacy of paganism within the Church. It is a time that begins the reaping of a terrible sowing.

The insidious heart of a French Cardinal, a man of mysterious dealings, has set the elements of evil astir. In order to save Henry's England Ban Talah must first save the Lady of the Land from the bindings of the Cardinal's sorcerous, wintery enchantment, a spell that is also a wicked inheritance of ills against the healers of her people. This is a tale of how one woman led her people in loyalty to a King and the Church a respect in her people, driving all that she fought for into all that she also fought against. A woman whom all called: Ban Talah.

ISBN: 978-1-61929-186-7
eBooks 978-1-61929-185-0

Twice Bitten
by R.G. Emanuelle

Fiona lost her mortality unwillingly to a woman she once loved. Now she wanders through the decades, a vampire in search of a soulmate. After 200 years, she thinks she's found her, in an upper-class family in New York City at the turn of the 20th century. Her name is Rose, and if only she will come to her willingly, Fiona will have her eternal companion. But Rose loves another, so Fiona sets in motion a twisted scheme that involves the woman Rose loves and a betrayal that will lead Rose into transformation. Will Rose succumb to Fiona's machinations and forever lose the woman she truly loves? Or will she find a way to foil the vampire's devious plan and save her soul-and her beloved's life? She's running out of options and, worse, out of time.

ISBN: 978-1-61929-088-4
eBooks 978-1-61929-089-1

Shadowstalkers
by Sky Croft

The mission of a shadowstalker is simple: stalk, hunt, and kill creatures of the night, while protecting the innocent, unsuspecting public who have no idea of the horrors that lurk in the darkness.

For the Valentine women, shadowstalking is a way of life. Supernatural threats lie in wait around every corner, and danger is a regular occurrence.

Though the mission is simple, Cassie Valentine finds her life is anything but. Not only is she in love with her best friend, but past mistakes haunt her dreams.

Along with her mother, Eve, and her younger sister, Vicki, Cassie must learn to negotiate the perilous terrain of day-to-day life, while also coming to terms with the past.

Will Cassie be brave enough to overcome her fears and give love a chance? Or will the Valentine family fall when a legendary foe resurfaces?

ISBN: 978-1-61929-116-4
eBooks 978-1-61929-117-1

OTHER REGAL CREST PUBLICATIONS

Brenda Adcock	Pipeline	978-1-932300-64-2
Brenda Adcock	Redress of Grievances	978-1-932300-86-4
Brenda Adcock	The Chameleon	978-1-61929-102-7
Brenda Adcock	Tunnel Vision	978-1-935053-19-4
Charles Casey	The Trials of Christopher Mann	978-1-61929-086-0
Michael Chavez	Creed	978-1-61929-053-2
Michael Chavez	Haze	978-1-61929-096-9
Sharon G. Clark	Into the Mist	978-1-935053-34-7
Eric Gober	Secrets of the Other Side	978-1-61929-100-3
Charles Lunsford	Running With George	978-1-61929-092-1
Helen M. Macpherson	Colder Than Ice	1-932300-29-5
Linda Morganstein	Harpies' Feast	978-1-935053-43-9
Linda Morganstein	On A Silver Platter	978-1-935053-51-4
Linda Morganstein	Ordinary Furies	978-1-935053-47-7
Andi Marquette	Land of Entrapment	978-1-935053-02-6
Andi Marquette	State of Denial	978-1-935053-09-5
Andi Marquette	The Ties That Bind	978-1-935053-23-1
Kate McLachlan	Return of An Impetuous Pilot	978-1-61929-152-2
Kate McLachlan	Hearts, Dead and Alive	978-1-61929-017-4
Kate McLachlan	Rescue At Inspiration Point	978-1-61929-005-1
Kate McLachlan	Rip Van Dyke	978-1-935053-29-3
Damian Serbu	Dark Sorcerer Threatening	978-1-61929-078-5
Damian Serbu	Secrets In the Attic	978-1-935053-33-0
Damian Serbu	The Vampire's Angel	978-1-935053-22-4
Damian Serbu	The Vampire's Quest	978-1-61929-013-6
Damian Serbu	The Vampire's Witch	978-1-61929-104-1
Damian Serbu	The Pirate Witch	978-1-61929-144-7
S.Y. Thompson	Under Devil's Snare	978-1-61929-204-8
S.Y. Thompson	Under the Midnight Cloak	978-1-61929-094-5
Mary Vermillion	Death By Discount	978-1-61929-047-1
Mary Vermillion	Murder By Mascot	978-1-61929-048-8
Mary Vermillion	Seminal Murder	978-1-61929-049-5

About the Author

S. Y. Thompson resides in Texas with her menagerie of animals. She fills her days with writing and playing with her Yorkie and six cats.

VISIT US ONLINE AT
www.regalcrest.biz

At the Regal Crest Website You'll Find

- The latest news about forthcoming titles and new releases

- Our complete backlist of romance, mystery, thriller and adventure titles

- Information about your favorite authors

- Current bestsellers

- Media tearsheets to print and take with you when you shop

- Which books are also available as eBooks.

Regal Crest print titles are available from all progressive booksellers including numerous sources online. Our distributors are Bella Distribution and Ingram.

CPSIA information can be obtained
at www.ICGtesting.com
Printed in the USA
FFOW02n1440180914
7409FF